WRITE
TURNS

WRITE TURNS

New Directions in Canadian Fiction

RAINCOAST BOOKS

Vancouver

Raincoast Books acknowledges the ongoing support of the Canada Council for the Arts; British Columbia Arts Council; and the Government of Canada through the Department of Canadian Heritage Book Publishing Industry Development Program (BPDIP).

First published in 2001 by
Raincoast Books
9050 Shaughnessy Street
Vancouver, B.C.
V6P 6E5
www.raincoast.com

Edited by Joy Gugeler
Cover design by Peter Cocking
Cover photo by Stone/JFB
Text design by Val Speidel

1 2 3 4 5 6 7 8 9 10

National Library of Canada Cataloguing in Publication Data

Main entry under title:

Write turns

Fiction by graduates of UBC's Creative Writing Program.
ISBN 1-55192-402-1

1. Short stories, Canadian (English)* 2. Canadian fiction (English)—21st century*. I. University of British Columbia. Dept. of Creative Writing.
PS8321.W738 2001   C813'.010806   C2001-910865-6
PR9197.32.W74 2001

At Raincoast Books we are committed to protecting the environment and to the responsible use of natural resources. We are acting on this commitment by working with suppliers and printers to phase out our use of paper produced from ancient forests. This book is one step towards that goal. It is printed on 100% ancient-forest-free paper (100% post-consumer recycled), processed chlorine and acid-free, and supplied by New Leaf Paper; it is printed with vegetable-based inks by Houghton-Boston. For further information, visit our website at www.raincoast.com. We are working with Markets Initiative (www.oldgrowthfree.com) on this project.

Printed and bound in Canada

CONTENTS

INTRODUCTION

Joy Gugeler

AS WITH MOST ROADS, LESS TRAVELLED OR OTHERWISE, THE PATH
to the writing life is characterized by varying speeds, unexpected
detours, perilous drops and dizzying ascents, but it is always a
path that one travels alone. Some writers choose to foster their
talents in isolation, rarely looking up from the sweat-stained draft
of the latest manuscript; others choose to gather in cafes, libraries
and bookstores, sharing secrets, birthing characters from the
chatter, worrying titles on their tongues like talismans; still others may follow that road to School, where would-be novelists,
poets, dramatists or journalists submit their work to the scrutiny
and encouragement of the experts who have gone before them.
There is no ideal formula, no ideal author, no ideal listener who
will polish a piece to perfection or provide guarantees of fame,
fortune or critical acclaim. There is only a gift, a craft and a will
to tell a story. And there is choice, always choice.

The fifteen writers included here have chosen to attend the
University of British Columbia for a Masters of Fine Arts in
Creative Writing in the hopes that the two-year degree would, as
Linda Svendsen, the current chair of the program said, "get it said
better, truer." Each has graduated in the decade between 1990 and
2000, the thirty-fifth anniversary of the department founded by

Earle Birney in 1965. When Birney opened its doors he said he wanted, "one course I can believe in, the first stone in a little shelter for the creative-writing student naked in academia." The department's silver anniversary was marked by the anthology *Words We Call Home*, a 375-page compendium published by UBC Press and edited by Svendsen with work by sixty-nine writers including George Bowering, Robert Bringhurst, Frank Davey, Gary Geddes, Jack Hodgins, Daphne Marlatt, Erin Moure, Morris Panych and Fred Wah. A *Calgary Herald* review raved, "If you are interested in the cutting edge of Canadian literature, then this is a collection for you to seek out and savor."

In the interim years the cutting edge has sharpened and the MFA program has grown to offer courses in numerous genres—screenplay, radio drama, creative non-fiction, short fiction, long fiction, poetry and playwriting. It has also maintained a well-respected and student-run literary magazine, *Prism international*, now celebrating its fortieth anniversary, and has completed its third year of a week-long summer writers' conference called Booming Ground. The program, as described by Jack Hodgins, one its most visible alumni, is founded on the premise "that beginning writers can shorten their apprenticeship by working with more experienced writers and with a small group of other beginning writers."

Perched on the blustery cliffs overlooking the Strait of Georgia, the Vancouver studio has been said to contribute to a renaissance that the *Vancouver Sun* described as a "post-national, post-industrial Pacific Rim cultural experiment" creating a new wave of Vanlit in the Canlit scene. Like its post-secondary counterparts offering graduate and undergraduate programs in creative writing in other regions of the country—the universities of New Brunswick, Windsor, Concordia, York, Calgary, Victoria—and like its American and British equivalents—the universities of Iowa, Columbia,

Stanford, Radcliffe, East Anglia and Trinity College—UBC offers a peer workshop setting, access to established writers and mentors (Andreas Schroeder, George McWhirter, Keith Maillard, Peggy Thompson, Linda Svendsen, Brian Wade and others), some tricks of the trade, technical tips, motivation and comaraderie. In combination with other programs that nurture all nature of talent— evening courses at community colleges, weekend retreats, writers-in-electronic-residence and summer workshops (Banff, Sage Hill, Humber—UBC has earned its place on the literary map and as a result has become the subject of media-inspired navel gazing, forelock tugging and fingerpointing.

In the media, both advocates and detractors have called the program: a "literary hothouse," a "so-called talent incubator," a "diploma mill," and in recent years a middleman for agents and publishers interested in adopting the Hollywood-style star system that a *Vancouver Sun* reporter wrote will identify "the young, the hot and the marketable, and push them into becoming personalities." While none of the writers here would likely invite this kind of introduction, reporters happily refer to them as a pack of accomplished twenty- and thirty-somethings. Skeptics, competitors and nay-sayers refer to them as a "precious mob", "the most vaunted", "the New Faces" and "the It crowd of young novelists rolling off the assembly line." Meanwhile articles about the size of advances and flush foreign rights deals litter the arts pages and one begins to wonder if discussion about the poetry of the finely-turned line is being sacrificed to make room for handwringing about the bottom line.

Somewhat predictably, the coverage has taken on the appearance of a witch hunt/love-in with many of the reports neglecting to focus on the works themselves, which, carry the real argument. *The National Post* claimed the program "has always had a reputation as a rigorous training ground but, over the last few years, it has made itself known as a literary candy factory, churning out one publishing industry darling after the next" while the *Globe* volleyed with, "Whether by coincidence or some sort of self-fulfilling contrivance, depending upon whom you ask, a steady stream of bright lights continue to zoom out of the program straight into envy-inducing contracts." Needless to say, the debate has been heated, public, self-perpetuating and on occasion vacuous, but the gossip and name-dropping has fueled that elusive engine of sales: buzz.

The furor, warranted or not, has also reignited the age-old question of "nature versus nurture": Can writing be taught rather than caught? It is a question that will not be answered with a unanimous yes or no, nor does it have to be. Those who do opt for schooling, though, are increasingly aware of the world of commerce impinging on the sacred domain of art. Some graduates of the program say the competition for book deals distracts writers from their focus on the text, that as *The National Post* asserted, the "frenzy of interest in signing up budding authors has deprived them of an environment in which they can undergo the painstaking and slow process of improving their craft." Those who spurn writing schools say the program gets the pick of an already talented crop and falsely takes credit for predictable successes. As graduates' names begin to pepper the shortlists for the country's top prizes—the Governor General's, Giller, Journey, Trillium, Danuta Gleed, Amazon/Books in Canada, Chapters First Novel—and gain the coveted attention of publishers abroad scoping Canadian recruits on the Booker, the Orange and the Commonwealth lists—the envy, the sales and the gossip abound. For many of the writers discussed in these articles and who appear in these pages, the papparazzi's obsession with rival camps is embarassing and misses the point: the fiction itself. In a marketplace dominated by big stores and small reviews, most writers are more interested in a response to their craft than their profile.

And so to the stories, that most elastic of forms stretching to accommodate a remarkable variety of visions, voices and subjects of scrutiny. How then to decide who to include? When the department put forward a pre-selected bundle of stories and asked me to make the final cut, I had the unenviable task of chosing *only* fifteen from an impressive and wide-ranging stable of writers, each deserving of attention. Assessing polish, tone, ingenuity and style, I arrived at the current Table of Contents. Another anthology, equally inviting, could easily be made of those remaining. It is my hope that readers will concur that the fifteen pieces collected here are deserving by *any* criteria. Ranging from the playful to the speculative, from the humorous to the horrifying, from the introspective to the illuminating, these works linger long after the last line, unfurl days later in conversation with a friend, and, like any garden of earthly delights, appeal to all the senses, but can only be truly appreciated bloom by bloom.

In *Hagiography* Aislinn Hunter tells the story of Sophie, a defiant God-fearing Catholic girl working as a ticket taker at a Triple X theatre, "at the peak of her sexual repression" and James, a young seminarian at St. Patrick's college in Dublin whom she might marry, should circumstances and fate intervene. They both love God and may come to love each other as well. "There is, in truth, a lot of love going around – mostly, but not entirely, of the holy kind." Hunter's story is rife with wry wit and the carefully placed cultural jab, playfully stepping outside of the ring to address the reader, hint at other possibilities, and underline just how arbitrary are the contrived events of life and story.

Across the Atlantic another young woman witnesses lust unfold, experiencing it vicariously in *Love Line*, a story in which Debbie Howlett adopts the voice of a precocious teenaged voyeur, Diane Wilkinson, as she maps the subtle faultlines in her Montreal family's suburban home. When her uncle, notorious for his half-cocked scams and "that funny business," arrives with his Las Vegas showgirl only to dally with Diane's Brownie leader and live up to her mother's low expectations, Howlett masterfully mimics the assured tones of mature conversation and sly innuendo yet clings to the naivete that protects Diane from her elders' duplicity and disappointment.

In *Black* Annabel Lyon dissects still another facet of childhood in a mesmerizing modern love story that recasts the family in detail-perfect language: "Lorelei the beauty queen had butterfly brains and the prettiest damn fingernails Morris had ever seen. She also had a baby girl who looked like she'd stepped off the top of a Christmas tree and was still floating down. They were like something from a magazine and Morris wanted to cut and paste himself right into their lives. He braided himself then and there into their histories, so that a year later, when Lorelei, who was mad as a star, took off, Morris and Suzy were left in a twist." As the story flashes backward to this moment and forward to a series of funerals Lyon reconfigures Suzy's life with a dazzling accuracy, confounding expectations and plunging us face-first into the pool of her discontent.

In the fourth in a series of stories with teen protagonists, this too set in the fraught hours that preceed an expected death, Kelli Deeth veers into darker territory with *Pet the Spider*, a disturbing account of Leah and Loretta's simultaneous attraction to and repulsion from Loretta's elderly and paralyzed aunt who has come from Scotland to die. Leah's brutal obsession with the woman is a stark portrait of disrespect and abuse, chillingly familiar. Leah knows she is staring into her own future when she confronts Aunt Phyllis in the final scene: "When I looked at her flat eyes, they expressed vast loathing and I was not spared."

Perhaps the most horrifying story in the anthology is *Dogs in Winter*, Eden Robinson's account of a young girl's repeated suicide attempts in order to escape the fate of her deranged mother, a serial killer who has raised her on the stench of blood and left her to live with the threat of retribution and inheritance. Robinson's prose is relentless and unadorned, shocking with simplicity, impossible to ignore. Here is childhood robbed: "Death should have a handmaiden: her pale, pale skin should be crossed with scars ... her dress should only be splattered artistically with blood, like the well-placed smudge of dirt on a movie heroine's face after she's battled the bad guys and saved the world."

But life's accidents can be both real and imagined, as Madeleine Thien's story *Dispatch* affirms. A wife, discovering her husband's unfulfilled longing in a pleading love letter, both assuages and indulges her grief by fabricating a dream in which her presumed rival is killed in a car crash. As she plays out the fantasy and watches the suffering of others in newscasts, she attempts to return to a state of relative peace. "At night, in the glow of the screen, you type to the up, down of your husband's breathing. It's difficult to look at him in these moments. His face is so open, so slack-jawed, vulnerable and alone. Both of you have always been solitary people. Like big cedars, your husband says, bulky and thick, growing wider year by year. You are charmed by your husband's metaphors, the quiet simplicity of them."

The outside world encroaches through a different medium in Nancy Lee's *Associated Press*, the story of a woman torn between a danger-seeking photojournalist in war-torn corners of the globe and an upright homeboy with a secret appetite for rough sex. Lee's prose is fluid and addictive, it's liquor smooth but with a powerful kick. Devotion and pain become conflated: "Months of absence made that boy a perfect lover. Distance times longing times uncertainty. You had both learned that love at its best was slow and drawn out, stretched thin for sadness to show through."

With prose that catches in your throat, and fearless, brash and searing images, Zsuzsi Gartner's *boys growing* also walks through the shadowy underworld of addictive attraction, telling of a high school teacher put off by the scent of men her own age, but animally attracted to her virile male students in a string of short-lived affairs with boys devoted to their mamas. Gartner's protagonist hunts: "Small boys who didn't get to sleep that night, their nostrils thick with blood sport, their trigger fingers, their everything, twitching. Bones growing faster than their skin. You could hear it—a terrible sound, canvas sails tearing on a tall ship at sea, a border guard grinding his teeth. Boys growing."

Terence Young also goes back to school in *Too Busy Swimming*, though on the other side of the law, relating the parallel stories of a husband testifying against colleagues accused of pedophilia and his wife who cleans the home of a gunshot suicide. It is a story of unimaginable circumstances and rare moments of bravery told with note-perfect dialogue and an ear attuned to the vivid and resonant phrase: "People say children are the glue that keeps a couple together. Maybe we're all the more amazing, then, living under the same roof without the benefit of adhesives. Or maybe it's just a matter of time."

Murray Logan's *RIP, Roger Miller* also plumbs the depths of a man withered by circumstance, not childless, but having lost a child to divorce, the drink and discouragement. Holed up in a camper in his friend's barn, poisoned by rum and losses he can't name, he reclaims dignity through revised memories. Logan's prose is understated, quiet, heavy in the pauses between action and deed as he tries to recall his son: "Memory is funny that way, filling in details, colours, T-shirts that never were ... he's always that same age, and he's always wearing that same damn T-shirt."

In *Blue Line Bus* Rick Maddocks writes of another hapless wanderer who abandoned a child, a Grateful Dead groupie busing to Victoria from Ontario's tobacco country who meets her son's father in a diner only to have a litany of her failings hurled at her before she boards. Maddock's ear for idiom is uncanny, the music in his prose like a daydream:. "She looked at him suddenly, so close, his face loose and honest and pricked with cold. 'You're such an idiot,' she said. And she was laughing up into the sky then, up over his shoulder, his light brown hair, the branches bared themselves grey in the sunlight and leaves fell in the shushing water like yellow and red flakes of rain and got carried away on the water that shivered over the white stones."

In *Letters to the Future* Andrew Gray drops in on a gypsy of a different sort, a two-bit scammer who seduces a librarian for the spoils of time capsules, a gravedigger looking for sentiment buried or lost or forgotten. Infused with self-mocking humour and a sense of the absurd, Gray ponders large questions in small moments: "What makes one person able to do something others can't? Julia Casket getting married at ninety-six, for example, or a bank robber sticking up the local credit union. It's a matter of will, being able to cross the line."

Anne Fleming's George is a middle-aged man who does have the will to rob a bank, if only to do "Something that whenever he thought of it afterwards would tug his lips in a mysterious smile, something that on this deathbed he'd crook his finger to draw them closer and confess in a sly happy whisper. Something that would make a good story." When George's wife is hit by a car on her bicycle and his son contracts AIDS, George is forced to rise above widowhood and prejudice. Fleming's characters are wondrously complex, the miracle of their contradictions fascinating.

Like George, Alison Acheson's Nellie is alone and weary of absence, loneliness and the eternal search for an elusive peace; she is a stranger in her own home. "*What an odd place,* she found herself thinking as she stood in her living room. Though she'd never thought that before. Now she thought, *This home is not meant for one person. Not meant for two either, or a family of more. It is meant for visitors.*" Dissatisfied with her own barren world she creates another in a birdhouse on her balcony, forming an unexpected alliance with her neighbour Simon over the care and feeding of her new companions. Acheson story revels in the subconscious and asks us to look twice at everything.

The final story in the collection likewise pairs two unlikely naturalists, though wisks us to Singapore circa 1860. In *Seven Years with Wallace* Adam Lewis Schroeder paints a heartbreaking portrait of a British colonialist about to board a steamer for his British homeland and the Dyak guide who has faithfully served him without pay or respect in the hopes that this alliance will ferry him to England as well. Devastatingly, Schroeder tells a truer story. Ali is refused entry to an elite hotel due to his attire and Wallace, typically, both defends and patronizes his charge. "Really, like a gentleman? We have spent years sleeping on beaches, my man, praying that another snake was not going to drop onto our heads. This lad was given a ... a human skull to play with as a child. We have been in utter wilderness nearly every day of the past seven years and now I wonder if he would like to sleep in a proper bed. He is not the Duke of York, granted, but I would dare say neither are you!"

And so the stories go—each a convincing rebuttal to accusations that these writers are hype without substance, each attesting to the strength of a new generation of Canadian talent poised to take their place aside others on the international scene to whom they've been compared, writers like Lorrie Moore, Pam Houston, Amy Tan, Melissa Banks, Rick Moody, Nathan Englander, David Eggers, Nick Hornby, Will Self and Zadie Smith. As with all writing, the reader is the final judge, so perhaps it is apt to end with an invitation: Read on, discover what lies around the next corner; it may be the sharpest right turn you've ever made.

Hagiography

Aislinn Hunter

SOPHIE BELIEVED SHE HAD BEEN CALLED BY THE DIVINE TO WORK at the Ormand Quay Triple X Cinema. First of all, she was good with numbers.

"Four pounds a ticket, times two shows, equals eight pounds. Add popcorn" (stale and overly salted) "at fifty-five pence— equals eight pounds fifty-five pence total."

She smiled brightly and put the gentleman's money in the old tin cash box.

"Next?"

Second, she was a devout and God-fearing Catholic girl who at twenty-one was at her peak of sexual repression. Divinity, Sophie and her mother decided, had called her to test herself. Besides, the only other places that were hiring in all of Dublin were the pubs, and Sophie's mother didn't care for the drink at all.

Sophie liked candy-apple red lip colour and short skirts that swirled around her ordinary thighs as she walked down O'Connell Street to work. She had learned to think of herself as plain and had given up all hope of ever being beautiful. It was, she reasoned, her individual features that never quite seemed pulled together. Often she caught sight of her reflection in shop windows: nose too long for her face, lipstick on her teeth, frizzy brown hair popping out of her barrettes. Behind the Plexiglas in the ticket booth, however, she felt desirable. She ignored the water stains marking the peeled yellow wallpaper and the cigarette burns along the counter. She sat up straight and focused on the task at hand.

The flicks at the Triple X ran at nine and eleven. There was always a fair enough crowd, especially for the American imports. "The Irish like nothing better," Peter the projectionist liked to remark, "than American smut. Reminds us of our blessed sanctity." He said this every time an American film was showing, chuckling more to himself than to anyone else. Sophie knew the Western pornos were Peter's favourites, better than the British films they usually showed. The American films were said to be the most outrageous. Films like *Way Down South* and *Cowboy Riders* were considered classics.

* * *

"Four pounds, please," Sophie says to the next man in the queue. Tonight she is feeling kind of pretty in her mother's light blue summer dress and knitted shawl. She leans toward the cut oval in the Plexiglas, slipping her hand underneath it to take the fellow's fiver. "Grand," she smiles widely, "one pound's yer change." She gives him back his coin, lets her fingers rest on his hand momentarily.

* * *

This is not about him. There are many men, mostly in their forties, whose hands Sophie brushes from the comfort of her red vinyl stool. This is not about numbers, unless numerology dictates fate and every cash transaction in the ticket booth or in Dublin leads to it. This is not about sex, although eventually we'll get to that. There is a young seminarian at Saint Patrick's College. His name is James, after the biblical James; we are, after all, in

Ireland. Young James loves God, also feels compelled by Grace, Divinity, his ma, what have you, to his vocation. The Lord, he believes, is his shepherd, there is nothing he should want. He will come to want Sophie.

*   *   *

James first meets Sophie on an April day, halfway down Grafton Street. He's bent over the cobblestones, tapping his finger on the ground.

"All right there?"

First he sees her ankles, sloppy flats, and then his head follows his eyes up her bare and goose-pimpled leg to her thick waist, round breasts and finally her face. It's pinched.

"All right or not? Are you daft?"

People pass by them. James clears his throat, shifts so Sophie's blocking the sun again.

"Sorry?"

"Did you lose something?"

He looks at the cobblestones in front of where he's kneeling.

"Ah, no."

Sophie, puckering her lips, surveys the street. People come and go from shops and offices.

"So?" she folds her arms. "Do you need a hand or not?"

"Something's written here," he says.

"Oh." She leans over and her blouse and cardigan open a bit. Sure enough, there are illegible scribbles over three of the stones.

"I can't read it," he sighs.

Standing up next to her, James feels tall and lanky. His dark fringe flops in front of his eyes and he brushes it aside impatiently. Sophie looks at him for a moment as if he is familiar, but not quite.

"All right," she sighs, "good enough, then." And she strides away.

James and Sophie both love God. And they both love their respective parents who love God more than Sophie and James ever could. Both families share a number of traditions: confession and communion, charity work with those less fortunate and the quiet kind of self-flagellation that comes from wondering if you love God enough. James is ready to give himself to God. But something about Sophie has bowled him over. There is, in truth, a lot of love going around — mostly, but not entirely, of the holy kind.

*　*　*

Later that week Sophie locks the ticket booth and sneaks up to the projection room for the first time in the seven months she's worked at the Triple X. She can't quite put her finger on it, but she's feeling a little unsettled. Maybe, she reasons, it was not being able to read that scrawl on the stones on Grafton Street. As if she's missing a sign.

Two light knocks on the projection room door get no response, so Sophie lets herself in. Peter's mangy head is pressed close to the projector and he's looking through the hole around the lens. He's got his hand around his penis, which surprises Sophie because she'd never really considered the possibility of it before. Averting her eyes, she takes in the nudie pin-ups tacked over the wood panelling.

"Humph." She clears her throat loudly. "Peter?"

"Yeah?" He barely turns toward her.

She's curious about the film but doesn't want to actually look at it. That, she figures, would be a sin.

"What?" He's impatient.

"Is it any good?"

*　*　*

James is good. Clean undies every day, never curses, respects his mother, does up the dishes after dinner, helps old ladies and so on. He makes the long trek from his flat in Parnell Square to Saint Patrick's College in Maynooth every day. He speaks both Irish and Latin. Coming home he recites the Bible under his breath, crossing in front of the pawnshops and military surplus stores that blanket Capel Street. He has memorized Genesis and the Revelations, the Psalms, Matthew and Mark. Today, a Sunday, he peers through the window of a sun-filled bakery and, seeing the scones, decides to indulge.

"Two, please."

"One pound sixty."

Through the shop window, between shelves loaded with sourdough and rye, he spies Sophie.

"Keep it," he says and leaves without his change, without his scones.

She would be perfect, he thinks, his pace quickening to catch up to Sophie, perfect on a carousel, sitting sidesaddle on a creamy palomino, her halo of hair catching the sunlight, her arm swinging open to him as she kicks off her loafers. She would be perfect if he could place her there in real life, at the carnival that came to Bray every summer when he was growing up. It was the most complete part of his childhood, the most freedom he'd ever felt. Flickering lights strung up like stars from Bray Head to the causeway and dozens of rides, side shows. Going round on the carousel, you could sometimes get a glimpse into the fat lady's tent, catch sight of her large, drooping breasts before the tent flap closed behind another customer. At the carnival, whole worlds that James had never considered were revealed. On top of the ferris wheel, James, only twelve, looked down at the smallness of the people below. He raised his arms to the sky, knowing there was nothing left between him and heaven. It was then, on that ferris wheel, that James first knew God.

*   *   *

At Ha'penny Bridge he is almost beside her. Unsure if he should actually touch this woman, he simply lopes along at a distance, thinking of ferris wheels and cotton candy, the pink of her cardigan. The more he muses, the more he wants to touch her.

"Ms.—" His hand—long, clean fingers—reaches out to her shoulder as she turns onto the sidewalk, but she picks up her pace before he can reach her. Sophie, oblivious to James' presence, looks both ways then trots across the street and enters a narrow utility doorway. NO ENTRANCE is written boldly above the door handle in black spray paint. Above his head to the left James sees the marquee.

Triple X.

Water Orgy and *All Wet*. Double bill.

Flummoxed, James takes a step back, rereads the sign. He decides he'll wait.

*   *   *

These are the options that are open to him: James can leave and pretend he didn't see Sophie. He can retrace his steps, go back to the bakery and then enter in under the ringing bells above the door. Embarrassed, he can ask the counter girl if she remembers him, and if so, could he still take the scones. Or, James could go in through the NO ENTRANCE doorway and seek out Sophie. He could put his hand out to her and bring her out of the Triple X and into the bright cast of the day. But it is a foreboding door and the fear of being seen stops him.

*   *   *

"Peter?" Sophie sees the projectionist down the faintly lit hallway.

"Over here, darlin'."

"Cheques?"

"Sam's got 'em." He jabs his thumb toward the office.

Sophie moves to squeeze by Peter, who is reclining against the wall outside the office doorway. He takes a deep drag of his cigarette, then flicks the ashes over the carpet, running his hand up Sophie's leg when she makes her way past him.

"Really?" she smiles, jabs him hard with her knuckle.

"All's fair," he mumbles, "all's fair."

Outside, Sophie hustles toward home, opening her envelope to check her wage card. James is following her. She adds up the figures in her head, mumbles little bits, "times eight … for taxes." Stuffing the envelope into her handbag, Sophie misses the light and steps out off the curb. It is mid-morning now and the traffic is thin. Nonetheless a lorry is barrelling toward her and, of course, the driver has his mind on other things.

*   *   *

The predicament is this: Sophie is still oblivious to her calling. James, however, is not. He loves Sophie more than he loves God and they've only just met. The lorry is barrelling down.

*   *   *

The lorry is barrelling down. The lorry driver has six children and a wife who cross-stitches and embroiders beautifully. It is not a happy home, but it is typical, and "typical" is well documented and quite routine in this country. Sophie steps out, typically. The driver has just noticed a spot on his trousers and is looking at it, wondering how it got there and if his wife can get it out.

Sophie steps off the curb.

James, as we have noted, is a bit too far behind.

There is the sound of brakes, there is a fantastic pause, there is a "No!" from the depths of James' soul, which is quite deep. "No!" again. The lorry driver swerves. Sophie is pulled off the road by a strong, ruddy hand. It is not James' hand.

*   *   *

Sophie marries Eamon, who is a friend of the fellow who saves her life, the fellow with the strong, ruddy hand. They date for two years and have sex on their wedding night and once a week after. It is blasé at the best of times. Sophie leaves her job, fore-going her calling, her Plexiglas shrine. She is no longer a virgin, so the temptation, the test the Triple X represents, no longer seems necessary. She starts going to the pubs, although her mother threatens to disown her. In her spare time Sophie gives cooking classes at the local Catholic Women's Association.

On a Tuesday, some four years into their marriage, Eamon is at the garage working late. That night Sophie is at home rifling through donations for the CWA's annual book sale. She happens upon a story in an American fashion magazine in which the heroine is bedded by a Montana plains man. Sophie discovers masturbation. Her happiness lasts close to six months.

*   *   *

But this is not about Sophie and Eamon. This is about James. Let's say the man with the ruddy hand was preoccupied, thinking about his pal Eamon who owns a garage.

*   *   *

The man with the ruddy hand is preoccupied, thinking about his pal Eamon who owns a garage. Eamon is fixing the ruddy-handed man's Austin. Thinking about where the money will come from, the man with the ruddy hand scuffs his toe on the pavement while he waits for the light to change. The lorry driver is looking at his pants.

Sophie steps out.

A "No!" rips through the skies and meets with the small, slender hand of one James MacNeill as he pulls on the shoulder of a woman in a pink cardigan. He loves her, but he doesn't even know her name.

*   *   *

Over scones with jam and tea at Bewley's (coming to a perfect four pound total), the conversation centres around not the almost accident, not numerology or *Water Orgy*, but on having a calling. Sophie leans forward across the table, still exhilarated by the "No!," the rush of attention, this lanky man folding her into his arms right there on O'Connell Street. Sophie sees Divinity in James, not just in his love of God, in his thin, white seminarian collar, but in his adoration of her, in the "No!" from the depths of his soul. Sophie is leaning across the table, her blouse and cardigan opening slightly. Her feet are grazing the floor and she's watching James watch her, suddenly aware of her own beauty, even in this brightly lit café. Settling back into her chair, Sophie thinks about how perfectly it fits her body, how throne-like it is, this dark wood chair on the James Joyce floor of Bewley's Café. She reaches her hand across the table to James. She is not giving him popcorn or change. It is an offering.

James the seminarian beams up at Sophie; she is breathtaking. He is nervous because he has never wanted anything this much in his life. With his finger he traces the water mark his tea cup has left. Round and round that finger goes, like a lazy sideways ferris wheel. James notices it becoming, in its roundness, the eye of God. God is watching them, as we all are, the two of them finally together, there, in Bewley's Café. Her hand stretches out farther toward his, the offering. His hand sliding across the table to hers, fingers touching first, then palms. His sleeve blurring the water mark, the ferris wheel, the all-knowing, all-seeing eye.

Love Line

Debbie Howlett

OUR DAD'S BROTHER IS LENNY WILKINSON AND HE LIVES IN THE
United States of America. We don't see him very often, once every
five years, but he turned up that August with a woman named
Laura. Uncle Lenny says that Laura is his new wife. Then he pats
her on the bum, right in front of my brother and me.

"Wife, eh?" Mum says to Dad, under her breath.

Dad says, "Now, Ruth," but you can tell he doesn't believe it,
either.

Dad and Uncle Lenny shake hands like strangers. "I told Laura
you'd read her palm," Uncle Lenny says, first thing.

My father likes to read our neighbours' palms after church on
Sundays when he isn't working on boilers. He met our mother
that way, the year the Canadian Nationals landed her in an
Olympic-sized swimming pool on the outskirts of Montreal. He
swam into her lane during a free swim and sent her duck-diving
deep to avoid him. Mum was still swimming synchro then, representing her country in the singles competition and travelling
from meet to meet with Granny, her chaperone and coach.

Soaking wet and shivering all over, Dad traced her love line
with a finger and told her it was like looking into a mirror. "I'm
here," he told her. "And here and here and here." Mum married
him in July that same year, in the parish of St. Ignatius, in the

middle of a heat wave, because she loved him and she was going to have his baby and it was 1959.

Laura holds out her hand to Dad, but he just shakes it instead. "There'll be plenty of time for palm reading," Dad says to her.

Uncle Lenny owns a company called Hocus Pocus in the state of Nevada. The company supplies magicians with what Uncle Lenny calls "tricks of the trade."

Uncle Lenny is just in town for a few days and needs a place to stay. "What do you say, Freddy?" Uncle Lenny says to Dad. Mum and Dad and Uncle Lenny are getting reacquainted again in Uncle Lenny's car while Wayne and Laura and I are sitting on the front stoop. Wayne tells us that Mum and Uncle Lenny and Dad used to be friends, but they're not friends anymore.

Laura says, "Why not?"

Wayne shrugs his shoulders and says he was too young to remember.

Mum raises her voice and I hear her say something about "that funny business." Then she says, "How long are you staying?" She is smoking in the back seat of Uncle Lenny's Rambler, listening to him and leaning forward on her elbows. The engine is humming, but the car isn't going anywhere. It has been places, though, and to prove it, Uncle Lenny has plastered the bumper with stickers from as far away as Fort Lauderdale and British Columbia and Lake Tahoe.

"Just a couple of days," Uncle Lenny says. He opens the car door and steps out into the bright yellow sunlight. "You two think about it," he says. He shuts the car door, tight. Then he takes three giant steps toward us. Beside me, Laura yawns. She and Uncle Lenny drove all night to get here.

Mum flicks her cigarette out the car window and it lands on the hot pavement next to the one she flicked out a few minutes ago.

"Can you take us around the block, Fred?" she asks, buckling up. She wants to mull things over. Dad slides over into the driver's seat. He places his hands at ten and two on the steering wheel, then slips the car into reverse. As he backs down the driveway, he stares out the windshield at me and Wayne. I wave.

* * *

Dad and Uncle Lenny have a reunion in the basement of our house with a couple of six-packs of Molson Canadian while Laura takes a catnap in my room. Mum says it reminds her of the old days.

"What old days?" I ask her. We are in the kitchen listening to Dad and Uncle Lenny ham it up downstairs. I am timing soft-boiled eggs to earn my cooking badge for Brownies and Wayne is eating them.

Back then, Mum says Uncle Lenny made his living renting out tables at the Magic City Pool Room. She says that she and Dad and Lenny used to do stuff together when Lenny lived in the city still. Wayne wants to know what kind of "stuff."

"Parties, dances, that kind of stuff," she says.

"Dad used to dance?" asks Wayne. We've seen Mum dance with Father Paul and Mr. Lester and everyone at the St Patrick's Day dance every year; but we've never seen her dance with Dad.

Mum says softly, "Your father watched."

The buzzer on the timer goes and I fish the egg out of the water with a spoon. It has a crack in it already and long white tentacles reach out from under the shell.

Wayne says the last one was runny.

Mum and I watch as Wayne slices off the top half of the egg. It comes off like a hat.

Wayne says, "So far so good."

Mum makes a joke and calls Wayne "an egg-spert." We all laugh until we hear a little crash downstairs that wakes Laura up and sends Mum flying. Wayne and I follow Mum, with straight faces. Uncle Lenny is on the floor, holding his sides because something's very funny. Dad is there, too, laughing and carrying on with a can of beer in his hand. They broke a lamp. Mum's favourite.

*　*　*

Before dinner, Mum sews on the little brown patch with the golden pot on it, even though my third attempt at the egg wound up hard-boiled. She puts it next to the one I got for thriftiness. Laura sits next to Mum, leaning back on her chair. She is brushing out her hair, which is still wet from the Mr. Bubble bath she took. She's using my squirrel comb.

"What's this one for?" she asks me. She points at a badge with a broom on it. She thinks my uniform is cute.

"Housekeeping," I say. Then I tell Laura how it took me a week of sweeping and vacuuming to get the badge. "It was the toughest one," I say. "I had to clean the whole house."

"Howse," she says, imitating me. She has an American accent that Mum says sounds crass and stupid. Laura thinks we sound British.

Mum and Laura don't exactly hit it off. Mum says that Laura is tacky. She tells Dad that Uncle Lenny could have done better.

"Better?" Dad says, only half-listening to her.

"Much better," she says, then storms around the house, fuming silently.

I like Laura. She is very pretty and she has a nice laugh that echoes through the house. She laughs a lot, especially around Dad, who she thinks is a scream.

Mum says, "He's a laugh, all right."

Dad raids the linen cupboard for a towel he can wrap around his head like a turban, then comes into the kitchen.

"What do you think?" he says to Mum.

Mum says, "Not much," without looking up from her sewing. She is still mad about that lamp. Laura roars.

I say, "I like it."

The turban is Uncle Lenny's idea. "Everyone does this stuff in Reno," Dad says.

"This isn't Reno," Mum says.

Uncle Lenny comes into the room with another can of beer. He blows a kiss in Laura's direction and Laura pretends to catch it in the palm of her hand. She presses her palm up to her mouth.

"Johnny Carson does this turban stuff on *The Tonight Show*," Uncle Lenny tells us. He tucks a piece of the towel behind Dad's ear so it's tight. "It kills 'em."

Wayne says, "Who's Johnny Carson?"

"Haven't you ever seen *The Tonight Show*?" asks Uncle Lenny.

Wayne and I shake our heads, staring at Dad. We are the only house on our block with an outdoor aerial and Mum says it is an eyesore. The aerial picks up three crummy channels in good weather; two in rain. It is finicky. On Saturdays, Dad hogs the changer and sends our aerial spinning out of control, while Wayne and I fetch cigarettes and beer from the *dépanneur* on the corner. From a distance our house always looks as if it is preparing for flight. We can hear the whirring of the antenna two blocks away.

On the way back Wayne always says, "Ahem, pilot to co-pilot, pilot to co-pilot." He speaks into his clenched fist and clears his throat.

I am the stewardess, offering "Beer, cigarettes?" to the passengers, or sometimes I am the co-pilot. It doesn't matter; the game always ends the same way. During takeoff, the house, with Dad in the cockpit, careens off course and slams into the St. Lawrence River.

The rest of the houses on the block are connected by underground lines and they get cable TV. Even the Lesters get cable TV. We get two English stations and one lousy French one.

"What you kids are missing," Uncle Lenny says, whistling through his teeth. "Believe you me."

Uncle Lenny tells me and Wayne that Johnny Carson is a late-night talk show host who is better than Ed Sullivan. Mum says to Uncle Lenny that no one's better than Ed, then she tells Dad that he looks silly.

*   *   *

In the basement, Uncle Lenny and Laura put on a magic show. Uncle Lenny is the magician and Laura is his assistant. "What do you want me to do, Lenny?" Laura says, but he doesn't give her anything specific to do, so she just stands around wearing a fancy sequined hat, waving her arms every once in a while and sending feathers sailing in all directions.

Before the show, Dad and Uncle Lenny carted boxes from the trunk of his car into our house. "This stuff is great," Dad told Uncle Lenny. He poked at the stuff in the boxes, until Mum came down the stairs. Then he took his place in the audience beside her.

The first thing Uncle Lenny does is make a Canadian dollar disappear.

"How did you do that, Uncle Lenny?" Wayne wants to know.

Uncle Lenny says, "Easy," but when he looks up his shirt sleeve, it is empty. "Where the hell did it go?" he says. Wayne and I help him look for the bill, but we don't find it. Dad says it'll turn up sooner or later.

For his next trick, Uncle Lenny cuts a deck of cards in half and gets Wayne to pick a card. Wayne shows it to me and Mum, but not to Uncle Lenny. It is the four of spades. Wayne gives Uncle Lenny back the card and Uncle Lenny cuts the deck again. Laura gives it a tap. Then Uncle Lenny holds his hand up to his forehead for a moment and closes his eyes. "Is this your card?" he says, showing us the palm of his hand with the four of spades lying face up.

We want to know how he does that one, too. He says, "That

one is simple." He knows which card Wayne will choose by the way he cuts the deck, then he puts a dab of Krazy glue in the palm of his hand, so when he gets the card back, it sticks.

Next, Uncle Lenny pulls an egg out of my ear.

"Neat," I say. Wayne and Dad and I clap while Uncle Lenny takes a bow, but Mum says she's seen it all before.

* * *

Uncle Lenny is Dad's younger brother, but Dad hadn't laid eyes on him in over five years the day he turned up in the Rambler. During dinner, Dad asks Uncle Lenny what he's doing so far from home. He says, "I'm travelling."

"Travelling where, Len?" Mum says. She looks at him across the table. Wayne says she hasn't warmed up to him yet.

"Around," Uncle Lenny says, with a mouthful of food. Then he says to her, "Mmmmm." We are eating lamb chops, even though it is only Wednesday, because Uncle Lenny and Laura are here. We are even having wine with dinner, a bubbly with a picture of a duck on the label. According to Uncle Lenny, it is one of Laura's favourites.

"Must be nice," Dad says, meaning travelling. Then Uncle Lenny says he has an idea for a syndicated TV magic show he is sure he could sell to the CBC.

Dad says, "A magic show, eh?"

"I'm still only thinking," Uncle Lenny says.

"Good luck," Mum says. "Times are tough."

Uncle Lenny looks at Dad. "Is that something you might be interested in, Freddy?"

From where I'm sitting between Laura and my brother, I know Dad's considering it.

"You'd get to be the star of the show, of course," Uncle Lenny says. "You could predict the future, say, by looking into a crystal ball."

Dad looks at his palms. "The future, eh?"

"It's a safe bet." Uncle Lenny tells us he knows all about safe bets, odds-making. He's chummy with blackjack dealers and keno runners, but swears on a stack of Holy Bibles that he himself never gambles on anything but a sure thing.

Uncle Lenny helps himself to another chop and splashes it with mint sauce. He says there's money in magic.

Mum wants to know how much money he is talking about.

"Piles," he says. For the rest of the meal, we chew without talking.

After Mum and I clear away the dinner plates, Uncle Lenny hands me two American quarters, and winks. The quarters are dirty. Then he asks me if my brother and I wouldn't be happier out in the front yard where it is still sunny and hot. I look over at Mum, who nods at me.

Wayne and I take our dirty quarters outside and sweat in the paved lot Uncle Lenny has called our "yard." Earlier that summer, Dad had concrete poured over our front lawn because he was tired of mowing it. In the still wet cement, my brother and I flattened out our palms. Tonight we take turns tossing our quarters into the handprints, while inside the house Uncle Lenny gives Mum and Dad the "hard sell." He wants Dad to invest in his magic company so the company can keep the TV show well supplied with two-headed coins, whoopie cushions, false-bottomed closets, you name it. Passing by the open window, I hear Uncle Lenny call it "up front money."

Wayne says in the five years that Uncle Lenny has been out of the city of Montreal, he has been around the world, maybe more than once.

"How do you know?" I say. Wayne says that Uncle Lenny told him so.

"Look here," Wayne says, digging in a pocket. He pulls out some matchbooks that Uncle Lenny gave him from a nightclub in Las Vegas, Nevada. The matchbooks have pictures of women on them, bare naked. Wayne shows them to me, but he's not supposed to show them to Mum. On the inside cover, the ladies have printed in their names and phone numbers, real neat.

"This is Cleo," Wayne says, showing off. Cleo has blonde hair to her waist and a nice set of teeth. "Kitty," Wayne says next. Kitty is brunette and from the neck up she looks like Mum, only friendlier. Wayne holds up another matchbook and says, "This one's name is Candy. Uncle Lenny says she's long-distance, but worth the nickel."

For a married man, I say Uncle Lenny sure has a lot of girl-friends. "Eh, Wayne?" I say.

Wayne says, "He sure does." Then he says that Laura looks a lot like the matchbook women. We pore over the matchbooks until Mum yells out the window that it's time for Brownies.

* * *

Uncle Lenny offers to give me a lift to Brownies, while Mum and Dad stay home to argue about the TV magic show. Dad wants to invest in Uncle Lenny's show, but Mum says no. Wayne says what she says goes.

In the church parking lot, Uncle Lenny spots Tawny Owl climbing out of her little Volkswagen and says, "Who's that, Diane?"

"That's just Tawny Owl," I say. Tawny Owl became our pack leader last month when Brown Owl quit in a huff.

"Hold on," says Uncle Lenny. He steers his car into the slot beside the statue of the Virgin and tells me he's coming in, too. I remind him that there are no boys in Brownies, but he says he doesn't mind. He says he thinks he'll like being the only boy in the troop.

"We're a pack," I say.

Our Brownie pack meets every Wednesday night in the church

basement, rain or shine. On the way in, Uncle Lenny says, "Christ, I haven't been in a Catholic church in years." I ask him, "What about when you got married?"

He looks my way, but doesn't say anything. Then he mumbles something about how he and Laura got married quickly in a little chapel off the strip in Sin City. "Nothing fancy, Diane," he says.

Uncle Lenny wants to stay with me at Brownies because he thinks it looks like fun. I ask Tawny Owl. She says OK, Uncle Lenny can stay.

"Thanks, Tawny," Uncle Lenny says, then he tells her he knew a nice girl named Tawny once.

"Is that right?" Tawny Owl says, smiling. Then she whispers to him that Tawny Owl isn't her real name.

"It ought to be," he whispers back. "It suits you."

When Uncle Lenny and Tawny Owl finish whispering, she invites him to sit in the Brownie ring, next to her. We all hold hands. I am across the room from them, between Patty and a Tweenie. I show Patty my cooking badge, but I don't let the Tweenie see it. The Tweenie is a French girl who isn't even a Brownie, but tonight's her big night.

Tawny Owl gives Uncle Lenny a big Brownie welcome and makes him take the pledge with us. Then we all sing and dance around the toadstool. We sing, "We're the Brownies, here's our aim, lend a hand and play the game." Uncle Lenny sings, too, even though he doesn't know the words.

Afterward, we break into smaller powwows to think up good deeds. Uncle Lenny stays beside Tawny Owl and helps her set up the enchanted forest on the other side of the basement. When they are finished, Uncle Lenny asks all the Brownies to form a circle again. His voice is high-pitched. We take our places while Uncle Lenny hands out flashlights. Then he switches off the lights.

During the Tweenie ceremony, we wave our flashlights around the room like fairy lights. I shine mine in the direction of Uncle

Lenny and catch him whispering something to Tawny Owl that makes her giggle and look away.

Once the Tweenies have walked through the enchanted forest, Uncle Lenny turns on the lights again. Tawny Owl calls him her little helper.

"There's magic in love," Tawny Owl says to the Tweenies. "Use it every day in all you do and see what wonderful things happen to you."

"A-men," says Uncle Lenny. At the end of the ceremony, Tawny Owl taps the Tweenies on the head and turns them into Brownies, while Uncle Lenny teaches them the Brownie handshake.

Patty's mother drives me home, after Uncle Lenny volunteers to stay and help Tawny Owl clean up the crepe paper river and the stepping stones.

"This could take all night," Uncle Lenny says to me.

When I get home, Dad is reading Laura's hand in the living room. He has taken off the turban and the two of them are having drinks on ice.

"Uh-huh," Dad is saying.

"Is something wrong?" Laura says. She tries to pull her hand away, but Dad hangs on to it.

"Look at that love line," he says. I am standing in the doorway. I cough. Dad looks up. He says, "Look at this, Diane." He drags his finger across her palm and asks me if I have ever seen anything like it. I shake my head, no. Laura's love line cuts her palm in two.

"Want to watch me read Laura's palm?" Dad asks me.

I say, "No, thanks," and head upstairs. In my room, I practise tying and untying the reef knot in my scarf until Mum comes in.

"Where's Lenny?" asks Mum. Her cheeks are flushed.

"I don't know," I tell her. I don't tell her that Uncle Lenny stayed for Brownies, though I don't know why not.

She tells me to get into bed, then after a few minutes, she

calls, "Lights out." I turn off the lamp beside my bed, but I don't fall asleep; I am too wound up. I am thinking about the magic show and Uncle Lenny and Mum and Dad and Laura and I am trying to piece it all together.

*　*　*

They're all in the kitchen the next morning when I get up: Mum, Dad, Wayne, Uncle Lenny and Laura. Laura is wearing Mum's good car coat over something strapless and Uncle Lenny is in the light blue seersucker suit he drove up in. I wave at Dad, but he is too wrapped up in something Mum is saying to him a few inches in front of his face.

When the telephone rings, they all stop talking and look at me. I get the phone. It is Tawny Owl. She says, "Good morning, Diane." Then she says she needs to talk to Lenny. I turn around and hold the receiver out for Uncle Lenny.

"Uncle Lenny," I say. "It's Tawny."

Mum says, "Give me that." She takes the receiver from my hand, grabs it, and then gives Tawny Owl a piece of her mind. When she hangs up, they go back to arguing about the magic business and about that other business Mum calls the funny business.

Uncle Lenny says, "Ruth, we're all family."

Mum goes, "Some family," pointing at Laura.

Everyone is quiet after that and Dad says he thinks Uncle Lenny and Laura ought to be on their way now because it is getting late.

Wayne and I hug Uncle Lenny and Laura out front, but Mum and Dad don't. Uncle Lenny tells Wayne and me that in the United States, they have thirty channels to choose from. "Or more," he says.

Uncle Lenny and Laura drive in a straight line away from us. They reach the end of our block before Mum realizes that Laura has gone with her good coat, the one she wears to church.

"Damn," she says, "I loved that coat." Then she says, "It's all your fault," looking at Dad.

Dad tells her he'll get her another one. But she's not buying it. She calls Laura a little tramp.

When Uncle Lenny's car is almost out of sight, Dad starts back toward the house and Wayne and I follow him. Mum stays where she is, watching her coat disappear until it is just a memory of a thing she once loved.

Black

Annabel Lyon

THE OLD WOMAN UPSTAIRS IS TAKING A LONG TIME TO DIE. Downstairs, Jones is making some phone calls. Jones calls Barry and Edith, and Tom and Anna, and Jack and Ruby and Glen. He calls Denise. He calls Larry and Kate and Bridget and Amy. He calls Foster. He calls Suzy and Morris.

"God, Jones," Morris says. "I'm so sorry."

"But will you come?" Jones asks.

Morris pulls on the phone cord, stretching Jones' voice out and letting it seize back to coils, a kid with bubblegum, finger to tongue. "Do you really think," Morris says, "at this point, I mean."

"Yes," Jones says.

"I mean, considering."

"Yes."

"Will Lorelei be there?"

"Lorelei, Lorelei," Jones says. "Are you coming or not?"

"Is this really the right time?" Morris says.

"I want to see everything go up in the air and come down again different," Jones says. "I think this is the thing I've been waiting for."

"This thing is your mother dying."

"Morris," Jones says. "You have to at least think about it."

"Suzy won't want to."

"I think you should be here for this," Jones says.

*　*　*

Suzy doesn't want to go.

"Come on, Suzy," Morris says. "Why are you being so difficult?"

"I just don't want to," Suzy says.

"You'll regret it later in life."

"No."

"We're going and that's final."

Morris is forty-three and Suzy is five.

*　*　*

There are complications. First, Suzy needs a dress.

"A dress!" Suzy shrieks, as though he has suggested a crucifixion or a gentle roasting. She runs around the house, flapping her arms. A dress!

Morris is dark but Suzy is blond. She has never worn a dress a day in her life.

"Come on, Suzy," Morris says. "It's not so bad."

"Have you ever worn a dress?" she asks.

"Yes," he says.

"How was it?"

"You get used to it," Morris says. "You have to get the right kind, that's all."

"What's the right kind?"

Black satin bias-cut with skinny little straps and a velvet train. Did he really, all those years ago? "Well, now," Morris says. "Let's see."

*　*　*

Morris and Suzy take the bus downtown. He pays and she looks out the window.

Morris thinks about dresses and little girls in dresses. He thinks about sturdy cotton, blue and white stripes, dresses Suzy could fall down in and people would worry about her first. Morris loves Suzy and wants her to be pretty and happy. He knows this is a contradiction and it distresses him pleasantly, like love. It draws his love for her out ahead of him in a long ribbon, trailing him along, flustered and anxious and determined to get things right.

Suzy thinks about construction paper and glue. She thinks about spreading a thin pool of glue into her palm and letting it dry and peeling it off again and how it makes a print of her skin, and how her palm is cool and sticky-dry afterwards. She thinks about scissors and the heavy feel of cutting and the sound, like a lion's snarling purr. She thinks about looping noodles of white glue all over the world.

They find Suzy's dress on a hanger on a rack in a large department store. Morris knows it when he sees it. The dress is plain yellow with a green satin sash and a bow above the bum. He selects yellow running shoes to go with the dress. Suzy steps from the cubicle, pretty as May, and lets the saleslady zip her up. Morris is delighted.

"What do you say?" he says to the saleslady. "I mean, what do you say?"

The saleslady looks at Suzy, who is kicking at herself in the mirror with the toe of her new running shoe.

"Thank you, Morris," Suzy says.

* * *

Another complication: will Suzy have to kiss the corpse? It happens that way in films. Angelic white-blond child is led to the open casket; creamy blond woman splinters, twenty years on, into something unrecognizable. Sometimes she will wear black, sometimes white; sometimes she will smoke, sometimes not.

Morris doesn't like to think of Suzy smoking, although he likes to think of the elegance of smoke in black and white.

He gives her a colour bath. Yellow hair, blue mat, orange towel, white hooded robe. A happy child's bath.

Morris sits on the toilet seat and watches Suzy play with her fish, a fat orange fish with yellow sunglasses. Inside its mouth sits a smaller blue fish with the pleasing form of a nut. Suzy pulls the blue fish out of the orange fish's mouth and lets them go in the water. The orange fish gobbles at the bathwater, eventually closing on the blue fish with a click.

Suzy has forty-seven bath toys—Morris has counted them. Today, she pulls the blue fish too hard and the ratchet jams, snapping the string. She pales, a fish in each fist.

"We'll find another one," Morris says quickly, wondering where Lorelei procured such a hideous toy. He offers Suzy one of the neglected forty-six, a turtle. She tries to stuff the turtle into the orange fish's mouth.

Tonight, and every night after tonight, Suzy must sleep with the fish. The orange fish does not worry her so much any more, but the blue fish weighs upon her heart like a stone. She puts it in her mouth, gags, takes it out. She sleeps with it against her lips, hoping her breath will keep it warm.

*　*　*

The house of Jones and his mother has the feel of a party, a laid-back Sunday-afternoon extended family get-together with stocking feet and beer cans and sports on TV for those that want it, but hushed in deference to the woman dying upstairs. It feels like a house full of people who just happen not to be in any of the rooms Morris wanders into. It hums, it buzzes, it breathes. Morris is surprised that Jones, being Jones, has achieved such a thing.

Morris divests Suzy of her coat and tells her to go play. He finds Jones and hands him a foil-wrapped banana loaf. Jones leads him into the kitchen, where a woman is talking on the phone.

"String him along," the woman says to the phone. To Morris she says, "Where's Suzy?"

"Hello, Lorelei," Morris says.

"Fuck that," Lorelei says. "Where is my child?"

Morris goes to find Suzy. She's in the den, playing with a beagle. "Time to go, Suzy," he says.

Back in the kitchen, the only person he sees is Jones, spiking ice cubes from a tray.

"Where did Lorelei go?" Morris asks. He looks around the room again in case she is hiding, but there is only Jones. Morris feels the phone staring at him suspiciously, as though it still holds her breath.

"She left," Jones says. "She had to go shopping." Jones and Lorelei are brother and sister.

Suzy got her blond from Lorelei, but Morris hopes that is the extent of it. Suzy blinks at Morris, waiting. She got her blue eyes from her real father, who is dead in Michigan. She got her vocabulary from Morris.

"Is everything OK out there?" Jones asks. "I don't know a lot about parties. Are we doing all right?"

"Smashing, Jones," Morris says. "Smashing."

Suzy soars back to the den, where the puppy is waiting for her. She pets the puppy. The puppy blinks. She scratches the puppy under the collar. The puppy likes that, too. She touches the puppy's ear with a fingertip. The ear flicks quick as a bug's wing, quicker than seeing. The puppy sneezes and Suzy is in love.

Outside, as the drinks go down, the guests start to slump a little less and throng a little more. A man standing near Morris points at the ceiling. "Have I got this right?" he asks Morris. "Is she actually dead up there?"

"I'm unclear on that point myself," Morris says. "You could ask Jones."

"The guy in the kitchen?"

Morris nods.

"That man."

Morris mingles. He meets the housekeeper, an Iranian girl with a long pour of hair on her like black honey. In the course of their conversation he learns she has no complete language. She was born in Tehran, but her family moved to Hamburg when she was two. At seven she was taken to Montreal, at twelve to Vancouver. Each language—Persian, German, French, English— was a box she tried to break out of, boxes nested each inside the next, like a Chinese puzzle. She is a delicious horror. Morris longs to lie beside her, to cage her in his arms like ivory and to whisper in her ear beautiful things she will not understand.

Jones tugs on Morris' sleeve.

"Yes, Jones," Morris says.

"She's dead."

"What. You mean, now?"

Jones nods. "What do I do?"

"What do you mean, what do you do?"

"With—it."

They look at each other.

"That's a damn good question," Morris says. "Did you make plans?"

"Rio," Jones says.

Morris stares.

"The other part, it kind of slipped my mind," Jones says. "Maybe if I get some more ice."

"Suzy?" Morris calls. "Honey? Start saying goodbye."

He goes to find Shiraz—he has an idea that is her name— and asks her to come home with him and Suzy, but she says no.

Morris goes to find Suzy. When he picks her up, her breath in his ear is a thick whisper about chocolate. "You and me both," he says.

He is turning her into her blue raincoat when she stops,

fists still poking the fabric for daylight. "I want to see Grandma," Suzy says.

There is an interesting silence.

"Grandma's sleeping, pretty," Jones says.

Morris can't believe it. Jones has a brain.

But Suzy is adamant; she is iron. She makes a break for the stairs and is snatched back by strangers.

"I know," Morris says. "Let's go for Chinese."

"Hurray!" Suzy roars.

"Sssh," Jones says, pointing upstairs and looking annoyed.

*   *   *

The first time Morris went for Chinese, he was six days old. His mother wore him on her chest in a tomato-coloured canvas sling. His parents were pathologically gentle people, walkers, sippers, smilers, tree-loving rainy-day pacifists, born fading. By the time he arrived, their lives were peanut-coloured, almost nude. In a baptismal moment his mother dripped sweet-and-sour sauce on his head, but she and his father were too engrossed in their respective fortune cookies to suspect meaning.

*   *   *

His most vivid childhood memory was of sickness, which he loved. He loved staying in bed all day, reading books, eating Jell-O, fish broth, globs of honey and aspirin crushed between two spoons. He loved the natural disorders of his body—vomiting, diarrhea, infections, swellings, fevers, pale sleeps and altered appetites. Because his parents did not believe in TV and because he had a window, Morris watched weather. He saw blushing sunrises, curtains of rain holding in the night, snow in the blue afternoons. He missed prodigious amounts of school, was top of his class and never wore a hat, in the hopes of catching something special.

*　*　*

In his bachelorhood, Morris would watch sports on TV. He watched blunt-headed events, car rallies and football. He watched women's triathlons from Hawaii, sun-slick virgins with space goggles and citrus neoprene and the strength of men. He watched figure skating. He listened to the hiss of skates, the music that didn't seem to fit with anything anyone was doing, the monsoons of applause. One afternoon he approached the TV and crouched before it, poked the skater gently with his finger and felt the prickling bite of static. She swooped and slithered. He studied her pixels. He imagined her laid out in his palm, a handful of dust. He imagined blowing her away. He backed away until she was a woman again, coronet and plumage. She glittered like sugar, like glass, spinning first one way, then the other. He couldn't turn her off. He let the afternoon go.

*　*　*

Morris once attended seminar in drag to see if anyone would notice. After graduation he got a job as a legal secretary. Eighteen years later, he got stuck in an elevator with a crazy woman and her two-year-old daughter. He told them his joke about the zebra. It was the beginning of the end.

*　*　*

Lorelei the beauty queen had butterfly brains and the prettiest damn fingernails Morris had ever seen. She also had a baby girl who looked like she'd stepped off the top of a Christmas tree and was still floating down. They were like something from a magazine, and Morris wanted to cut and paste himself right into their lives. He braided himself then and there into their histories, so that a year later, when Lorelei, who was mad as a star, took off, Morris and Suzy were left in a twist.

* * *

Sometimes Suzy is pie-happy. Other times she is the pale queen on the dark shore, watching for stone ships that never return. At four she ties her shoes, recites the alphabet and dreams of winged men with glass hands that shatter and bleed. Ice is her favourite food. Morris puts food colouring in the ice cubes they eat together for a bedtime snack. He watches Suzy suck, then bite down. Her pyjamas still have feet. She is the black queen, pale and dolorous in her steel crown, mouth running with colours.

* * *

When Suzy is five, she and Morris attend a party given in honour of, or in spite of, the death or dying of Suzy's maternal grandmother, Lenore. Death happens; trauma is narrowly avoided; bruised souls are slicked over with the balm of a good Chinese takeout and the inimitable joy of chopsticks in the hands of the uninitiated. Puppies are discussed.

* * *

When Suzy is thirteen, she and Morris will go to Jones' funeral. The service will be short and mercifully lacking in foolery — no poetry readings, mucus-riddled reminiscences or favourite pieces of cello music. Jones will lie quietly in his casket at the front of the church. On top of the casket will be propped a large black-and-white glossy, taken about fifteen years earlier, of Jones with a movie-star grin, syrupy eyes and feathered, frosted hair. Morris will spend most of the service pondering this photograph. He will conclude that Jones, being Jones, had it taken all those years ago with just this occasion in mind. Morris will surprise himself, at this point, by weeping.

Suzy will not cry. "I don't get this," she will say.

Jones will leave Suzy fifty thousand dollars, to be given over to her in a lump at the age of forty-four years. Jones will leave Morris wondering what space, if any, Jones' passing has left in the world.

* * *

When Suzy is sixteen and into black, Morris will overhear her talking on the phone. "This guy I live with," she will say, meaning himself, Morris. This will startle him, unduly, since it is only true.

Suzy will spend months of daytime in her room, door closed, blinds drawn. She never goes out; she never plays music. She has no boyfriends, girlfriends, clubs, interests or hobbies.

Morris asks her what she does in there.

"Think," Suzy says.

"I'm trying," Morris says. "Yoga? Taxes?"

"No, that's what I do. I think."

* * *

In university, Suzy will have a roommate who dyes her hair black every two weeks to hide her red roots. The roommate will have had an old Irish granny who told her she was damned to hell because she hadn't been christened. She said her hair was stained all the colours of sin because devils had crept into her mother's womb through the umbilical cord and kissed her scalp with mouths bloody from eating the flesh of the newly dead. The roommate's parents used to go away for the weekend, leaving granny to babysit.

Suzy will tell Morris about her frantic, spice-haired roommate. He will tell her how he had always wanted a band called Dropdead Redhead.

"Was I christened?" she will ask.

"Absolutely," he will say, wondering.

Suzy will write away for a copy of the parish records. One day a letter will come and she will burst upon Morris like a star, hurling a ball of crumpled paper in his face. "They called me Candace," she will spit.

"Well, look at it this way," Morris will say. "You're still a Pisces."

"I am a fucking fish named Candace," Suzy will say, her voice warped to a queerness, the closest she ever comes to tears.

Morris will wonder if he has ever loved her more than at this moment, his beautiful, misnamed undaughter.

*　*　*

In graduate school Suzy will thrive, in a sick way, in her philosophy of science seminar. She will tell Morris how every scientific phenomenon has an infinite number of logically possible explanations. She will liken facts about the world to dots on a graph, which can be joined by any number of different lines, representing theories. She will tell Morris how human relationships are like scientific theories, where every fact one person has about another is a dot, but the connecting lines exist only in one's head. No two lines are identical: love; a theorem; lines connecting lives; invisible threads looping through the universe, weaving a fabric of uncertainty and certain ignorance.

Morris will watch Suzy talk, Suzy of the black tunic and black leggings and the fine baby's hair. He will remember Suzy going into black, but he won't ever remember her coming out.

*　*　*

It is a fact about Suzy that she will never fall in love. People will come to her in fragments—a pleasing glance, the width of a hand, a tone of voice, a cast of thought—from which she cannot seem to cobble a passion. Or maybe it is that Suzy herself is fragmented, all shards and splinters, shivered by a world of farce and darkness. Or just that she is flawed: hair thinning like a banker's and a coldness of bearing she cannot sense and cannot lose.

* * *

During a bout of food poisoning, Morris will come over to make Suzy ruby Jell-O and hold her hand. While she is in the bathroom throwing up, he will look at her chick's hair on the pillow. Her hair is falling out.

When Suzy comes back she will look at the pillow. "Oh, that Candace," she will say.

* * *

When Suzy is thirty-six, she will go to Morris' funeral. She will wear a baseball cap because her hair is many different lengths, and in some places absent. She will not change her clothes for the occasion. She will smell strongly of herself. She will not cry.

* * *

Fifty years later, Suzy will be in her garden, weeding her borders. She will be remembering a time when she couldn't breathe if she saw a flower, when they were evil mouths that talked to her when she was alone, laughing and hissing, coloured cups brimming venom. How they waved their petals, furling and unfurling, blind twisting mouths, thrusting petulant lips. Now they will fill her head with a rush like rain, a song of threading voices. She will feel the grass about her, the looming blades, for she will have fallen—a stroke, they will say, sudden, they will say—and she will realize there was a time when she could look at a person's eyes and it was like looking into a house through an open window and then when it was like looking through glass.

Days will pass before they find her. It will have been a slow death. Eighty-six years is a slow death.

Suzy and Morris in the Chinese restaurant, blue and gold. Through the window, the oriental filigree of traffic on a late afternoon downtown, after rain.

"This is how you eat an egg roll," Suzy says. "This is how you eat chow mein."

Suzy is discovering chopsticks. She chews with her mouth open, concentrating. "Oh, peas!" she says.

Morris looks at the goop in Suzy's open mouth. "Here," he says, passing her a plate. "Some more of the green stuff."

"Why?"

"It's good for you."

"Why?"

"Eat."

Suzy giggles and throws a pea at his head.

Morris giggles. Truly, he thinks, *I am a terrible parent.*

She throws all her peas at him, then pokes at her plate with the chopsticks for something golden and crunchy. "Can I have a puppy?" she asks.

"Sure," Morris says.

Always here, always now, he thinks, watching her eyes pool to glory. *Always remember me this way. Because the day I am dust this is all you will have, and it will not be enough.*

"Doggy bag?" the waiter says.

Suzy, alarmed, looks at Morris.

"Yes," he says. "Yes, please."

Pet the Spider

Kelli Deeth

I HELPED LORETTA RAKE THE LAWN, WHICH WAS COVERED IN leaves. Loretta's Aunt Phyllis sat through the sliding glass doors watching Magnum P.I., which she did in the afternoons. She had an illness, which left her unable to move, and Loretta said she had come from Scotland to die.

"Can we feed her?" I said.

"Feed who?"

"Your aunt."

"You mean go within ten feet of her?" Loretta said, biting her lip, raking furiously, because her father, Mr. Beatty, was meticulous about his lawn.

"I'll feed her, you can watch."

"Whatever gives you a thrill."

Inside, Aunt Phyllis sat in her wheelchair, gazing out onto the backyard, her hair combed down over her eyes and ears.

"And we could fix her hair," I said. I wheeled the wheelchair into the kitchen, which Mrs. Beatty had recently painted red and white.

"Do I look like a beauty technician?" Loretta said. "You going to a dance, Aunty?"

Aunt Phyllis groaned and I smoothed her hair.

"Just for herself," I said.

"Aren't you a ball of fun," Loretta said.

I took a carton of strawberry ice cream out of Loretta's jammed freezer. I thought Aunt Phyllis would like strawberry ice cream because it suggested femininity and delicacy.

I sat in the chair before her and spooned it into her mouth. I dabbed at the sides of her mouth with a serviette.

"She understands," I said.

"Two plus two," Loretta said. "Come on Aunty, hold up your fingers." They lay still in her lap. I thought she was trying.

"You can tell when she makes noise," I said. "I think."

"Aunty just likes to be heard. You should hear her go to the bathroom."

Aunt Phyllis' eyes moved slowly to Loretta and I could tell Loretta had gone too far, been cruel. Aunt Phyllis' eyes were almost closed.

Loretta put her arm around Aunt Phyllis' neck, kissed her cheek repeatedly. Aunt Phyllis panted.

"She doesn't like that," I said.

"I love you, Aunty," Loretta said, squeezing harder. "I'm sorry, Aunty." Loretta's voice was high, hyper.

"You're making it worse," I said.

Loretta was laughing, trying to catch her breath. "Oh, Aunty, you crack me up."

I spooned in more ice cream, trying to show her that I knew she was uncomfortable and probably hated Loretta.

Loretta caught her breath, put her hands over Aunt Phyllis' ears.

"Aunty, would you tell me if you could understand?"

I watched Aunt Phyllis' fingers. Instead, Aunt Phyllis closed her mouth.

"Watch," I said. "Is your husband dead or alive?" I watched the fingers—moving a finger up meant yes. But they remained still on her thigh. Mrs. Beatty said she was losing the ability to move even those.

"She's decided it's nappy time." Loretta kissed the top of Aunt Phyllis' head, rolled her into the living room. Loretta lifted one arm and I lifted the other, then we pulled her onto the couch and tried to sit her up straight. I turned her head toward the television and placed a pillow behind her neck.

Loretta changed the channel to a soap opera everyone in the family assumed Aunt Phyllis was interested in, even going so far as to assume she had a crush on a character.

While Loretta went into the kitchen to pour us pop and to fill a bowl with chips, I entered Aunt Phyllis' empty bedroom. It smelled of floral freshener, stale air and a decaying sweet smell, even though the window was open. The wallpaper and curtains were mauve and the two dressers were white with fancy, gold drawer handles. I opened the closet and saw Aunt Phyllis' clothes, a brown blazer, dresses with belts, clothes belonging to her when she could speak and walk. It was an Aunt Phyllis I could barely imagine, one who could enter a room of her own accord. I closed the closet and went to the dresser. On a lace doily, the kind that Mrs. Beatty fashioned herself, sat a black and white picture of a man and a woman. They were the same height and wore long, wool coats. The man had his hand on the small of her back and the woman, her hair pulled back, a black hat on her head, was smiling with an expression of gratitude.

I went back into the living room and sat beside Aunt Phyllis. I did something daring, something I didn't even think about, just did. I placed my hand on her shoulder, to tell her I cared. But it startled her and she made a snorting sound of fear and alarm. I took my hand away quickly.

* * *

The wind was coming down from the north, but it had not yet snowed, only looked every day as if it would. It was the time of year when my mouth tightened on the walk to school.

Sitting in my Grade 8 classroom near the end of the day, looking out the window, I tried to imagine, as I often did since Aunt Phyllis had come from Scotland, what it would be like to be unable to move. But the noise of the classroom made concentration difficult.

After school, I wanted to go to Loretta's, so I could feed Aunt Phyllis. I wanted to have some sort of conversation with her. I wanted to know how she felt about death, if she was scared to die.

"Why can't we go to your house?" Loretta said. "I'd like to see your brother jam. Maybe he can teach me how to play."

"Tomorrow," I said. My brother and Dan, who were both in Grade 11, had skipped school and gone to Toronto for the afternoon and wouldn't be jamming.

Inside, I saw Aunt Phyllis' head first, the scalp visible. Her gaze was focused on Magnum P.I. Mrs. Beatty, who took care of her during the day, was pulling knee-highs onto Aunt Phyllis' legs.

"Keep her while I go to the IGA," Mrs. Beatty said.

"I'm not a babysitter," Loretta said.

Mrs. Beatty slipped her bare feet into sandals, though it was autumn.

"Spare me your tongue."

She slammed the door.

I rested my hands on the handles of the wheelchair and smelled old skin, a salty, horrid smell. "She needs a bath," I said, firmly.

"There are some things I don't do," Loretta said. "I don't get near naked bodies."

"But how would you feel?"

"I would have a vodka and orange juice," Loretta said. "Nothing wrong with a little dirt."

"She needs a bath," I said. I did not look forward to seeing her without clothes on, but there was a part of me that had to know, had to know what it would look like, be like—I had to go through with it.

Loretta turned off the television with her toes.

"If I help you, we watch your brother jam for three days in a row. Deal?"

"Why do you want to see him so bad?"

"I have my romantic future to consider," Loretta said.

"Fine." It suddenly occurred to me that I should ask Aunt Phyllis if she wanted a bath, but something told me it was safer to assume, that when it involved dirt and a body, you had the right to assume. I rolled her into the bathroom, onto the pink bath mat, and after that, I avoided her eyes; they were bright, glaring.

I ran warm water, not too hot, and I wondered if I were Aunt Phyllis, would I want a bath, or would I just want to be left alone.

I squeezed in bubble bath.

"A bubble bath," I said, smiling at Aunt Phyllis, trying to appear light-hearted, friendly, because giving a bath was an act of compassion. But Aunt Phyllis' face hung, her mouth tugged downward, as if she were trying to figure something out, trying to listen. I had the sudden sensation that Aunt Phyllis could read my mind—that she knew that it was wrong. I should ask. Aunt Phyllis would think hateful things about me—that I was cruel, that I knew better, but didn't care.

I tried to pretend that it was just a bath, just a bubble bath. Aunt Phyllis would want to be clean and I had been compassionate enough to notice.

I took an arm and Loretta took another arm of the heavy pink sweater and when we pulled it off, Aunt Phyllis' hair rose in static electricity. I kept my eyes on Loretta's face, which was scrunched up.

Her bra was lace and her breasts sagged in it like water balloons. There was an added intensity to Aunt Phyllis' eyes. She hated me. She would kill me if she could.

I was not sure I could carry on and felt like vomiting.

"Flabby," Loretta said.

"She understands," I said.

"You know I love you, Aunty," Loretta said, pulling Aunt Phyllis' head to her own breasts. "I'm just teasing you because you have a bit of flab."

"One day this will happen to you," I said.

Loretta frowned, bit her red lipstick.

"You going to take it off?"

"We have to."

"Go ahead," Loretta said.

"I'm thinking."

"She's getting cold."

"Why can't you?"

"Who wanted to give her a bath?"

The word bath helped me remember our mission and that's what it was: a mission. My eyes fell on Aunt Phyllis' pink arms, the diamond on her ring finger. Someone had loved her.

"Fine," I said. I leaned forward, got my arms behind Aunt Phyllis' back and unclipped the bra. As I pulled it off, gently, Aunt Phyllis hummed in a high voice, an angry whine. That she hated me could not be mistaken.

"Do the rest," Loretta said. "And hurry before the water gets cold. Would you want to take a bath in cold water?"

I could not possibly turn back. It was my fault Aunt Phyllis was half undressed and I would have to go through with it, get it over with.

I grabbed Aunt Phyllis' burgundy slacks around the waist and pulled, the underwear with them. I turned my mind into a complete blank, a whiteness that allowed for no feeling. My eyes saw things I refused to absorb. Helpless things, a bright pink body, thin legs, grotesque helplessness. I would punish myself for what I had no right to see.

We each peeled down a knee-high.

Loretta spoke in a kind, strained voice. "All right, honey, just take a deep breath while we lower you in."

My throat was closed. I simply performed my duty. I lifted her under one arm, under one leg, using the muscles in my back to hold her in a standing position. We moved her toward the tub, sat her on the rim. We slipped her legs over, then both lifted either side of her, lowered her into the tub. Suds floated flat in the water.

Loretta soaped her. "You're going to smell so pretty," she said.

Aunt Phyllis was sitting in the water, getting soaped, and I was responsible. Loretta soaped her legs, her breasts, her bum, then quickly and brutally in the spot I could not look at. Aunt Phyllis was dying and couldn't move and there was nothing I could do.

I tried to do what Loretta did easily. I kissed Aunt Phyllis on the back of the head. "Don't worry."

*　　*　　*

Aunt Phyllis began to cough in the night, Loretta said, and Mr. or Mrs. Beatty, or Loretta, had to get up and shake her to stop her from choking on her own saliva. Mr. and Mrs. Beatty said Aunt Phyllis was waiting to die.

But I didn't want to give up. One weekend, I slept over at Loretta's house. At dinner time, Mr. and Mrs. Beatty, Loretta and Aunt Phyllis and I sat at the round table. Everyone but Aunt Phyllis ate scalloped potatoes, green beans and pork chops. Mr. Beatty wanted Aunt Phyllis at the table so that she wouldn't feel left out.

Mr. and Mrs. Beatty talked about the fish and chip store they had recently bought. Apparently, the cook kept showing up drunk and couldn't hit the toilet when he peed. Mrs. Beatty said they should never have bought the place and Mr. Beatty said, "That's enough."

"Do you wish you could eat a pork chop?" Loretta said to Aunt Phyllis, whose eyes appeared to be closed. The slits widened.

"Leave her alone," Mr. Beatty said. "She's bad enough off without you waving pork chops in her face."

"I was just asking her if she missed them," Loretta said, her body tensing.

"She'll enjoy her applesauce later," Mrs. Beatty said.

"I wasn't saying she wouldn't," Loretta said.

"I don't think we should have her eat with us anyway, Tom," Mrs. Beatty said.

After dinner, when Mr. Beatty had gone to the fish and chip store, Mrs. Beatty sat with her arm tightly around Aunt Phyllis on the couch and every once in a while she would give her a kiss. Sometimes Loretta would get up and give her one.

"She'll die at home, at least," Mrs. Beatty said, pulling Aunt Phyllis close to her.

"Then God can take her to the bathroom," Loretta said, changing the channel with the remote. "Right, Aunty?" she said, but her tone suggested that Aunt Phyllis couldn't have understood what she had said.

I studied Aunt Phyllis, wanting to say something kind.

"Her hair looks nice today," I said.

"It should," Mrs. Beatty said. "It took me all morning to get her head under the tap."

I wanted to say something to her, to show her that I knew she did not want to die.

When the movie was over, Mrs. Beatty said, "Help me put her to bed." She got up stiffly, holding her back.

"Not now," Loretta said. "We'll do it later."

"Be quiet with the chair," she said.

For a while, we sat and watched videos, colours flashing, but we could barely hear the television, because the sound was so low.

"I think she wants to go to bed now," I said.

"No," she said. "Aunt Phyllis wants to party."

Loretta and I looked at her for a second and then Loretta said,

"Whatever. All I see are skinny chicks in tight clothes, anyway."

The noise in Aunt Phyllis' throat started when we lifted her. I accidentally elbowed her in the side and she made a high-pitched yelp. Then we had her awkwardly in the chair, one hip higher than the other, and she was huffing as if we'd attacked her. Mrs. Beatty banged on the wall, the sign to be quiet.

"Give me a break," Loretta said, under her breath. "Thanks, Aunty."

Loretta wheeled the chair and I walked in front, removing boots and Loretta's textbooks from the path. Once we had her rolled into the bedroom with the door shut behind us, we turned on the light, which revealed the high bed, the flat pillows that could not have been comfortable.

Loretta wheeled the chair around the far side of the bed where there was a narrow space between the bed and the wall. They put her to sleep on that side so she would be closer to the radio, which was set on a shelf beside the bed, along with the dolls, china dolls, that Loretta had brought in from her room when she heard that Aunt Phyllis was coming from Scotland.

We each took an arm and lifted her, kicked the wheelchair out from under her with our feet. We struggled to keep her up and she made the vicious sound a dog a might make, a low violent sound, and she was still fighting for breath.

Then there was a knock on the front screen door and Mr. Beatty's voice, "Would someone open the damn door?"

Loretta, who was always afraid of making her father angry, said, "Take her for a minute." I leaned against the wall and settled Aunt Phyllis on my leg. The fact that I was leaning against a wall made her weight manageable. But she was still a pressing force and she couldn't hold her head straight and it fell back in my face, so all I could smell was her white hair.

"Just wait a minute," I said kindly.

Then I felt it, hot liquid spreading down and out across my leg, all over my thigh, down to my knee.

Loretta came back in. "Loser," she said, about her father. Then she took Aunt Phyllis' other arm and we lifted her, pushed and pulled and shoved her, onto the bed, which creaked. She didn't make sounds.

I didn't look down at my soaked thigh and Loretta did not notice it. She noticed the urine when we pulled down Aunt Phyllis' green track pants, but she only held her breath. We both knew that we should have wiped her down, but neither of us mentioned it. We pulled her top efficiently off her head and let her lie there with nothing on while we took her sleeveless night-gown out of the top drawer and unfolded it. Then we pulled it without tenderness over her head and bent her arms any way we had to in order to get them through the sleeve holes.

With the nightgown on, she lay stiffly, her breathing a little calmer. My thigh was sticky and warm and the stench of urine was rising from my jeans.

I had to look at her face, to get a good look at it, to see if she knew what she had done to me and to see if she had done it on purpose, to hurt me, to make me feel bad, and to make me know that she knew exactly what was going on, and had the whole time, to let me know that she wanted me to leave her alone. When I looked at her flat eyes, they expressed vast loathing and I was not spared.

* * *

Loretta and I went to bed in her double bed, which was really a pullout couch, one she could fold up during the day. Loretta soon began snoring, loud grinding snores. I couldn't sleep because all I could smell on my hands was Aunt Phyllis' skin. I left the room quietly and stood at Loretta's kitchen window, which looked onto the neighbour's kitchen window. Inside two panes of glass, a spider waved his leg.

I sat in the vinyl kitchen chair and pretended to be paralyzed. It took all my concentration to imagine, to feel that I could not move anything, even if I had to. I breathed deeply, kept every muscle still, until I was paralyzed. Anyone can do whatever they want, I thought. I can't move.

I wanted to move. I stood at the window where winter would be coming, winter that would fill every crack and hole. But it wasn't winter yet: somehow that meant I still had time. It wasn't over for me and I shivered at the thought, a shiver in my chest, from somewhere deep, permanent, felt only when it wanted to be. In the window, the spider was in the same place, but balled up, as they almost always were, and I pet it through the glass.

Dogs in Winter

Eden Robinson

AUNT GENNA'S POODLE, PICNIC, GREETED PEOPLE BY HUMPING their legs. He had an incredible grip. A new postman once dragged Picnic six blocks. Picnic bumped and ground as they went; the postman swore and whacked at the poodle with his mailbag.

Picnic humped the wrong leg, however, when he burst out of our lilac bushes and attached himself to one of Officer Wilkenson's calves. I was lounging on the porch swing, watching hummingbirds buzz around the feeder. On that quiet, lazy summer afternoon, traffic on the nearby highway was pleasantly muted.

"Whose fucking dog is this?" A man's yell broke the silence.

I sat up. A policeman was trying to pry Picnic off his leg. Picnic was going at it steady as a jackhammer.

"Frank! Get this thing off me!" the policeman said to his partner, who was unhelpfully snapping Polaroids.

The policeman lifted his leg and shook it hard. Picnic hopped off and attacked the other leg. The officer gave Picnic a kick that would have disabled a lesser dog. Not Picnic. I brought them the broom from the porch, but not even a sharp rap with a broom handle could quell Picnic's passion.

"Oh, my," Aunt Genna said, arriving on the porch with a tray of lemonade. She had rushed inside when she saw the police officers coming because she wanted to get refreshments. I didn't know it at the time, but they kept returning to ask if Mama had contacted me since her jailbreak. I just thought they really liked Aunt Genna's cookies. She was always hospitable, the very picture of a grand Victorian lady, with her hair up in a big salt-and-pepper bun on top of her head. The lace on her dress fluttered as she put the tray down and rushed to the walkway where the policemen stood.

"Is—this—your—dog?" the policeman hissed.

"Why, yes, Officer Wilkenson." She knelt to help them pry Picnic from the policeman's foot. "I'm so sorry. Are you hurt?"

"Can you just hold it for a moment?" Officer Wilkenson's partner said to Aunt Genna, holding up his Polaroid. "I want to get you all in."

* * *

There is a lake I go to in my dreams. Mama took me there when I got my period for the first time.

In the dream, she and I are sitting on the shore playing kazoos. Mama has a blue kazoo; mine is pink. We play something classical. Crickets are chirping. The sun is rising slowly over the mountains. The lake is cool and dark and flat as glass.

A moose crashes through the underbrush. It lumbers to the edge of the lake, then raises its head and bellows.

Mama puts her kazoo down quietly. She reaches behind her and pulls a shotgun from the dufflebag. She hands me the gun. We have trained for this moment. I steady the gun on my shoulder, take aim, then gently squeeze the trigger.

The sound of the shot explodes in my ear. A hole appears between the moose's eyes. I don't know what I expected, maybe the moose's head to explode like a dropped pumpkin, but not the tidy red hole. The moose collapses forward, head first into the water.

"Let's get breakfast," Mama says.

Wearing my blue dress, I walk calmly into the lake. The pebbles on the shore are all rose quartz, round and smooth as Ping-Pong balls. As I go deeper into the lake, my dress floats up around me. When I am in up to my waist, I see the moose surfacing. It rises out of the water, its coat dripping, its eyes filled with dirt. It towers over me, whispering, mud dribbling from its mouth like saliva. I lean toward it, but no matter how hard I try, I can never understand what the moose is saying.

*   *   *

Paul and Janet are the parents I've always wanted. Sometimes I feel like I've stepped into a storybook or into a TV set. The day we were introduced, I don't know what the counsellors had told them, but they were trying not to look apprehensive. Janet was wearing a navy dress with a white Peter Pan collar. Light makeup, pearls, white shoes. Her blond hair was bobbed and tucked behind her ears. She looked like the elementary schoolteacher that she was. Paul had on stiff, clean jeans and an expensive-looking shirt.

"Hello, Lisa," Janet said, tentatively holding out her hands.

I stayed where I was. At thirteen, I felt gawky and awkward in clothes that didn't quite fit me and weren't in fashion. Paul and Janet looked like a couple out of a Disney movie. I couldn't believe my luck. I didn't trust it. "Are you my new parents?"

Janet nodded.

We went to McDonald's and I had a Happy Meal. It was my first time at McDonald's. Mama didn't like restaurants of any kind. The Happy Meal came with a free toy — a plastic Garfield riding a motor scooter. I still have it on my bookshelf.

Paul and Janet talked cautiously about my new school, my room, meeting their parents. I couldn't get over how normal they seemed. I didn't want to say anything to them about Mama. If I did, they might send me back like a defective toaster.

*   *   *

The first time I saw Aunt Genna, the sun was high and blinding. She came out to the porch with lemonade and told her poodle Picnic to leave me alone. Picnic jumped up on me, licking my face when I bent to pet her. I ran across the yard, squealing and half afraid, half delighted. Aunt Genna tucked her dogs up with quilts embroidered with their names. She served them breakfast and dinner on porcelain plates. Aunt Genna took me in when Mama went to jail that first time, took me in like another stray dog, embroidered my pillow with my name, served me lemonade and cookies in miniature tea sets. One of her dogs—Jenjen, Coco or Picnic—was always following her. Although she was born in Bended River, Manitoba, she liked to believe she was an English lady.

We had tea parties every Sunday after church. Aunt Genna brought out her plastic dishes and sat the dogs on cushions. Jenjen and Coco loved teatime. I would serve them doggie biscuits from plates decorated with blue bears and red balloons. Picnic didn't like to sit at the table and would whine until Aunt Genna let him go to his hallway chair.

Since I wasn't allowed to have real tea, Aunt Genna filled the silver teapot with grape juice.

"How are you today, Lady Lisa?" She would ask, in her best English accent.

"Oh, I'm quite fine," I would say. "And yourself?"

"Quite well, except that I have gout."

"Oh, how awful! Is it very painful?"

"It makes my nose itchy."

"Would you like a scone?"

"I'd adore one."

It was at one of these tea parties that I first asked about my parents. Jenjen was gnawing at her biscuit, spreading crumbs on the table. Coco and Picnic were howling. I poured grape juice for both of us, then said, "Are my parents dead?"

"No," Aunt Genna said. "They are in Africa."

I put down my cup and crawled into Aunt Genna's lap. "What are they doing in Africa?"

"They are both doctors and great explorers. They wanted so very much to take you with them, but there are too many snakes and tigers in Africa. They were afraid you'd be eaten."

"But why did they go?"

"They went because they were needed there. There are very few doctors in Africa, you see, and every single one counts."

"But why did they go?"

"Lady Lisa," Aunt Genna said, kissing the top of my head. "My Lady Lisa, they didn't want to leave you. Your mother cried and cried when they took you out of her arms. Oh, how she cried. She was so very sad."

"Then why did she go?"

"She had no choice. Duty called. She was called to Africa."

"Was my father called, too?"

"Yes. Your mother took him with her. They went together."

"When are they coming back?"

"Not for a long, long time."

I put my arms around her and cried.

"But I will always be here for you," she said, patting my back. "I will always be here, my Lady Lisa."

Aunt Genna told me other things. She told me there were monsters and bogeymen in the world, but all you had to do was be a good girl and they wouldn't get you. I always believed Aunt Genna until Mama killed her.

*　　*　　*

Janet liked these weird art movies that never made it to the Rupert theatres. She was always renting stuff with subtitles, dark lighting, talking heads and bad special effects. This one was called *Street Angel* and I secretly hoped it would have some sex, but when the movie opened in a squalid hut, I wondered if Janet would believe me if I said wanted to do homework. For the first few minutes nothing happened, except this grimy, skinny kid scrounged through garbage heaps for food. In the background there where all these dogs getting kicked and shot and run over. Then the kid was in an alley and it began to snow. I stayed very still, not really paying attention to the end, my mind stuck on the scene where this old dog collapsed and the rest of the pack circled, sniffing its body. A skinny brown mutt nipped at the old dog's leg. The dog growled deep in its throat and staggered to its feet. I knew what was coming. I knew and couldn't stop watching. The mutt ripped into its stomach. The scene went on and on until the dog stopped yelping and jerking on the ground, its eyes flat as the mutt dragged its intestines away from the feeding frenzy. The boy kicked the pack aside and stood over the body. He picked up a cigarette butt and stuck it in the dead dog's mouth.

*   *   *

I saw Mama on a talk show one day.

She was hooked in from her cell via satellite. Another woman, one who had murdered her mother and grandmother, sat in front of the studio audience, handcuffed to the chair. Next to her was a girl who had drowned her baby in a toilet, thinking it had been sent to her by the devil.

Mama wore no makeup. Her hair was pulled back and grey streaks showed through the brown. She looked wan. Sometimes when she gestured, I could see the belly shackle that bound her wrists to her waist.

The talk-show host gave the microphone to a man from the audience who asked, "When was the first time you killed?"

For a long time Mama said nothing. She stared straight into the camera, as if she could see the audience.

"I lost my virginity when I was twenty-seven," Mama said.

"That wasn't the question," the talk-show host said impatiently.

Mama smiled, as if they hadn't got the punch line. "I know what the question was."

I shut the TV off.

How old was I the first time I saw Mama kill? I can't remember. I was small. Not tall enough to see over our neighbour's fence. Our neighbour, Mr. Watley, built a fence to keep kids from raiding his apple orchard. It was flat cedar planks all the way round to the back, where he'd put up chicken wire. When the fence didn't keep them out, he bought a pit bull, a squat black-and-brown dog with bowlegs.

I had to pass Mr. Watley's house on the way from school. I could hear the dog pacing me, panting loud. Once, I stopped by the fence to see what would happen. The dog growled long and low. The hair stood up on the back of my neck and on my arms and legs.

"Who's there?" Mr. Watley called out. "Sic 'em, Ginger."

Ginger hit the fence. It wobbled and creaked. I shrieked and ran home.

After that I walked home on the other side of the street, but I could still hear Ginger. I could hear her when she growled. I could sense her pacing me.

None of the kids liked to play at my house. No one wanted to go near Ginger.

A carload of teenagers drove by Mr. Watley's house the morning Mama killed. They hung out the windows and one of them came up and pounded on the fence until Ginger howled in frustration. When Mr. Watley opened the door, they threw beer bottles. He swore at them. I heard him from my bedroom. Down in the yard, Ginger kept ramming into the fence. She'd run up to it and try to jump and hit it. The fence shuddered.

"Stay away from that man," Mama said to me before I left for school. "He's crazy."

All day long at school I'd been dreading the walk home. I waited on the other side of the street, just before Mr. Watley's house. My Thermos rattled in my lunch box as my hands shook.

Ginger barked.

I waited until I saw Mama peeking out of the kitchen. I felt a bit safer, but not much. I ran. Maybe it was stupid, but I wanted to be inside. I wanted to be with Mama. I remember looking both ways before crossing the street, the way I'd been taught. I ran across the street with my Thermos clunking against the apple that I hadn't eaten and hadn't been able to trade. Running, reaching our lawn and thinking, I'm safe, like playing tag and getting to a safety zone where you can't be touched. I remember the sound of wood breaking and I turned.

Ginger bounded toward me and I couldn't move, I just couldn't move. She stopped two feet away and snarled and I couldn't make any muscle in my body move. Ginger's teeth were very white and her lips were pulled back way up over her gums.

I found my voice and I screamed.

The dog leapt and I banged my lunch box against the side of her head and her jaws snapped shut on my wrist. There was no pain, but I screamed again when I saw the blood. I dropped the lunch box and Ginger let go because Mama was running toward us. Mama was coming and she was shrieking.

It was unreal then as it is now. Mama and Ginger running toward each other. They ran in slow motion, like lovers bounding across a sunlit field. Mama's arm pulled back before they met and years later I would be in art class and see a picture of a peasant woman in a field with a curved knife, a scythe, cutting wheat. Her pose, the lines of her body, would be so like Mama's that I would leave the class, run down the hallway to the bathroom and heave until I vomited.

Mama slid the knife across Ginger's scalp, lopping off the skin above her eyebrows. Ginger yelped. Mama brought her knife up and down. Ginger squealed, snapped her jaws at Mama and crawled backward. Up and down. Mama's rapt face. Up and down. The blood making spatters on her dress like the ink blots on a Rorschach test.

* * *

The moose's short neck makes her unsuited for grazing; consequently she is a browser. Her preference runs to willow, fir, aspen and birch, as well as the aquatic plants found at the bottom of lakes. The moose is quite able to defend herself; even grizzly bears and wolf packs think twice before attempting to kill the largest member of the deer family. Much of the moose's time is spent in the water. She is an excellent swimmer, easily covering fifteen or twenty miles. She is a powerful traveller on land, too, trotting uphill or jumping fallen branches hour after hour.

During the rutting season, her mate, the bull moose, is one of the most dangerous animals, frenzied enough to inflict death or dismemberment on those who stand between him and her and incapable of distinguishing between friend and enemy.

* * *

A man and a woman came into our backyard. The woman knelt beside me as I lay back in my lawn chair, feeling the drizzle on my face. She touched my hand and said, "Your mother's been asking about you."

Her hair and skin were tinged blue by the diffused light through her umbrella. She showed me a card. I didn't bother reading it, knew just by looking at her perfectly groomed face that she was someone's hound dog.

"Janet's in the house," I said, deciding to play dense. It never worked.

Her hand squeezed my arm. "Your real mother."

I wondered what she did when she wasn't trying to convince people to visit serial killers in jail. Sometimes they were writers or tabloid reporters, grad students, the merely morbid or even a couple of psychics. I wondered why they always came in pairs and what her partner was thinking as he stood behind her, silent. Only the sleaziest ones came after me like this, not asking Paul or Janet's permission, waiting for a time when I was alone.

Mama kept sending these people to talk to me, to persuade me to come visit her. I suspected that what she really wanted was a good look at my face so she'd know whom to come after if she ever got out.

"She misses you."

I turned my face up to the sky. "Tell her I miss Aunt Genna."

"You don't really want me to tell her that, do you?"

I closed my eyes. "You're taping this, aren't you?"

"Lisa," the woman held on to my arm when I tried to sit up. "Lisa, listen—it would only take a day, just one day out of your life. She only wants to see you—"

I jerked my arm away and ran for the house just as Janet came out.

"Who are they?"

The man and the woman were already leaving. They could try all they liked. I wasn't ready to see Mama and maybe never would be. But I didn't want any questions either. "Just Jehovah's Witnesses."

I saw the woman waiting outside school the next day, but pretended not to notice her. Eventually she went away.

* * *

I was fourteen when I first tried to commit suicide. I remember it clearly because it was New Year's Eve. Paul and Janet were at a costume ball and thought I was with a friend. Paul was a pirate and Janet was a princess.

They drove me to my friend's house. Paul put his eye patch on his chin so it wouldn't bother him as he drove. I sat in the back, at peace with myself. In my mind I was seeing my foster parents at my funeral, standing grief-stricken at the open casket, gazing down at my calm face.

When they let me off, I walked back home. I brought all Janet's Midol and all Paul's stomach pills upstairs to my bedroom, where I had already stashed two bottles of aspirin. I went back down to get three bottles of ginger ale and a large plastic tumbler.

Then I wrote a poem for Paul and Janet. It was three pages long. At the time it seemed epic and moving, but now I squirm when I think about it. I'm glad I didn't die. What a horrible piece of writing to be remembered by. It was something out of a soap opera: "My Darling Parents, I must leave / I know you will, but you must not grieve" sort of thing. I guess it wouldn't have been so bad if I hadn't made everything rhyme.

I emptied the aspirin into a cereal bowl. Deciding to get it all over with at once, I stuffed a handful into my mouth. God, the taste. Dusty, bitter aspirin crunched into my mouth like hard-shelled bugs. My gag reflex took over and I lost about twenty aspirin on my quilt. I chugalugged three cups of ginger ale to get the taste out of my mouth, then went more slowly and swallowed the pills one by one.

After the twenty-sixth aspirin, I stopped counting and concentrated on not throwing up. I didn't have enough money to get more and I didn't want to waste anything. When I got to the bottom of the cereal bowl, I'd had enough. I'd also run out of ginger ale. Bile was leaking into my mouth. Much later, I discovered that overdosing on aspirin is one of the worst ways to go. Aspirin is toxic, but the amount needed to kill a grown adult is so high that the stomach usually bursts before toxicity kicks in.

My last moments on earth. I didn't know what to do with them. Nothing seemed appropriate. I lay on my bed and read *People* magazine. Farrah was seeing Ryan O'Neal. Some model was suing Elvis's estate for palimony. Disco was dying. A Virginia woman was selling Belgian-chocolate-covered caramel apples at twelve dollars apiece to stars who said they had never tasted anything so wonderful.

At midnight I heard the fireworks, but was too tired to get out of bed. I drifted into sleep, my ears ringing so loud I could barely hear the party at our neighbour's house next door.

Sometime during the night, I crawled to the bathroom at the end of the hall and vomited thin strings of yellow bile into the toilet.

All the next week I wished I had died. My stomach could hold nothing down. Janet thought it was the stomach flu and got me a bottle of extra-strength Tylenol and some Pepto-Bismol. To this day, I can't stand the taste of ginger ale.

*　*　*

By some strange quirk of fate, Mama came for me not long after the SPCA took Picnic away. People had complained about Picnic's affectionate behavior and when Officer Wilkenson got involved, it was the end.

Aunt Genna was weeping quietly upstairs in her bedroom when the doorbell rang. She was always telling me not to let strangers in, so when I saw the woman waiting on the steps, I just stared at her.

"Auntie's busy," I said.

The woman's face was smooth and pale. "Lisa," she said. "Don't you remember me, baby?" I backed away, shaking my head.

"Come here, baby, let me look at you," she said, crouching down. "You've gotten so big. You remember how I used to sing to you? 'A-hunting we will go'? Remember?"

Her brown eyes were familiar. Her dark blond hair was highlighted by streaks that shone in the sunlight.

"Aunt Genna doesn't like me talking to strangers," I said.

Her face set in a grim expression and I knew who she was. She stood. "Where is your aunt?"

"Upstairs," I said.

"Let me go talk to her. You wait right here, baby. When I come back, maybe we'll go shopping. We can get some cotton candy. It used to be your favourite, didn't it? Would you like that?"

I nodded.

"Stay right here," the woman said as she walked by me, her blue summer dress swishing. "Right here, baby."

Her high heels clicked neatly as she went upstairs. I sat in the hallway, on Picnic's high-backed chair. It still smelled of him, salty, like seaweed.

Something thunked upstairs. I heard a dragging sound. Then the shower started. After endless minutes, the door to the bathroom creaked open. Mama's high heels clicked across the floor again.

"I'm back!" Mama said cheerfully, bouncing down the stairs. "Your aunt says we can go shopping if you want. She's taking a bath." Mama leaned down and whispered, "She wants to be alone."

She had my backpack over one shoulder. I jumped down from the chair. Mama held out her hand. I hesitated.

"Coming?" she said.

"I have to be back tonight," I said. "I'm going to Jimmy's birthday party."

"Well, then," she said. "Let's go buy him a present."

She led me to her car. It was bright blue and she let me sit up front. I couldn't see over the dashboard because she made me wear a seatbelt. Aunt Genna's house shrank as we drove away. I remember wondering if we were going to get another dog now that Picnic was gone. I remember looking down at Mama's shoes and seeing little red flecks sprayed across the tips like a spatter painting I'd done in kindergarten. I remember Mama giving me a bad-tasting orange juice and then I remember nothing.

*　*　*

"Yuck," I said. "I'm not touching it."

"No problem," Amanda said. "I'll do it."

Amanda was everyone's favourite lab partner because she'd do absolutely anything, no matter how gross. We looked down at the body of a dead fetal pig that Amanda had chosen from the vat of formaldehyde. We were supposed to find its heart.

"Oh, God," I said, as Amanda made the first cut.

For a moment, I was by the lake and Mama was smearing blood on my cheeks.

"Now you're a real woman," she said. Goose bumps crawled up my back.

"I don't know how you can do that," I said to Amanda.

"Well, you put the knife flat against the skin. Then you press. Then you cut. It's very simple. Want to try?" I shook my head and crossed my arms over my chest.

"Chickenshit," Amanda said.

"Better than being a ghoul," I said.

"Just my luck to get stuck with a wimp," she muttered loud enough for me to hear as she poked around the pig's jellied innards, looking for a small purple lump.

I sat on my lab stool feeling stupid while Amanda hunched over the pig. Not all the chopping and dismemberment in the world could make her queasy. Mama would have liked her. She straightened up and shoved the scalpel in my face, expecting me to take it from her.

At that moment, I saw the scars on her wrist. When she noticed me staring, she pulled her sleeve down to cover them.

"I slipped," she said defensively. "And cut myself."

We faced each other, oblivious to the murmur of the class around us.

"Don't you say anything," she said.

Instead of answering, I unbuttoned the cuff of my blouse and rolled it up my arm. I turned my hand over so the palm was up.

*   *   *

The second time I tried to commit suicide was when I was fifteen, a year after my attempt with the aspirin. This time I had done my homework. I knew exactly what I was going to do.

I bought a straight-edged razor.

Janet and Paul were off to the theatre. I waved them goodbye cheerfully as they raced through the rain to their car.

I closed the front door and listened to the house. Then I marched upstairs and put on my bikini. I ran a bath, putting in Sea Foam bubble bath and mango bath oil. I stepped into the tub, then lay back slowly, letting the water envelop me as I watched the bathroom fill with steam.

The razor was cold in my hands, cold as a doctor's stethoscope. I held it underwater to warm it up. Flexed my arms a few times. Inhaled several deep breaths. Shut the water off. It dripped. There was no way I could die with the tap dripping, so I fiddled with that for a few minutes.

Got out of the tub. Took a painkiller. Got back in the tub. Placed the razor on the crook of my elbow. Hands shaking. Pushed it down. It sank into my skin, the tip disappearing. I felt nothing at first. I pulled the razor toward my wrist, but halfway down my forearm, the cut began to burn. I yanked the razor away.

Blood welled in the cut. Little beads of blood. I hadn't gone very deep, just enough for the skin to gape open slightly. Not enough to reach a vein or an artery.

I was shaking so hard the bubbles in the tub were rippling. The wound felt like a huge paper cut. I clutched it, dropping the razor in the tub.

"I can do it," I said, groping for the razor.

I put it back in the same place and pushed deeper. A thin stream of blood slithered across my arm and dripped into the tub. It burned, it burned.

Paul and Janet came home and found me in front of the TV watching Jimmy Stewart in It's a Wonderful Life. It always makes me cry. So there I was, bawling as Paul and Janet came through the door. They sat on either side of the armchair and they hugged me.

"What is it, honey?" Paul kissed my forehead.

"No, really, I'm OK. It's nothing." I said.

"You sure? You don't look OK," Janet said.

I rested my head on her knees, making her dress wet. Paul and Janet said they wanted to know everything about me, but there were things that made them cringe. What would they do if I said, "I'm afraid Mama will find me and kill me"?

"I'm such a marshmallow. I even cry at B.C. Telephone commercials," is what I said.

Paul leaned over and smoothed my hair away from my face. "You know we love you, don't you, Pumpkin?"

He smelled of Old Spice and I felt like I was in a commercial. Everything would be perfect, I thought, if only Canada had the death penalty.

* * *

In a tiny, grungy antique store in Masset on the Queen Charlotte Islands, I found the moose. Paul and Janet had brought me with them to a business convention. Since the finer points of Q-Base accounting bored me silly, I left the hotel and wandered into the store.

Nature pictures and small portraits of sad-eyed Indian children cluttered the wall. The hunchbacked owner followed me everywhere I went, saying nothing. Not even hello. I was about to leave when I saw the moose.

"How much is that?" I asked, reaching for it.

"Don't touch," he grunted at me.

"How much?" I said.

"Twenty."

I handed him the twenty dollars, grabbed the picture and left.

"What on earth is that?" Janet asked when I got back. She was at the mirror, clipping on earrings.

"Oh, nothing. Just a picture."

"Really? I didn't know you were interested in art. Let me see."

"It's just a tacky tourist picture. I'll show it to you later."

"Here," Janet said, taking the package from my hands and unwrapping it.

"Careful," I said.

"Yes, yes." Janet's mouth fell open and she dropped the picture onto the bed. "Oh my God, that's disgusting! Why on earth did you buy it? Take it back."

I picked up the picture and hugged it to my chest. She tried to pry it from me, but I clung to it tightly. Paul came in and Janet said, "Paul, get that disgusting thing out of here!"

She made me show it to him and he laughed. "Looks very Dali," he said

"It's obscene."

"This is from the woman who likes Pepsi in her milk."

"Paul, I'm serious," she hissed.

"Let her keep it," Paul said. "What harm can it do?"

Later I heard him whisper to her, "Jan, for God's sake, you're overreacting. Drop it, all right? All right?"

I still have it, hanging in my bathroom. Except for the moose lying on its side, giving birth to a human baby, it's a lovely picture. There are bright red cardinals in the fir trees, and the sun is beaming down on the lake in the left-hand corner. If you squint your eyes and look in the trees, you can see a woman in a blue dress holding a drawn bow.

* * *

Amanda's house was the kind I'd always wanted to live in. Lace curtains over the gabled windows, handmade rugs on hardwood floors, soft floral chairs and dark red cherry furniture polished to a gleam.

"You like it?" Amanda said, throwing her coat onto the brass coat stand. "I'll trade you. You live in my house and I'll live in yours."

"I'd kill to live here," I said.

Amanda scratched her head and looked at the living room as if it were a dump. "I'd kill to get out."

I followed her up the stairs to a large, airy room done in pale pink and white. I squealed, I really did, when I saw her canopied bed. Amanda wore a pained expression.

"Isn't it revolting?"

"I love it!"

"You do?"

".It's gorgeous!"

She tossed her backpack into a corner chair. I flopped down on the bed. Amanda had tacked a large poster to the underside of her canopy—a naked man with a whip coming out of his butt like a tail.

"It's the only place Mother let me put it," she explained. "Cute, huh?"

Downstairs, a bass guitar thumped. A man shrieked some words, but I couldn't make them out. Another guitar screeched, then a heavy, pulsating drumbeat vibrated the floor, then it stopped.

"Matthew," Amanda said.

"Matthew?"

"My brother."

Amanda's mother called us to dinner. Matthew was already heading out the door, wearing a kilt and white body makeup. His hair was dyed black and stood up like the spikes on a blowfish. When his mother wasn't looking, he snatched a tiny butterknife with a pearl handle and put it down his kilt. He saw me watching him and winked as he left.

"So where do your real parents come from?" Amanda's mother said, pouring more wine into cut crystal glasses.

There were only the four of us. We sat close together at one end of a long table. My face flushed. I was feeling tipsy.

"Africa," I said.

Amanda's mother raised an elegant eyebrow.

"They were killed in an uprising."

She still looked disbelieving.

"They were missionaries," I added. I took a deep drink. "Doctors."

"You don't say."

"Mother," Amanda said. "Leave her alone."

We were silent as the maid brought in a large white ceramic tureen. As she lifted the lid, the sweet, familiar smell of venison filled the room. I stared at my plate after she placed it in front of me.

"Use the fork on the outside, dear," Amanda's mother said helpfully.

But I was down by the lake. Mama was so proud of me. "Now you're a woman," she said. She handed me the heart after she wiped the blood onto my cheeks with her knife. I held it, not knowing what to do. It was warm as a kitten.

"I think you'd better eat something," Amanda said.

"Maybe we should take that glass, dear."

The water in the lake was cool and dark and flat as glass. The bones sank to the bottom after we'd sucked the marrow. Mama's wet hair was flattened to her skull. She pried a tooth from the moose and gave it to me. I used to wear it around my neck.

"I'm afraid," I said. "She has a pattern, even if no one else can see it."

"Your stew is getting cold," Amanda's mother said.

The coppery taste of raw blood filled my mouth. "I will not be her," I said. "I will break the pattern."

Then I sprayed sour red wine across the crisp handwoven tablecloth that had been handed down to Amanda's mother from her mother and her mother's mother before that.

After a long, shimmering silence, Amanda's mother said, "I have a Persian carpet in the living room. Perhaps you'd like to shit on it." Then she stood, put her napkin on the table and left.

"Lisa," Amanda said, clapping her hand on my shoulder, "you can come over for dinner anytime you want."

*   *   *

Mama loved to camp in the summer. She would wake me early and we'd sit outside our tent and listen. My favourite place was in Banff. We camped by a turquoise lake. Mama made bacon and eggs and pancakes over a small fire. Everything tasted delicious. When we were in Banff, Mama was happy. She whistled all the time, even when she was going to the bathroom. Her cheeks were apple red and dimpled up when she smiled. We hiked for hours, seeing other people only from a distance.

"Imagine there's no one else on earth," she said once as she closed her eyes and opened her arms to embrace the mountains. "Oh, just imagine it."

When we broke camp, we'd travel until Mama felt the need to

stop and settle down for a while. Then we would rent an apartment, Mama would find work and I would go to school. I hated that part of it. I was always behind. I never knew anybody and just as I started to make friends, Mama would decide it was time to leave. There was no arguing with her. The few times I tried, she gave me this look, strange and distant.

I was eleven when we went through the Badlands of Alberta and while I was dozing in the back, the car hit a bump and Mama's scrapbook fell out of her backpack.

I opened it. I was on the second page when Mama slammed on the brakes, reached back and slapped me.

"Didn't I tell you never to touch that? Didn't I? Give it to me now. Now, before you're in even bigger trouble."

Mama used the scrapbook to start our fire that night, but it was too late. I had seen the clippings, I had seen the headlines and I was beginning to remember.

That night I dreamed of Aunt Genna showering in blood. Mama held me until I stopped trembling.

"Rock of ages, cleft for me," Mama sang softly, as she cradled me back and forth. "Let me hide myself in thee."

I closed my eyes and pretended to sleep. Mama squeezed herself into the sleeping bag with me and zipped us up. I waited for her to say something about the scrapbook. As the night crawled by, I became afraid that she would never mention it, that I would wait and wait for something to happen. The waiting would be worse, far worse, than anything Mama could do to me.

* * *

Amanda and Matthew had a game called Take It. The first time I played, we were behind a black van in the school parking lot. They stood beside me as I rubbed a patch of skin on my calf with sandpaper until I started to bleed. The trick of this game is to be extremely high or just not to give a shit.

Amanda squeezed lemon juice onto my calf. I looked straight into her eyes. "Thank you," I said.

Matthew pulled a glue stick out of his schoolbag and smeared it on my calf. "Thank you," I said.

Back to Amanda, who had been poking around in the bald patch of earth by the parking lot and had come back with a hairy spider as large as a quarter. It wriggled in her hands. *Fuck, I thought. Oh, fuck.*

She tilted her hands toward my calf. The spider struggled against falling, its long, thin legs scrabbling against her palm, trying to grab something.

Long before it touched me, I knew I'd lost. I yanked my leg back so that the spider tickled the inside of my leg as it fell, missing the mess on my calf completely. I brought my foot up and squashed it before anyone thought of picking it up again.

*   *   *

When I was twelve, I took the Polaroid picture Officer Wilkenson had given me to a police station in Vancouver.

In the picture, Aunt Genna and Officer Wilkenson are both blurs, but there is a little brown-haired girl in the foreground clutching a broom handle and squinting into the camera.

I showed the Polaroid to a man behind a desk. "That's my Aunt Genna," I said. "My Mama killed her, but she's not in the picture."

He glanced at the picture, then at me. "We're very busy," he said. "Sit down." He waved me toward a chair. "Crazies," he muttered as I turned away. "All day long I got nuts walking in off the street."

A policewoman took me to another room, where a grave-looking man in a navy blue suit asked a lot of questions. He had a flat, nasal voice.

"So this is you, right? And you say this is Officer Wilkenson?"

He made a few calls. It all took a long time, but he was

getting more and more excited. Then someone else came in and they made me say it all over again.

"I already told you. That's Aunt Genna. Yes," I said, "that's the officer. And that's me."

"Holy smokaroonies," said the navy blue suit. "We've got her."

*   *   *

The third time I tried to commit suicide, I found out where Paul kept his small automatic at work. It was supposed to be protection against robbers, but it wasn't loaded and I had a hard time finding the ammunition. When he was busy with an order, I put the gun in my purse.

This time I was going to get it right.

I remember it was a Wednesday. The sky was clear and there was no moon. I didn't want to mess up Paul and Janet's house, so I was going to do it at the Lookout Point, where I could watch the waves and listen to the ocean.

I left no note. Couldn't think of anything to say, really. Nothing I could explain. There was already a queer deadness to my body as I walked up the road, trying to hitch a ride. This was the last time.

Cars passed me. I didn't care. I was willing to be benevolent. They didn't know. How ironic, I thought, when Matthew pulled over and powered down his windows.

"Where to?"

"You going anywhere near Lookout?"

"I am now."

I opened the door and got in. He was surprisingly low-key for Matthew. He had on a purple muscle shirt and black studded shorts.

"Going to a party?"

"Yeah," I said. "Me and a few old friends."

Something British was on the radio. We drove, not saying anything until we came to the turnoff.

"You were supposed to go left," I said.

Matthew said nothing.

"We're going the wrong way," I said.

"Yeah?"

"Yeah. Lookout's that way."

"Yeah?"

"Matthew, quit fucking around."

"Ooh. Nasty language."

"Matthew, stop the car."

"Scared?"

"Shitting my pants. Pull over."

"You know," he said casually, "I could do anything to you out here and no one would ever know."

"I think you'd better stop the car before we both do something we might regret."

"Are you scared now?"

"Pull the car over, Matthew."

"Babe, call me Matt."

"You are making a big mistake," I said.

"Shitting my pants," he said.

I unbuttoned my purse. Felt around until the smooth handle of the gun slid into my palm. The deadness was gone now and I felt electrified. Every nerve in my body sang.

Matthew opened his mouth, but I shut him up, slowly leveling the gun at his stomach.

"You could try to slap this out of my hand, but I'd probably end up blowing your nuts off. Do you know what dum-dum bullets are, asshole?"

He nodded, his eyes fixed on the windshield.

"Didn't I tell you to stop the car?" I clicked off the safety. Matthew pulled over to the embankment. The radio played "Mr. Sandman." A semi rumbled past, throwing up dust that blew around us like a faint fog.

He lifted his finger and put it in the barrel of the gun.

"Bang," he said.

Mama would never have hesitated. She'd have enjoyed killing him.

I had waited too long. Matthew popped his finger out of the barrel. I put the gun back in my purse. He closed his eyes, rested his head on the steering wheel. The horn let out a long wail.

I can't kill, I decided then. That is the difference. I can betray, but I can't kill. Mama would say betrayal is worse.

*   *   *

A long time ago in Bended River, Manitoba, six people were reported missing:

Daniel Smenderson, 32,	last seen going out to the nearby 7-Eleven for cigarettes
Angela Iyttenier, 18,	hitchhiking
Geraldine Aksword, 89,	on her way to a curling match
Joseph Rykman, 45,	taking a lunch break at the construction site where he worked
Peter Brendenhaust, 56,	from the St. Paul Mission for the Homeless
Calvin Colnier, 62,	also from the St. Paul Mission

*   *   *

After a snowstorm cut off power to three different subsections near Bended River, a police officer, investigating complaints of a foul smell, went to 978 West Junction Road. A little girl greeted him at the door in her nightgown. The house was hot. He could smell wood smoke from the fireplace in the living room. Chopped wood was piled to the ceiling. As he stomped the snow off his boots, he asked if her parents were home. She said her daddy was in the basement.

"Where's your mommy?" he asked.

"Gone," she said.

"How long have you been here on your own?"

She didn't answer.

"Do you know where your mommy went?" he asked.

"A-hunting we will go," the little girl sang. "A-hunting we will go. Heigh-ho the derry-oh, a-hunting we will go."

He took her hand, but she wouldn't go down to the basement with him.

"Mama says it's bad."

"How come?"

"Daddy's down there."

As he opened the door, the reek grew stronger. Covering his mouth with a handkerchief, he took a deep breath and flicked the light switch, but it didn't work. He went back to the his car, radioed for backup and was refused. The other officer on the Bended River police force was on lunch break. So he got his flashlight, then descended.

And found nothing. The smell seemed to be coming from everywhere. Nauseated, he called out, asking if anyone was down there.

The basement had neatly tiled floors. Everything sparkled under the flashlight's beam. Faintly, beneath the overpowering stench, he could smell something antiseptic, like the hospitals used. There was a large, thick butcher's block with a marble counter against the wall in the centre room.

"It smelled something like rotten steaks," he told friends later. "But more like the smell my wife gets when she has her period."

There were only three rooms in the basement. A bathroom, a storeroom and the centre room with the marble counter. After checking them all twice, he noticed that the butcher's block was hinged. He heaved and strained but couldn't lift it. His fingers, though, felt a small button on one of the drawers. What did he have to lose? He pressed it.

The countertop popped up an inch. He tried to move it again and managed to slide it open. Beneath the butcher's block was a freezer. It was making no sound, no humming or purring. It was dead. The stench intensified and he thought he was going to faint.

He reached down and lifted the lid. For a moment, the skinned carcasses inside the freezer looked to him like deer or calves. Then he saw the arms and legs, sealed in extra-large plastic bags piled high.

Three days later, Moreen Lisa Rutford was charged with seven counts of murder. The bodies were identified only with difficulty, as they had no heads or fingers and Moreen refused to cooperate. The easiest to identify was David Jonah Rutford, Moreen's husband, who was missing only his heart.

*   *   *

Death should have a handmaiden: her pale, pale skin should be crossed with scars. Her hair should be light brown with blond streaks. Maybe her dress should only be splattered artistically with blood, like the well-placed smudge of dirt on a movie heroine's face after she's battled the bad guys and saved the world. Maybe her dress should be turquoise.

She should walk beside a dark, flat lake.

In the morning, with rain hissing and rippling the lake's grey surface, a moose should rise slowly from the water, its eyes blind, its mouth dripping mud and whispering secrets.

She should raise a shotgun and kill it.

*   *   *

Mama wore her best dress to go calling. She sat me at the kitchen table and we ate pizza, Hawaiian, my favourite. She was cheerful that morning and I was happy because Daddy was gone, so they hadn't argued. The house, for once, was quiet and peaceful.

She said, "I'm going to have to leave you alone for a bit, honey. Can you take care of yourself? Just for a little while?"

I nodded. "Yup."

"I made you some lunch. And some dinner, just in case I take too long. You know how to pour cereal, don't you?"

"Yup."

"Don't let anyone in," she said. "Don't go out. You just watch TV and Mama will be back before you know it. I got you some comics."

"Yay!" I said.

And I never saw her again until she came to get me at Aunt Genna's.

She kissed me all over my face and gave me a big hug before she left. Then she hefted her backpack onto one shoulder and pulled her baseball cap low over her face. I watched her bounce down the walkway to the car, wave once and drive away, smiling and happy and lethal.

Dispatch

Madeleine Thien

THE WAY YOU IMAGINE IT, THE CAR IS SPEEDING ON THE HIGHWAY. Over Confederation Bridge, street lamps flashing by. It's early spring and the water below, still partially frozen, shines like a clouded mirror. You saw this bridge on a postage stamp once. It is thirteen kilometres, made of concrete, and it is not straight. It curves right and left so that no one will fall asleep at the wheel. In the morning sunshine, the concrete is blindingly white.

"Here we go," Heather, the driver, says. She has a calm, collected voice.

Charlotte—you saw a picture of her once, dark-brown hair tied in a low ponytail—has her feet propped up against the dashboard. Her toenails are lacquered a deep-sea blue. In the back seat, Jean leans forward, nodding appreciatively at the coastal landscape. The earth is red, the way they imagined it would be. It is rolling and the colours segue together, red and coffee brown and deep green. A flower garden on a hill shapes the words, WELCOME TO NEW BRUNSWICK.

Beside the road there are cows standing in a circle, heads together, like football players in a huddle. Charlotte points through the windshield at them. "Strange sight," she says. Her words get lost under the radio and the engine accelerating, but the other two nod and laugh. They wave to the cows. The car is shooting down the highway, trailing over the yellow line and back again, down to a curve in the stretch of road where they slip out of sight.

*   *   *

This country is a mystery to you. The farthest east you have been is Banff, Alberta. To imagine these three women, then, Charlotte and Heather and Jean, you have to make everything up as you go. Take Atlantic Canada, for instance. You remember postcards of white clapboard churches, high steeples glinting in the sun. You've never met Charlotte, but you picture yourself with the three of them, driving by, snapping pictures. Along winding dirt roads, they chance upon coastal towns, lobster boats bobbing on the water. Or else abandoned canneries, paint bleached and peeling, the wood still smelling like the sea.

Instead of working, you daydream or sit cross-legged on the couch, roaming the television channels. For you, news is a staple food. There's a story about a freighter that sprang a leak crossing the Atlantic Ocean. Thousands of boxes fell into the water. Months later, the cargo—a load of bathtub toys—washes up on the shoreline. Children and adults comb the beach. "I am six and three-quarters years old," one boy tells the cameras proudly. "I have collected fifty-three rubber ducks." He smiles, his pockets and hands overflowing with yellow.

You're writing a book about glass, the millions of glass fishing floats that are travelling across the Pacific Ocean. They come in all shapes, rolling pins, Easter eggs, perfect spheres. And the colours, cranberry, emerald, cobalt blue. In North America, these glass floats wash up in the hundreds. Decades ago, boys and girls ran to gather them in, the buoys shimmering at their feet. They sold them for pocket money. Now, the floats are harder to come by. In the wake of storms, collectors pace the beach. Every so often, a rare one appears. Recently, on Christmas morning, a man and his granddaughter came across a solid black orb. Shine it as he did, the glass float remained dark as a bowling ball. The float has no special markings and, to date, its origins are unknown.

For hours, you stare at the computer screen, thinking about the load of bathtub toys. You have far too much time on your hands. Sometimes a thought settles in your mind like a stray hair and refuses to leave. Like now, you remember your husband coming in after a jog in the rain. He went straight into the bathroom. When you heard the sound of water drumming against the bathtub, you snuck inside, steam and hot air hitting your lungs. For a full minute, you watched your husband shower, his back to you. The skin on your face broke into a sweat. You watched his body, the runner's muscles, the tendons. You reached your hand out and placed it flat against his spine, where the vertebrae curved into sacrum. He didn't even startle.

You think now that he always knew you were there. You think of the million ways he could have read this gesture. But what did you mean, putting your hand out? Perhaps you only wanted to surprise him. Perhaps you only wanted to see if through the steam and heat he was truly there, or just a figment of your imagination.

*   *   *

Sometimes when they're driving, no one wants to stop. Like they're married to the highway, the exit signs flashing past. They're thousands of exits away from Vancouver.

It's food that lures them off the road. A Tim Hortons at the side of the highway, beckoning. You watch them giggle into a booth, Styrofoam cups of coffee balanced in their trembling, stir-crazy fingers. The first half-dozen doughnuts go just like that. Heather lines up for more. "Get the fritters," Jean says, laughing, her voice shrill in the doughnut shop. "I just love those fritters." Heather buys a dozen. They're sugar-crazed by the end of it, strung out on the sidewalk in front, their legs stretched in front of them.

At night, the three of them pile into a double bed. "I've forgotten what the rest of my life is like," Heather says. They've each written up a handful of postcards, but have yet to send them off.

Charlotte lies back on her pillow. Her hair has come loose from its elastic band and it floats down beside her. "Don't you ever wonder what it would be like not to go back?"

"If I had a million dollars," Heather says.

"Don't you ever think, though, overland, we could drive to Chile. If we just started going in a different direction. Instead of going west, we could be in Chile."

The next morning they continue west and no one complains. Outside Thunder Bay, they pull over at the statue of Terry Fox. Charlotte sits down on the stone steps and cries. She can't stop. "It's the fatigue," she tells them, struggling to catch her breath. "God, I'm tired of sleeping in motel rooms every night. Let's pull out the tents and camp. To hell with indoor plumbing. Can't we do that?" The tears are streaming down her face, mascara thick on her cheeks.

Later on, in the dark of their tent, she tells them how she remembers the day he died. When she describes it—how she stood at her elementary school in a jogging suit, listening to the announcement on the radio, watching the flag lowered to half-mast—she feels her life coming back to her. Bits and pieces she thought were long forgotten. Before that moment, she was too young to fully understand that death could happen. But then the young man on the television, the one with the curly hair and the grimace, he died and it broke her heart.

* * *

Your husband has the body and soul of a long-distance runner. He is a long-haul kind of man. Even asleep, he has that tenacity. At a moment's notice, he'll be up again, stretched and ready. Unlike you. When you lie down, you doubt your ability to up yourself again. You are the Sloppy Joe of women. You watch TV lying on the couch, you read in bed, curled up on one side. Sometimes, when the lights are out, you drag your computer into bed with you. While your husband snores, you write about the woman who owned four thousand glass floats. An arsonist torched the building she lived in. The apartment collapsed but, miraculously, no one was killed. The morning after, passersby came and picked the surviving balls from the rubble—black and ashy and melted down.

At night, in the glow of the screen, you type to the up, down of your husband's breathing. It's difficult to look at him in these moments. His face is so open, so slack-jawed, vulnerable and alone. Both of you have always been solitary people. Like big cedars, your husband says, bulky and thick, growing wider year by year. You are charmed by your husband's metaphors, the quiet simplicity of them.

Your husband has never been unfaithful to you. But only a few months ago, you found the letter he had written to Charlotte. They had grown up together and, in the letter, he confessed that he loved her. Your husband left the letter, and her reply, face up on the kitchen table. You imagine the instant he realized, standing on the warehouse floor, broom in one hand. He tried to call you, but you just stood there, letting the telephone ring and ring. When you read his confession on that piece of looseleaf, your husband's perfect script stunned you. You thought of his face, his brown eyes and the receding slope of his hairline, the way he sat at the kitchen table reading the paper, frowning, his lips moving silently to read the words.

The woman, Charlotte, had written back. She had told him to pull himself together. She'd returned his letter, telling him that their friendship would never recover. And then he left both letters on the kitchen table. Not maliciously. You refuse to believe he did it maliciously. Your husband is not that kind of man. He is the kind of person who honours privacy, who can carry a secret until the end. Shell-shocked and hurt, he must have forgotten everything.

You've imagined it perfectly. Before he left for work, he took both letters and laid them on the kitchen table. He read them over and over. He'd offered to leave his marriage for her, but she had turned him down flat. Pull yourself together. He made a pot of coffee and poured himself a cup. He put on his shoes, then his jacket. The envelope was on the counter. He folded it up and tucked it in his pocket. Hours later, while his mind wandered back and forth, he pulled it out, only to discover the envelope was empty. The letters were still face up on the kitchen table, where his wife, sleep-creased and hungry, had found them. He called, but the phone just rang and rang.

That night, you went out and didn't come home. You climbed on a bus and crossed the city, crying intermittently into the sleeve of your coat. At a twenty-four-hour diner, you ordered a hamburger and fries and sat there until dawn, when the early risers started showing up for breakfast. You read the paper from the night before and then the paper from that day, cover to cover, and then you walked home, through the tree-lined streets and the slow muscle of traffic heading downtown. At home, your husband was already gone. You turned on the TV, then you lay down in bed and slept for hours.

You've pictured it from beginning to end, upside and down, in every direction. You've pictured it until it's made you sick and dizzy. Your husband has never been unfaithful to you, but something in your life is loose now. A pin is undone. When he came home and lay down beside you, you told him, "We'll work things out," and he, ashen-faced, nodded.

His skin was pale in the white sheets and you hovered above him, kissing his skin, trying not to miss anything. You have never been unfaithful. That's what you were thinking every time you kissed him. Look at me, you thought. I have never been unfaithful, and here I am, kissing you. You looked straight at him. Your husband's heart was broken and it wasn't you who did it. That's what you thought, when he pushed his face against your chest, his body taut and grieving.

* * *

There's a memory in your mind that you can't get rid of. The two of you in bed, lying next to one another like fish on the shore, watching images of Angola. Out on Oak Street there's the white noise of traffic, endlessly coming. Catastrophe. Your husband said that line again, "Too many cameras and not enough food," and the two of you watched a woman weep. She wiped her eyes in her dirty handkerchief. And you, on the other side of the world, on another planet, watched soundlessly.

Instead of writing your book, you are watching the midday news. Like some kind of teenage kid, you're lying on the couch, the remote cradled on your stomach, hand in the popcorn. The world is going to hell in a handbasket. You think this, but never say it aloud because it's terrible to be so cynical. But look at the world. While your city works its nine-to-five, bombs detonate, planes crash, accidents happen. You sound like your mother. While your marriage stutters on, revolutions rise and fall, blooming on the midday news like some kind of summer flower. There's dinner to be made. Lately you have discovered your weak heart. Instead of sitting at the kitchen table writing your book, you're watching flood waters in Central America, you're watching Dili, people in trucks with rifles strung on their arms. You've never even heard a shot fired. You know you think about your marriage far too much. You know that, given the chance, you will sit all day on your couch like this, watch what happens in another country. There is a woman clinging to a rooftop. A flood in Mozambique. A lack of supplies, everything coming too late. By morning, the water may rise over the spot where she sits. You want to get on a plane. You who have always wanted to please people, you want to sandbag and work. You know what you think of this woman on the rooftop—she did nothing to deserve this. But what would she think of you? She would look at you with disbelieving eyes. She would look at you with only the faintest expression of pity.

*   *   *

Through small-town Ontario, the three women snap photos of water towers. While you watch from the background, Charlotte climbs through the passenger window, her body swaying reck-lessly out. When she ducks back in, her hair is wild, blown frizzy around her head. She smiles a lopsided grin.

Past hockey arenas and high-steepled churches, blue sky over dry fields, they're singing along to the radio. Looking forward to night, when they will pitch their tent under cover of stars, break out the beer bottles that clank in the trunk. They can see them-selves dancing carelessly in the hot evening. Charlotte, drunk and spinning, saying, "Girls, I've known you all my life. What would I do without you, girls?" How bittersweet it is, when she says that. How she wonders what it would be like to be nineteen again, or twenty-one. But she'll settle for this, curled up with her friends in front of the fire. When they arrive in Vancouver, her life will return to normal. Heading home to Saskatoon again, catch-ing up on all the time she's missed.

*   *   *

You're afraid of why it comes to you, clear as a picture. You tell yourself you're bound to Charlotte, but what you're afraid of is this: instead of getting on with your life, you're following her. To make sure that she's gone. To chase her out of your life. In all these vivid imaginings, you are the spectator, the watcher, the one who refuses to leave until the last act. You move through your emotions, anger settling on you like some forgotten weight. It makes you watch until the end.

So badly, you want to be the person who grieves for her. Not the envious one, the one whose heart has toughened up. You're standing on the road. There's even a space for you. A bus stop, of sorts, lit up with harsh fluorescent lights. You never stray from it. No matter what, come hell or high water, come death or disease, you'll stand there watching it all unfold.

*   *   *

When you see the accident, you know it must have happened a hundred times before. The stretch of highway heading to Lloydminster, straight as an arrow. Wide open, it tricks the driver into believing she's awake.

You almost convince yourself you're there, that it's you, semi-conscious in the driver's seat: exactly when you realize that the car is out of control, that it cannot be undone, exactly when, you're not sure. Even the impact seems part of your dream. It knocks you out. But not before you see Charlotte, sitting beside you, the slow-motion crumbling of the passenger side. Her sleeping body, belted in, thrown sideways. She's in your lap, slouched awkwardly against your body. You know you're going under. The car. You have the sensation the car is closing in. Then you don't even know it, you're under, the three of you in your seats.

Later on, Heather can only say, "We were speeding and the car slipped out of control." Hundred and forty kilometres on a flat stretch of highway. Over the ditch and straight for a tree on the border of a farmhouse.

When the crash comes, this is what you see: lights flashing on all around; houses you couldn't see for the dark snapping to life; all these people, half-dressed, hurrying out into road, running in the dewy grass.

The car is wrapped around the tree, the interior light miraculously blinking.

* * *

You don't want to be lovesick. You dream yourself sitting in an orange rocking chair, a steaming cup of coffee resting on the arm, the chair tipping back and forth and nothing spills. As if you could do that. Keep moving and the tiny thing you balance, the thing that threatens, stays secure. You love your husband, love him in a way that makes you heartsick. You think it is irrational to feel this way, to be so overwhelmed by the small tragedies of your life when all around you there are images of men and women and children. In Dili there are the ones who never ran away to hide in the mountains. You pray for them in the best way you know how. You picture them standing on the street on a summer day, dust against their feet. You picture them safe. Before you know it, your hands are clasped in front of your face. It takes you aback, the way you sit there, shocked and unhappy.

Hardly a month passed between the time you found the letters and the night the accident happened. In the morning, your husband heard the news by phone. He stayed on the phone all morning, calling one person then another. He knew them all, Jean and Heather and Charlotte, childhood friends from Saskatoon. You learned that after the car hit the tree, Jean and Heather stood up and walked away. In shock, Heather started running, straight down the road. An elderly man, still dressed in pyjamas, guided her gently back to the site.

It was Heather who called your husband. "Charlotte was asleep the whole time," she told him. "She never felt a thing."

If your husband grieved, he did the gracious thing and refused to show it. When you asked him how he felt, he held himself together. "I don't know," he said. "It's over."

The expression on his face was closed and you knew better

than to push. You left him alone in the apartment. It's space that he needs and that's what you give him. No confrontation or rehashing of that small betrayal, though each day you tilt between anger and sorrow. You expect his grief, are willing to understand it, even. Still, he refuses to part with it—his private sorrow is not on display for you. It belongs to him alone.

These days, he spends hours reading the paper. But you can tell that it's only a cover. Like you, he's thinking. Your house is a silent place. The two of you, solicitous but lost in thought, the radio constantly murmuring in the living room. And because you believe in protocol, in politeness and respect, you don't ask him and you never mention her name. When you dropped those letters into the trash, you were telling him the terms of your agreement. Don't mention it, you were saying. Pretend it never happened. Both of you like two cedars, side by side and solitary.

You'd never met Charlotte. You worry that it's sick, this fascination with her life. But in the middle of the day, your hands poised over the keyboard, you have a vivid image of her in the passenger seat, asleep and dreaming. Something in you wants to reach your hand out, the way children lay their fingers on the television screen. When the car leaves the road, you want to nudge it back. Point it back on course. Let it not end like this.

Really, you are just a bystander. It's your husband who should be there, standing in the road. You in the background, curious. It's your husband whose emotions run deep, who weeps the way he never did in real life. If this were a picture, you would be a blur in the background.

*   *   *

Saskatchewan is a photo to you, a duotone of blue and gold. Wheat fields bent against the wind or motionless in the heat, a freeze frame. There's a picture of Charlotte when she was sixteen, a lovely girl standing outside of a barn, laughing, dark hair shaking against the blue sky. You have never been to Saskatchewan. Imagine a sky so huge it overwhelms you. Wheat vast as the desert. You picture Charlotte on a dirt road somewhere, a road that cuts through a field. This is the way that you remember her, because between you and your husband, she will always have a kind of immortality.

For a long time you think of her as the kind of person you would like to be. She is a farmer's daughter, a one-time schoolteacher, a bus driver. You think of her as a dreamer. People are drawn to her. They say, "She really knows how to live." Even you, in your make-believe world, are drawn to her. You watch the way her hands move, not gingerly, not tentatively. You hear her voice. It booms through space.

You play a game with her. The kind of game friends play to pass the time. If I was an animal, what kind of animal would I be? You tell her she is an elephant, a tiger, a gazelle. Your husband, she says, is a camel. He is a long-haul kind of man. But what are you? A tern, she says. You do not know what this is. A bird, she says. It flies over the sea. It is swift in flight. You imagine it is the kind of bird that could fly forever. Given the choice, it would never land. You say this is a fault and she laughs. She says you see the negative in everything. She has a smile that fills the room. What kind of person are you? There's some part of you that's glad she's gone. Glad that all those qualities, that smile, that confidence, couldn't save her.

*   *   *

You make a list of all the things you're afraid of: nuclear catastrophe, childbirth, war, a failed marriage. As if there is any equality between these things. You know that writing them out will not make them go away. But the list worries you. You don't want to be selfish. Walking along your Vancouver street, you press a blueberry muffin into the hand of a young man sitting on the sidewalk beside his dog. There's an apple in your coat pocket you're saving for someone else.

At home, you and your husband lie beside each other in bed, sunlight streaking through the blinds. You lie motionless like people in shock. A part of you knows that you're doing everything wrong. You know it, but still, you're sitting at the kitchen table each day, working hard. While researching Japanese glass floats, you come across the ama—divers in Japan's coral reefs who, with neither wetsuits nor oxygen masks, search the water for abalone. For up to two minutes at a time, these women hold their breath underwater. Their lung capacity astonishes you. Some of the ama are as old as sixty. Imagine them dotting the water, chests bursting for air, going on about their daily work.

*   *   *

One night, when neither of you can sleep, you take a late-night walk together. Through sidewalks coated with autumn leaves, you walk hand-in-hand. It is three in the morning and the streets are empty. A car turning the corner sweeps its lights across you, then disappears. You can hear it travelling away from you, you listen until the sound evaporates. At one point, in a gesture that reminds you of children, your husband swings your hand back and forth, and your joined arms move lightly between you.

The road you are following goes uphill, ending in a circle of mansions. There is a small green park in the centre and this is where you and your husband stop, turning slowly, examining the houses, trying to guess if the mansions are really abandoned as they appear. Nothing stirs. Out here, in this dark patch of land, it's easy to believe that only you and he exist. In the quiet, your husband hums softly, a tune you can't identify. He catches your eye and stops abruptly. You look at him with so much grief and anger, it surprises you both, what you can no longer withhold.

He tells you that it is unforgivable, what he has done. But he cannot go back and he does not know how to change it.

Something in your body collapses. It just gives way. Maybe it is the expression on your husband's face, telling you that there is no longer any way out. You tell your husband you've been seeing strange things, imagining cities you've never visited, people you've never met. You say, "I cannot go on like this anymore," and your own words surprise you, the sad certainty of them.

He paces behind you, nodding his head, then begins walking the perimeter of the park. As he walks away from you, your husband raises his voice, as if he believes that no one can hear him. Perhaps he no longer cares if anyone does. He tells you more than you can bear to hear. He says that when he read Charlotte's letter, he was devastated. He wished her so far away that he would never see her again. He talks and he cannot stop. He says he is afraid of being alone, afraid of making terrible mistakes. He is ashamed of being afraid.

This is what you wanted, finally. Here is his private grief, laid out in view of the world. But your chest is bursting with sadness. You are not the only ones affected. There is still that woman who haunts you. What will she think of all your efforts, your tossing, your fear and guilt? How long will she remain with you?

Out front, the houses are still. You stand on your side of the park, watching for signs of movement, expecting the lights to come on, expecting people to come hurrying into the road.

In the end, you know that the two of you will pick yourselves up, you will walk home together, not because it is expected or even because it is right. But because you are both asking to do this, in your own ways, because you have come this far together.

For a long time you stand this way, the two of you hunched in the grass. In your mind's eye there are people all around the world turning, diving, coming up for air. Your husband and you in this quiet circle. He crouches down to the ground, face in his hands. There is Charlotte, asleep and dreaming in a car moving through the Prairies. Your husband comes to his feet and looks for you, through the dark and the trees. One perilous crossing after another.

Associated Press

Nancy Lee

THAT BOY WORKS AS A PHOTOGRAPHER FOR THE ASSOCIATED PRESS.
He is at home in a suite at the Marriott Hotel in a city whose
name sounds like machine gun fire. Through e-mail he sends you
photos of human rights violations: the scarred backs of Chinese
women, a severed hand at the side of the road, a secret mass
grave. You send him photos of local atrocities: your father's retirement cake in the shape of breasts, your aunt's feet after bunion
surgery.

That boy is more social conscience than you can bear. His love
letters are fervent diatribes, global history lessons. He woos you
with the warm blood of political uprising, the testimonials of
broken refugees. Devotion disguised as the pain of strangers,
something coded and hidden in newspaper clippings, wire service
announcements. When he does think to mention the small of your
back, the smell of your skin, his words are few and precious, grains
of rice, drops of clean water.

In your last message, you wrote: *A terrible thing has happened here,
too. I've been selected for jury duty. A man has killed prostitutes and buried them
in his backyard. There will be crime scene photos.*

You sent that message three days ago. You have not heard
from him in five weeks, since he responded to the retirement
cake photo with a curt "ha, ha." You know he isn't dead; he

checks in with a supervisor at the AP every day. You want to call it irresponsible, selfish, but while he risks his life to capture what is important and unknown, you live in a two-bedroom condominium with heated tile floors. Everything he does seems forgivable.

*   *   *

There are no new messages on the server.

*   *   *

This boy, with his high-rise view suite, black leather furniture and state-of-the-art home theatre system is seducing you the old-fashioned way.

You had chosen the perfect outfit for court, a tailored black suit, a steel-grey blouse, serious but impartial. Your makeup was decidedly neutral. The air in the courtroom was warm and over-used. The lawyers shuffled papers as the accused was led to his seat. He was older than you had expected, clean-scrubbed, almost bald, dough-faced, with small eyes that receded like pressed raisins. The judge entered; you stood, then sat. Then, after some mumbled statements by the prosecutor and nods from the defence counsel, the judge looked over his glasses and thanked you for your time. You were confused. The lawyers shook hands amicably, clapping each other on the elbow. The defendant, cuffed and shackled, played with his fingers, unfazed. You looked to this boy, the well-dressed stereo salesman beside you. He was softened by your alarm, tried to reassure you. "It's a little known fact that most criminal cases are settled before lunch."

Outside the jury room, you stalled, studied the geometric patterns in the carpet, wondered about sneaking into another trial. You imagined opening statements, objections, false testimony, blood-stained evidence. This boy felt responsible for you, you could tell. As he stretched into his raincoat, he hovered, as if waiting to see how long you would stay. When no one else was left, he offered to walk you to your car, then at your car, to buy you lunch. Lunch stretched out past dark and now you are in his apartment.

South African Chardonnay in hand-blown glasses, Nina Simone in quadraphonic sound. You let your head loll back against the sofa, indulge in the ease of its smooth surface. You watch him lounge in his chair, polished black hide pulled tight over a chrome skeleton. This boy wears expensive cologne, gets his hair cut before he really needs to, tries clothes on in a change room before buying them. He smiles in a way that shows you he will never really look old. You know everything about him. You tell yourself he isn't your type; you don't like dark-haired men, men with skin so clean-looking you suspect they lack scent or heat.

He reaches under the coffee table and pulls out a box. "Do you like trivia?" he asks.

You smile despite yourself. "Yes."

He hands you a stack of cards. "We'll have a contest. First one to get ten in a row, wins."

The idea of competing engages you; you could use a victory, even a small one. You shuffle the cards in your hands. "Wins what?"

He smiles. "We'll decide that after."

You reach for your wineglass.

He turns over the top card in his deck. "What is the capital of Indonesia?"

You try to swallow before you laugh and end up coughing. Chardonnay rises up into your nasal cavity. The alcohol burns. You snort, then start to giggle uncontrollably. He laughs with you, his eyes curious. You wave your hands in front of you, shake your head, try to calm yourself. "Boy," he says, "you must really know this one." This makes you laugh harder. You curl over yourself, your hand at your stomach. The moment you feel tears in your eyes, you know you will let yourself lose this game, sleep with this boy.

*   *   *

There are no new messages on the server.

*   *   *

Months of absence made that boy a perfect lover. Distance times longing times uncertainty. You had both learned that love at its best was slow and drawn out, stretched thin for sadness to show through. Each moment you spent together held within itself a nagging seed, a small, hard reminder of what you would inevitably lose. The sensation of your fingertips touching, life vibrating from one skin to another, seemed at the same time an immeasurable gift, an unbearable injustice. Sometimes it took you days to undress each other.

Your bodies moved on each other with calculated stealth, invasion, capture and surrender. You lingered wherever the territory seemed foreign, the damp skin behind his knees, the pale insides of his wrists. He unfolded you like a map. Searched for subtle changes in the landscape, tan lines, new body lotion, a scratch from the neighbour's cat. Your couplings remained wordless. No room between you for declarations, he insisted, only understanding. The entire vocabulary of common love was inappropriate for what you had together. When you felt those words rising inside you, you held them back like stale breath. Sometimes they managed to leak out, as mewing when you cried, as gasps when you were ecstatic.

You were someone else when that boy was in town. You took vacation time from your job at the library and forgot that you worked there. You attended political talks and rallies, watched slide shows of world suffering. Your legs and underarms were waxed. Your hair was trimmed and highlighted in a way that made you look, you thought, more optimistic, proactive. You read at least two newspapers every day. You went to basketball games, watched him lean forward in his seat and nod intently while everyone around you stood and cheered. You listened as he rattled off player stats and conference rankings; you heard him say that this was the one thing he missed about the city. You lay naked in front of his camera, stared into the eye of his lens, tried to project who you were when you were with him, hoped that it would bloom on the paper as something disturbing and spectacular, something from which he would try, but fail, to turn away.

*   *   *

There are no new messages on the server.

*   *   *

This boy wants to tell you he loves you even though you've only spent four nights together; you can tell. But you know by the careful way he makes dinner reservations, by his gracious habit of being on time, that he will wait until you are ready to hear the words, four weeks, maybe six.

The first night he is in your apartment, he cooks dinner in your kitchen. He looks at home, doesn't panic when he can't find turmeric in your cupboard. He interrogates you as he dices and juliennes, his slender hand working your knife into the hearts of vegetables. You dodge his questions. Duck and cover. You are accustomed to listening and thinking carefully, painfully about what has been said; answering has always made you nervous. "Who was your first best friend?" he asks, handing you a slice of jicama. "I don't know," you shrug. He looks at you strangely. You chew; your mind sifts for something engaging, articulate. "What do you think of East Timor?" you ask. He shakes his head. "It's awful. I guess." You nod. He smiles without looking at you, which, you've learned, is the physical cue that he's about to make a joke. "I'll start researching it tomorrow if it's important to you." You pick up a garlic clove and hurl it at his head; it bounces off his temple. He slams the knife down. "OK, that's it." He chases you around the counter until he has you pinned against a wall with your wrists behind you. He presses into you, you press back. He brushes the hair out of your face, moves his open lips to your neck and whispers slowly, "Tell me. The name. Of your first. Best friend."

*   *   *

There are no new messages on the server.

*   *   *

While you are brushing your teeth and he is shaving in the bathroom mirror, this boy asks whose clothing takes up a third of your bedroom closet, whose boxes and equipment fill your hallway storage space. You say they belong to a man, a friend. "What kind of friend?" he asks. "The kind that works overseas," you reply.

You stare at his reflection in the mirror and watch tense lines cut down to his jaw as he rinses his razor under the tap. You are surprised to see that expression on someone else. You've worn it so often, you sometimes slip into it accidentally, catch it reflected in the windows of cars, mirrored elevator walls.

Your own face is slack, as if your muscles have gone to sleep. This, too, is unfamiliar.

He sees your face in the mirror and stops shaving. "What?"

You continue brushing, very slowly as you weigh the pros and cons of saying simply, "Nothing." You slide the toothbrush out of your mouth and spit into the sink. "I know what you're thinking."

He snickers. "What am I thinking?"

You turn and look straight at him, wanting him to know that you are connecting with him, relating to him, not mocking him. "You're telling yourself—leave it alone, leave it alone—over and over again."

He stares at you, shakes his head, throws his razor into the sink and walks out of the bathroom.

* * *

There are no new messages on the server.

* * *

You weren't really interested in that boy until he told you he was leaving town. He was the too casual and tousled blond beside you in a rodeo-bar-turned-trendy-hangout. A going-away party for a fashion reporter, a button-down Ralph Lauren gay friend named Thomas who was, at that moment, riding a sluggish mechanical bull and twirling his suit jacket above his head. You were half tanked and more than half bored. The conversation with "Runs-Hands-Through-Hair," the indigenous nickname you had thought up for him in a desperate effort to keep yourself amused, was stilted and depressing. He wanted to talk about Pinochet. You wanted to talk about why you hated country music, all those lost wives and dogs and trucks. After several attempts at attack, you both capitulated, nodded politely when the other spoke, sipped your drinks in armistice.

After an hour, you cut in on Thomas's account of his latest nineteen-year-old, a Scottish model with a mop of red hair and an endearing Italy-shaped birthmark on his right hip, perfect for Milan. You Euro-kissed him goodbye. Pulled your coat on as you walked to the exit. That boy was standing on the street, finishing a cigarette. He offered to share a taxi.

When he mentioned returning to Mexico, you imagined white sand beaches, blended drinks, cerviche, cheap hotels, burning tequila. You leaned your head against the taxi window, let his voice hum in the background and thought about slipping into a bath, washing away the smell of rodeos and politics. You were surprised when the taxi pulled up to his building, a new brick townhouse near the centre of the city. You had cast him in a less cosmopolitan setting, a low-rent ethnic neighbourhood popular with the college crowd, an old house, a single room. He invited you in for coffee, to look at his photographs. You were curious. You guessed at something *National Geographic*: majestic cliff-scapes, waterfalls, the craggy faces of friendly market vendors. Instead, you found a small, one-legged Mexican boy, shirtless with a bandana around his forehead, kissing the barrel of an automatic rifle. The decapitated bodies of three freedom-fighters at the roadside, their heads snatched as trophies, the hand of one victim making the shape of a gun. An old woman crying out, cradling the body of a young woman whose torso had been blown open by explosives, the brilliant midday sun catching the young woman's wound like an oozing tropical fruit.

He placed a mug of coffee on the table in front of you and nodded at the pictures. "It isn't how most people think of the world."

You nodded, half agreeing with him, half acknowledging the embarrassing truth about yourself: you never really thought of the world. You rarely watched the evening news, only read the entertainment section of the paper. It wasn't that you didn't want to know what was going on, but that you couldn't make sense of it. The world had become too tangled for you to unravel in the half-hour before dinner, coups, rebellions, interventions, peace-keeping. Complex systems to manage hunger and violence and exploitation, but not end it. This is what bothered you most, that there was no conceivable end.

You caught him glancing at his own photographs, his lips pressed tight. You noticed his blond hair was peppered with gray just above his ears, incongruous with his age — which you had noted as you admired the myriad stamps in his passport — thirty-one. He struck you as the kind of person who could age overnight. Perhaps after a long trip, extended time away, he would return and seem worn, closer to expiration, sudden lines on his face, a distance in the way he thought about a question before answering. Was it already happening? You felt unexpectedly sad. Before you could think about what you were doing, you reached out your arm and slipped your hand inside his. He looked to you for just a brief second with a small, private smile. You took a deep breath. With his eyes back on the photos, he squeezed your hand, ribbons of warm muscle.

You sat down together on the couch. He explained each photo, his voice quiet and articulate. He rested his arm on the back of the couch behind your neck, his body inches from yours. He watched you as you looked at his photographs, which made it difficult for you to watch him. You imagined that under his white shirt, his frame was taut, trained. When he smiled, his pale grey eyes warmed the angles of his face and you saw for the first time that his lips were smooth and fleshy, like a boy's.

By three a.m. you had heard all about the Zapatistas and their struggle for independence. You were drawn in by their hidden faces, their deft manoeuvres in the night.

You spent every night together; you called in sick four days in a row. The weekend before he left, you drove together to a bed and breakfast in the mountains. On an eighteenth-century silk brocade divan, in front of a window overlooking a glacier lake, you asked him if you could join him in Mexico. You made it sound casual, like you were planning to go there anyway. And you were, someday. He stared out the window as if on the lake there was something familiar, something he knew he would see at this place. You breathed as slowly and as quietly as you could. His face was relaxed, his mouth turned up slightly at the corners, a half smile. You took that as a good sign. He had been thinking about it, too. His eyes stayed on the lake as he spoke, "This is something I do alone." You turned to look at the lake instead of him. Didn't want him to see the tension in your mouth, your jaw. Didn't want him to read your thoughts.

* * *

There are no new messages on the server.

* * *

You call this boy because you should, because you haven't been completely honest. He arrives with flowers, birds of paradise. You've set the coffee table with two bottles of red wine and two glasses. You sit on opposite ends of the couch. You tell him the entire story from beginning to end. Twice you cry uncontrollably. He says nothing, but nods often, pries the soggy tissues out of your palm and replaces them with fresh ones. Refills the wineglasses before they threaten to empty. You both fall asleep on the couch.

* * *

The next day, you send the following message: I can't compete with all the trouble in the world.

* * *

Seeing this boy as often as you do, you worry about the dense scrub of familiarity, an overgrowth of tender comfort that will lead to apathy, and inevitably, contempt. You know sex is the place where it will germinate, root itself. You are vigilant. You read women's magazines for advice on frequency, intensity, variety: the trick to keeping a relationship hot is to save up your tricks; every third time incorporate something new.

But it is by accident, not during one of your "every third" times, that you strike the mainline to this boy's desire, expose what is raw in him with the slip of your hand. It begins when you undress him one night and jokingly wrap his leather belt around your wrists. He moves on you swiftly, one hand at his zipper. He pushes your arms above your head, draws the belt so tight it bites your skin. Opens your legs with his knees, shifts his weight to one side, works himself past the crotch of your panties. He covers your eyes with his hand, holds you captive until it is over.

Nights later, he turns you naked on your stomach. Traps you between his legs while he loops his belt around your neck, enters you slowly from behind. His body on you and over you again and again. You lose your heartbeat in his rhythm, then feel its return, throbbing in your neck and head as the belt tightens. He curls the tail of the belt around his fist, once, twice. You watch the bedroom wall advance, retreat, as your vision narrows, then brightens. You wonder in a moment of swoon if you will die here, a willing hostage in your own bed. You wonder how many women in the world die this way, blind and tied. He finishes abruptly; the belt goes slack. You watch colours dance on the inside of your eyelids as he kisses your neck, strokes your hair, slides down your body to finish you off.

This is how sex evolves between you. Loving torture. You invest in equipment: blindfolds, restraints. He learns to use a belt so that it stings without breaking the skin. You learn to admire the marks across your back, around your ankles and wrists. There is something divine and surprising in the mercy you show each other afterward. A sincere caretaking that is ciphered into everyday language as you soothe your limbs against the cool of the sheets, fluff pillows for one another, check for any true harm. Something as simple as this boy offering to get out of bed and make coffee, warms you like an unexpected gift.

* * *

You are lying on your side in the predawn morning, lulling between the blue light of your bedroom and a dream about microfiche. The phone rings and you reach for it, bring it to your ear, though ordinarily you would let the machine pick it up at this hour. There is a buzz and a click, then the sound of an open tunnel.

"Tell me you don't have cancer." It is that boy.

"What?" you ask, trying to ground yourself in time, space and context. "What?"

"Cancer."

You sit up. This boy is motionless, far away in sleep, his back to you. You speak softly, your lips close to the receiver. "I don't have cancer."

He sighs. "Thank God. While I was in Aceh I had this awful nightmare that you were dying and not going to tell me." He laughs and it sounds forced. This, you think, is his best effort at being light.

You are silent.

"I'm sorry," he says, "for not writing."

You hear the echo of your own breath in the phone, ragged and quick.

"Aceh's a mess. It's East Timor all over again. Worse. They're making an example of the Acehnese. They're—"

"Do you know what time it is here?" you ask.

"Yes. I'm sorry." He is silent. You hear him tap something in a broken rhythm, his finger or a pencil against a hard surface. He coughs. When he speaks again, he sounds tired. "Is he there?"

"Who?" You swallow to mask your voice.

"I don't know," he laughs, "anyone." The casual tone sounds awkward on him.

You cannot think of where to begin, how to explain, so you just say, "Yes."

The click when that boy hangs up is so quiet, you don't realize he's gone until you hear the hollow hum of air, feel the useless weight of the receiver in your hand.

You slip the phone into its cradle, turn and curl against this boy's back. You brush your foot against the sheet in small circles, a sleep habit left over from childhood. His hand reaches behind for your waist and pulls you close. You hunker down behind his shoulder, hide from the sun, a sliver of light above the windowsill.

*   *   *

You try to separate that boy from your life. The surgery is messy, like something severed in the jungle without anaesthetic. You mistrust your preferences, your habits, wonder which ones you adopted because of him. When did you start preferring americanos to cappuccinos? When did you decide fifty dollars was far too much to pay for dinner? In a grocery store line-up, you dig through your purse for your cheque book. You have already asked yourself if it was his suggestion to buy organic, to skip the cereal aisle and never buy peanut butter or oranges from Florida. Inside your purse, your palm catches the tip of an open lipstick, oily and cold. The checkout girl taps the counter impatiently with a pen. The man behind you mutters. You stare at the deep maroon smear across your hand, a wound without pain. Ask yourself, did I buy that for him? You tell this boy things are busy at the library. You stay late and roam the stacks, searching for topics that might interest you if you were the type to have interests. The history of carousel horses, small engine repair, winter gardening, the complete works of Dorothy Parker, Japanese paper art, the concise dictionary of Eastern mysticism, the songs of Bruce Springsteen, a century of fashion, a hundred and one metalwork ideas, the encyclopedia of Victorian upholstery. You start bringing books home, their weight somehow comforting in your arms. The books pile up on your floor like clumsy pagodas. In many books you find things left behind by previous readers: bus transfers, an unused teabag, shopping lists, candy wrappers, business cards, two fettuccini noodles and once, a fifty-dollar bill folded between two diagrams of origami frogs. And sometimes, shockingly, in the margins of books, doodles, random sketches of geometric shapes or cartoon faces in pencil or pen. Messages scratched into a dirt wall, the impenetrable hieroglyphs of those who came before you, searched for something in this same place.

In a book on kosher cooking you find a piece of paper folded as a bookmark. A list of names: six nuns and two priests. You recognize the list; you carried it yourself for a while. Abominable murders posted on the Internet. You tell yourself now you never really cared about those people; that love and propaganda are not the same thing.

At home, with this boy, you monitor your autonomy at all times. You balk when he buys theatre tickets without consulting you, snap at him when he suggests CDs for your meagre collection. You feel a need to establish definite boundaries, dig a trench in the comforter when you sleep in the same bed at night. You are vigilant; the integrity of the border may no longer be compromised. You sometimes imagine a halo of white chalk around your body as you walk through the apartment. Feel it between your fingertips and this boy's skin when you touch him, something dusty and smooth. He is understanding. Tells you he respects independent women. Wonders aloud if the two of you should move in together. You point to the piles of books on your floor and tell him there is hardly room.

*   *   *

If you had imagined some life for you and that boy, it was not the one you had. If you could do it over, you would be the kind of girl he would want to take with him. You would be stronger or smarter or angrier or harder. You scold yourself for being too yielding, too pliable. You remember his photos of the female Zapatistas, narrow, rigid women in fatigues and bandana masks, their eyes burning points of disobedience. Look in the mirror at your own eyes, vague, watery. Your body, still young but softening, curving gently in and out on itself, womanly. An easy body, a body to come home to.

You've been unusually tired in the mornings and evenings, prone to crying in the afternoon. You decide to join a gym. Start in the class that combines kick-boxing and aerobics. A sinewy man four inches shorter than you shouts in your face as you force your limbs into fierce upper cuts, jabs, hooks. You feel both keenly charged and on the verge of collapse as you duck, dodge and swing, duck, dodge and swing. Sweat gathers in a stream between your shoulder blades; you watch your arms lash out in front of you, tell yourself this is useful. This will come in handy someday.

*   *   *

You join this boy for dinner at a trendy, upscale restaurant, this boy and his friends. You are out of sorts when you arrive, pace the foyer and scratch at the fake gold leaf with your thumbnail until this boy comes out to use the phone. "I was just going to call you," he says, all surprise and relief. "I just got here," you say.

He leads you to the table. Everything in the restaurant is dark red: the carpet, the plush upholstery, the curtains that drip down sides of walls, the walls themselves, reddened with a paint so dark and matte, it sucks away at the room's already dim light.

The friends, three men arranged around a table, are easy to look at, the type who use hair products, wear dry-clean-only clothes. Two of them look a little younger than this boy; the third, older. This boy moves to fill your glass with wine. The older friend stops him, "Give her the good stuff." This boy fills his own glass with the remains of a cheaper Zinfandel, christens your glass with a more expensive Merlot.

The banter is light and energetic. Each friend draws you into alliance—a nod in your direction, a sidelong glance, a more direct, "Am I right?" from the older friend. You trail on the fringe of conversation, swallow your wine in mouthfuls. All the friends are attractive, all the friends are funny and sharp. This generic quality makes you stare at this boy until he is nothing but a blur between two faux finished pillars. You wonder if his friends share the same proclivities in bed. You think that you could probably sleep with any one of these men. Apart from some minor differences, age, hair colour, height, they seem interchangeable. You think that they would also like to sleep with you. At intervals, each one turns from the conversation to smile at you, hold your gaze for as long as he can, create the brief illusion that the two of you are alone. Two of them bump wrists in an attempt to refill your wineglass. They all laugh at your quips, mistake your apathy for keen wit. The message is clear, "If it doesn't work out for you two, remember us, we're just as good."

You peruse the menu. One of the younger ones leans over to you, "The décor in this place is something else, hey?" "Yes," you say, dryly, "I believe they call this period, early hemorrhaging." The friend chuckles. This boy stares at you with more than a hint of annoyance; you feel, momentarily, like a child.

After you've ordered, the conversation turns to electronics, DVDs, amps. You rearrange the napkin on your lap, study the other restaurant patrons: couples and groups who look far too young and coutured to be real. You wonder if they all give to Amnesty International.

You wish silently that you had met that boy's friends, anonymous phone voices who beckoned him out for drinks and card games. "You wouldn't enjoy it," he'd tell you. "They're crusty old photographers and pressmen. It's all shoptalk."

"There aren't any women?" you asked.

"Sure there's women," he told you, "but they're crusty, too."

On those nights, you thought about calling your own friends. Girls from the college library program, girls who worked with you. Friends you ran into on the street and exchanged phone numbers with, knowing full well neither of you had any intention of getting together. You couldn't be bothered to keep in touch; you ignored invitations, forgot birthdays. When you did call, you found yourself rambling to an answering machine; it promised to call back as soon as possible, but never did.

You spent those nights alone, imagined that boy in a smoky room, laughing. His head tilted back as he slouched in his chair. Relaxed in a way he never was with you. The people in the room were sharp and funny, informed. The women were never crusty.

The food arrives and the smell of it—garlic, anchovies, olive oil—causes a turn in your stomach. You excuse yourself from the table, move calmly through the restaurant to the ladies' room, a pulsing den of mirrors and chrome washed in lighter, pinker red. In the stall, you grip the cold tank of the toilet, lean your face down to the bowl and catch a whiff of bleach and air freshener. Your body unleashes two-and-a-half glasses of sanguine wine. After, you rinse your mouth and wash your face with cold water at the sink, pat yourself dry with a paper towel. As you reapply lipstick, you feel relieved that the alcohol is out of you. You tell yourself, it's better this way. This is no time to take up drinking.

* * *

By the week's end, this boy is frustrated by your cultivated despondency. You wander around his apartment, look under cushions, behind the television. You flip through magazines to watch the pages fan. He offers to fix you a drink, but you decline, pacing instead a track around his coffee table. He fixes himself one, a generous glass of gin; you haven't had sex for days now and he is edgy. He carries his drink to the coffee table and stands in your way. You stop in front of him. He runs his hand around the back of your neck and up into your hair, squeezes the base of your skull. "I know what might make you feel better."

He massages your scalp, gently pulling on the roots of your hair. You feel your skin loosening its grip on your bones. You lay your head back into his palm and let him hold you. Your shoulder blades relax back and down. His lips land on your collarbone;

his tongue follows his fingertips as they cautiously unbutton your blouse. His hand slides around your body to unhook your bra. You feel yourself hanging in air, your head tipped back, and wonder when he will let go, when you will fall. He keeps your head cradled in one hand as the other moves to your skirt, reaches up and under the hem. You stop him there, your hand grabbing down for his wrist and wrenching his arm up between you. He smiles at the speed and severity of your gesture.

You look at him as directly as you can. "I'm late."

*　　*　　*

There are no new messages on the server.

*　　*　　*

This boy holds your hand in the waiting room. Whispers he loves you. Gets up to check with the nurse about the time. Shakes his foot while he reads a magazine. You breathe deeply into your stomach, sure you can feel something there, something floating in a liquid pouch. You tell yourself there are already too many people in the world, too many hungry children. You sift through a stack of newspapers on the waiting-room table, pull out all the international news sections. Wars, disasters, atrocities calm you. It is exactly as you suspected, the world is no place to raise a child.

You stare at a colour photograph on the front page of a world news report: *Army helicopter hit by rebel ground fire crashes in jungle outside Aceh.* The image is the view from the jungle floor. Leafy trees and vines decorated with glinting pieces of fuselage. Here and there, dark red blooms hung from branches like great tropical flowers.

The doctor who performs your procedure is cheerful, tells a joke about three men with Alzheimer's who share a house; he makes the nurses laugh. He gives instructions in a cooing voice, as if you are a wounded child. *Slide down to the end of the table, good, good, feet on here.* He stops for a moment with your ankle in his hand, turns your leg to examine the fading marks. Looks at you softly, with his eyebrows raised as if asking if he should be concerned. You push a weak smile, he smiles back broadly and sets your foot in the stirrup.

Let your knees relax outward, that's it, good, you'll feel a little pressure, just my hand, good, perfect.

His voice is hypnotic in its warmth, its soothing timbre. You close your eyes and feel the glow of the examination lamps on your body. You try to draw in that focused heat, absorb it, as if it is the sun. The sounds of the room fall away in gentle increments. The chatter of nurses fades to a distant twitter, then comes back to you as the chatter of American girls on the beach, their busy hands spreading oils and lotions, adjusting straps and sunglasses. The whir of the machine hums and vibrates into the engine of a seaplane as it parts with the water, leaving a bright white cleft in the cyan tide. You are lying on the sand, the earth's warm pressure against your back, the comfort of the sun penetrating deep into your centre. Every now and then, someone, a cocktail waitress, a cabin boy, comes by to ask if you are all right, you tell them, yes, yes. As they move away from you, your head is filled with the sweetness of jasmine and tropical fruit. There are other sounds: the music of handmade instruments, the easy laughter of island wives, the clicks and clacks of an unknown language. There are painted birds, brilliant flowers. There are no rebels here, you tell yourself, no guerillas, no freedom fighters. No one dies here, no priests, no women. No children die here.

*   *   *

The sun is setting by the time this boy gets you home, a postcard sky melting with oranges and pinks. He feeds you Tylenol ss, tucks you into bed. Tells you he will stay on the couch, so you can get some rest.

You watch the phone out of the corner of your eye for a long time before turning onto your side and lifting the receiver. You dial numbers, listen for the chimes, dial more numbers. The switchboard operator at the hotel tells you he is usually gone by this time in the morning, but she tries his room anyway.

You let the phone ring, counting in your head; you've decided to hang up after seven. At six, a woman says hello.

"Oh," you say, "I must have the wrong room."

"Just a minute," the woman says. There is the sound of the phone being put down and picked up again.

"Hello?" It is that boy.

"Hello." You feel a numb outline around your arms and legs.

"Hello. How are you?"

"I saw your photo. In the paper. The helicopter." It is the rawness between your legs that you wish you were rid of, but the painkillers are slow.

"Yeah. What a mess. Can you hold on a sec?" The phone is muffled. You hear his voice, the woman's voice, his voice again, then a door slamming. "Sorry. Are you still there?"

You exhale. You cup your hand between your legs, press your knees together, squeeze the hospital maxi pad. Everything burns like an open wound.

"I'm glad you called. I was going to call you. I mean, I've been wanting to call you."

You roll onto your back, raise your knees to alleviate the pressure. The pain retreats and you are left with something dull but insistent.

"I've been thinking of coming back. Maybe next month for a couple of weeks."

You turn onto your side again, the pain itself far less trouble than its shadowy threat. You have nothing to say.

"Are you still there?"

You count to ten before answering.

This boy sleeps with a clear mind, dreams in quadraphonic sound. In the dark, you stare at his shoulder. You marvel that his body is so sharp, so vividly distinguishable from the rest of the world. Your own skin seems to blur into the air around you, wash into the sheets. You watch the flutter beneath this boy's eyelids. Run your fingers through his hair, damp around the temples like a feverish youth. You kiss the bridge of his nose.

Tomorrow you will tell him it's over. He will be stunned. He will negotiate, then shout, then cry. You will not know when to touch him. You will follow him around as he gathers his things and beg him to talk to you. He will call you something horrible and you will slap him so hard his mouth will bleed.

But by the end of it, sometime between ten and midnight, after a full day of emotional hostage-taking, without food or water, while you are filling a glass with ice and he is touching hydrogen peroxide to his lip, you will look at each other and see someone so unfamiliar, you will wonder if you are in the right apartment, the right country. It is then that you will both reach a settlement, decide to call a truce, lay down in each other's arms, and soon after, manoeuvre your way out, in the dark.

boys growing

Zsuzsi Gartner

I HAD FALLEN IN LOVE BY THEN WITH THREE DARK-HAIRED BOYS fiercely loyal to their mamas and I swore I'd never do it again. My own mama said: Never go out with a boy prettier than yourself.

I tried to listen to her, but a noise got in the way. Sound of my blood motoring through my veins. A dull roar. Sometimes that.

Sometimes nothing.

* * *

A Saturday before the first day back at school, Labour Day weekend. He filled up the tank of my car and then asked if he should check the oil, his hair flicking in and out of his eyes in a wind that seemed to be coming from all directions. Hot, weasly wind. The foothills smouldering. Too far away to see, wild horses ran— tails on fire, trailing smoke. But you could smell it. The whole city reeked of burning hair, cooked tar, sweat. Dull brown rivers of gophers, smoked from their holes, flowed across fields, small boys mowing them down with BB guns like they were on a buffalo kill. For a quarter a corpse. Small boys who didn't get to sleep that night, their nostrils thick with blood sport, their trigger fingers, their everything, twitching. Bones growing faster than their skin. You could hear it—a terrible sound, canvas sails tearing on a tall ship at sea, a border guard grinding his teeth. Boys growing. It kept me awake. Their mothers the next day would have to strip their beds and wash the sheets. Nervous mothers, wondering how babies grow up to be cowboys. Bewildered mothers, wondering how they didn't notice. One, one of them, dared press her face to the moist spot on the sheet, a faded sheet dancing with purple Barneys, and inhaled. Then her heart pinwheeled with guilt and shame filled her mouth like sand.

An elk calf came out of the scrub that Saturday at the edge of the barracks, angled across Sarcee Trail—horns bleating, metal kissing metal, siren wail—and down the ravine, long front legs buckling, spraying scree. It ended up caught in the school field, chest ripped open against a ragged hole in the fence, tranquilizer dart in its quivering left haunch, deep in its meat. On Tuesday I would find a thread of its heart still dangling from the fence.

How do I know it was the heart? I know.

He filled up the tank of my car and then handed me my change. His fingernails were cut short and amazingly clean. Later, I found out he went to the bathroom after each fill-up and scrubbed until his skin was almost raw.

I counted the change slowly just to keep him there. He was new in town. He was going to Diefenbaker, my school.

"Maybe you'll be in my class."

"Yeah, maybe." He shrugged. Green fruit. Motherless child.

That evening it looked to be snowing. Ash falling from the sky.

* * *

Boy #2 once told me this, as if he thought it was funny: "My mum would carve you up with a butcher knife if she knew."

"Would she," I said, as if I couldn't care less, barely looking up from what I was doing. "Oh, would she."

One other thing my own mama said: Always aim for effervescence.

Only now does the thought occur to me: It was him thinking he could carve me up. Boys are always more dangerous in hindsight.

Boy #2, though, he was a scary one.

*   *   *

Jennifer Hermann. Teresa Kowalsky. Eddie Lau. I called out their names, making eye contact when necessary, ignoring the grunters, the slouchers, the dispossessed. One more year of school and they'd all be sprung on the world and there was nothing I could do about it. Sioux O'Hearn. Brittany-Jane Staples. Rajit Singh.

Then the shock of his name in my mouth. I let it swell like a communion wafer and then pried it slowly off the roof of my mouth with my tongue.

Just outside the classroom window a thread of essential organ meat hung from a wire fence, twisting in the breeze. Gopher shit littered the field, crunching underfoot like dry dog food. Just south of the foothills, militiamen were shooting the wild horses.

The Hershey-sponsored world map rolled up to the top of the blackboard with a violent snap.

"Here," he said.

*   *   *

I can't remember exactly when the smell of men my own age began to be invasive. Like a jar of marinated artichoke hearts, like wet metal.

*   *   *

Boy #1 asked: "When I get a real gig, will you come and watch me?"

He was really a very unmusical boy. His mother encouraged him, though. The kind of bottom-dwelling burbot who thought it would be fun to have a rock star for a son. The father pushed a broom somewhere and left her fantasies unfulfilled. Mothers are so often unaware of the harm they do. At least that's what I used to think.

"It's not enough to want it," I told him.

Later, I saw him sometimes out of the corner of my eye, like one of those dark spots that appear after you've been out in the sun too long—slouching down the hall with his Walkman on, tapping on the lockers. Usually alone. After Kurt Cobain died, Boy #1 wore a noose around his neck for days, his hair in blueberry Kool-Aid-streaked dreadlocks down over his sorrowful eyes.

It was all I could do not to laugh.

* * *

That strand of elk heart from the fence? I took it home. Something to rub back and forth between my fingers. Something to do while I watched the changing weather.

* * *

I always wanted them to tell me about their girlfriends. I *encouraged* them. Girls like stick insects. But instead, this is what they did. They talked about their mothers. Even him. Ghost woman who choked me in my sleep with her perfume, something he remembered came in a bottle shaped like a cat. Her fur collar still cold from outdoor air when she came into his room to kiss him goodnight. He always pretended to be asleep. He knew that it pleased her.

All that energy boys use up trying to please their mamas. Could keep space junk in permanent orbit. Could.

There is stuff up there you would not believe.

* * *

The new science teacher was nothing if not persistent. Complimented me on my hair. The kind of crimson glow strontium nitrate gives pyrotechnics, he told me. (Originally from Minnesota, like most middle-Americans he had fireworks on the brain.) Before I could admit I found this moderately interesting, I moved quickly out of his airspace.

Grown men and their sorry skins. Don't they know?

*   *   *

Boy #3 said: "I like these lines around your eyes." And I hadn't even noticed them myself.

He was one smooth boy. He worked in a deli part-time and little stick insects came from miles just to hang around and watch him shave pastrami. I was sitting at the corner table one afternoon when a woman came in, much too elegant for the neighbourhood. She seemed to vibrate like a hydro line. Her hair was anchorwoman perfect. She made a big show of ordering, as if she wanted a sandwich as perfect as her hair. Boy #3 listed all the options, with or without this, with or without that. After she paid, she leaned over the deli counter— she was *that* tall—and kissed him on the cheek and told him not to be late for supper.

I said: "So why didn't you introduce me?"

He rolled his eyes up into his head.

I told him they'd stay stuck like that forever.

*   *   *

A weekend in early October. The new boy (he, him) was coming around often by then. He didn't talk much. Stood on the front steps of my condo and looked out toward the mountains. This was deeply satisfying. I'd had enough of restless boys, boys jittery with the future, boys who didn't know when enough was enough. The sky was so clear that I could almost forget how the air had looked in early September. Along the windowsills, though, there was a thin film of ash soft as mouse fur.

I just wished he wouldn't wash so often. Most of the time, he didn't smell like anything at all.

The mother, on the other hand, some nights she smoked me out of my own bed. Perfume in a cat-shaped bottle. Like hot stinking piss.

* * *

The science teacher wouldn't take no for an answer. Rang my classroom phone. Said, "$Sr(NO_3)_2$. Say, it's got a catchy beat!" One of the English teachers, the one with the limp and the pouchy smile, thought he was handsome in a secondhand, draft-dodger kind of way. "You're nuts," she said in the lunchroom. "If it were *me*." Her breath leprous with want.

She liked the way he made a poetry of science.

I could smell his wet rot. Creosote flesh. Gave me flash headaches, like being trapped in abandoned cabins while shifting timbers sweated sap. Like pressing my nose to a telephone pole. I had to stand upwind of him just to have a conversation.

* * *

Then there were the girls, the ones that leaned so close I could smell their smoky, minty breath as they explained why they couldn't stay for the test. Their thin lies whistled through my ears like razor kites. Stick insects with their arms pressed to their sides, never meeting my eyes. Outside there was an engine idling, torn vinyl seats, The Prodigy blaring from six speakers, "Smack my bitch up!" They're not the ones I had to watch out for, though. It was the huggers. The girls with naturally flushed cheeks. The Save The Planet girls with little platinum rings glinting in their navels. Curvy girls rampant with optimism.

Girls are growing from the minute they leave the womb. And if it's very quiet, you can hear it. A soft, continual *swish swish swish*. Like something cloaked in taffeta coming to get you in the night.

Boys growing. Now that can wake the dead.

*   *   *

He went for milk in the driving rain wearing only shorts and my trench coat, bare feet in Nikes, umbrella held so high above his head it did no good. I found this so endearing I would have chewed my right leg out of a steel trap to follow him if I had thought he wasn't coming back. On all fours, my own blood puddling off my chin.

Hot chocolate and a thin jolt, then backgammon with our eyes wide open, skulls flaring like jack-o'-lanterns.

I lined up all the other dark-haired boys I've ever loved and shot them like ducks in an arcade.

*   *   *

Boy #2, scary boy, said: "I need a sister."

I called him up at home one night and his mother answered. Just Boy #2 and her in the house. The father, he had done something foolish and irreparable some years ago involving his car, a garage and a hose. Nothing you could speak of. Boy #2, he was a hacker. Down in the basement, tooling around on his Pentium 166. Making decent money changing classmates' grades, deleting infractions. The whole public school system was going to him by then. Skin white as bleached cotton.

The mother answered with her very Swiss accent. I winced at the thought of cloth napkins folded with military precision, bed sheets pulled taut enough to bruise hips, bust skin at the bone. Cheese served mild, gutless. I recalled that she looked like an amphibian of some sort. Blood barely moving through her veins to that creaky, dark chamber of horrors, her heart. She said he was busy with his homework.

When he finally came to the phone, I said: "Hey there, it's your big sister."

The next night he put his foot through the door of my hall

closet. Splinters ringed his tapioca calf. Spiny blowfish. Pulled out all the kitchen drawers and threw them against the walls. Twist-ties rained from the ceiling. Grabbed a fondue fork and pressed it to my forehead, right between my eyes.

His mother had been listening on the other line.

* * *

Then him.

We watched the news together. He was utterly addicted to newscasts, drawn to the flickering wreckage of other lives. A moth to light. His mother had been newsworthy. Leapt to her death holding onto his spina-bifida sister, fluid leaking from both their brains.

One night there was an item on a new treatment. The rest of the evening he sat picking at the threads in the carpet until it was time to go to work.

I lifted his hair out of his eyes. But he looked right on through me.

* * *

The science teacher finally wore me down. Showed me the tattoo of a formaldehyde baby on his right arm and I agreed to go to a Halloween party with him.

* * *

Boy #1 said (more than once): "My mom loves this song."

I was taking a bath. He sat on the toilet lid, torturing my old Gibson acoustic. I flicked some bubbles at him and told him to stop. He started wailing away even louder, in his seriously unmusical manner. The bottom-feeder was in the tub, darting about under my knees, tonguing the bathtub ring, swallowing my soap, egging him on. Panic grabbed me right between my ribs, grip like an angry preacher, and squeezed. I realized if I didn't do something he would never stop, ever, he would play on in hell with his mother clapping and cheering, mouth moving like a catfish's, moustache quivering.

What happened next: I rose out of the water, a tsunami of rage, fifty feet tall, and grabbed the guitar out of his hands. I slammed it against the sink, swung it at the edge of the tub.

"Rock on," I said, handing the busted guts back to him as he started to cry.

* * *

Teaching the Elizabethans, I decided to make a small detour. The Elizabethans, as my students already knew (and seemed to approve), didn't bathe very often. Even the aristocracy was rather ripe.

I told them that men and women were attracted to each other's body odour. Someone made an inspired gagging noise and they all laughed. I told them that the Elizabethans would have considered deodorant a form of birth control. Even the dispossessed in their low-cloud formations at the back of the room found this amusing. I told them that when a noble woman took a fancy to a gentleman, she would carefully peel an apple and place it in her armpit for a number of days until it was deemed appropriately aromatic. (She could, I didn't add, choose to place it elsewhere.) Then she would present it to her suitor.

I said: "They called this a Love Apple."

"That," buzzed an agitated stick insect, "is like so, pardon me, incredibly fucking *gross*."

The exchange student from Osaka put up his hand and asked, "Please, Miss, will this be on the test?"

The whole class in the hall afterward, lockers open, surreptitiously sniffing their pits. And him skidding into the showers, clothes still in midair as the water pulsed on, scrubbing until blood beaded the surface of his skin.

* * *

In his wallet there was a photograph of a beach. In the background a fat man lay on a picnic table. In the foreground sat a small boy sucking in his smile, a woman half-hugging him, half-tickling him. Plastic shovel in his hand, blocking her face. She had her mouth to his ear and was telling him he'd made the best sandcastle in the world. That he would be an architect someday and build her a room touching the sky. Sunspots burned above their heads like painful lesions.

"With an elevator?" he asked.

With an elevator. She promised him *that*.

During the night she shredded the back of my couch, the wallpaper in the hallway, thin strips fluttering above the forced-air vent.

I paced the hall, quietly cajoling, *here* kitty kitty kitty.

* * *

The afternoon before the costume party I sat in the stands, hugging my knees and watching football practice. A new student teacher sat beside me, eager, slapping her hands together against the cold. "They look like aliens," she said, "running around down there."

The ground rumbled underneath my feet. Boys growing heavier as they ran, soon to crack the crust of the earth wide open.

I casually approached the field when the practice broke up and asked him a favour. I whispered it. Told him it was for a joke. His sudden laughter shaved my heart. Moth boy. It was all I could do not to put my hand to his cheek. Then I went home to dress for the party. The lawn was already frosted over. In the distance the mountains were white.

The science teacher took one look at me and said, "You're not going like that?" I wore faded blue hospital garb, white sneakers, a stethoscope around my neck, and on my face something to protect me from the nip of the night. He looked down at my doormat, scratched at something on his palm. He turned his head and stared toward the mountains. Then he said, "You do know that's a jockstrap, don't you?"

"Oh my God," I collapsed against him laughing, "OH MY GAWD! I thought it was a surgical mask."

It took him a few seconds, but he laughed, too. Although not when I said I was going to wear it anyway.

At the party there was some whispering and then I heard him say loudly, so everyone could hear, just in case there was any doubt, "She thought it was a surgical mask!" I twirled around, demonstrating my ignorance, pumpkin lights twinkling above my head, while formaldehyde man stayed as far away from me as he could. Apples bobbed in a bowl of spit.

The women, though. The women thought it was funny.

And all night long I was breathing deeply of his smell. I was the life of the party. Oxygenated. On.

Oh! How utterly convincing love can be. How utterly convincing!

Cat piss in a bottle. Against love like this, I thought, what small thing was that?

*   *   *

A Monday in November. I walked down the corridor at lunch, gnawing on my heart of elk. The floors gleamed, as they did every Monday. Ammonia still clung to the air, scouring my brainpan.

He was leaning against his locker. A girl stood in front of him, not a stick insect, not a curvy glory. A solid bound-for-Oxbridge type. Field-hockey calves. *A Confederacy of Dunces* clutched to her chest. She lifted his hair out of his eyes with the eraser end of her pencil.

I moved toward them. Don't tell me I didn't know what I was doing. I said, "Hi there!"

Then I hip-checked him. Ever so playfully, but it threw him off balance. The girl, she just stood there looking astonished.

* * *

I could have said: Close your mouth, young lady, before something flies in.

* * *

I could have said: Fish in a barrel. Formed the words with my mouth.

Too Busy Swimming

Terence Young

THE SCOTSMAN'S PALACE IS A NO-STAR, PLAID-TRIMMED, STUCCO motel on a busy road in the industrial district. I could have chosen a B&B by the park, or a room at the Save Inn, but the Palace fit the Victoria School Board's budget. It was close to a mall and away from all the tourist kitsch by the harbour. Teachers stayed there for conferences because it was cheap; they could save a few bucks on their per diem.

It was nearly midnight by the time I walked into the lobby. It had taken me five hours to cover sixty miles. In five hours I could have flown to Toronto. When I lived in Victoria, friends from the mainland always asked if I felt trapped living on an island. Now I understood the question. The clerk gave me a room over-looking the street, across from an all-night coffee shop crowded with taxi drivers and hookers. The coffee shop offered a breakfast deal for Palace guests.

In the morning, I called Doreen in Vancouver, then got a booth. Leona was already at the counter waiting for me. For a few months one winter, I had imagined leaving Doreen for her. She was one of those bullets a man has to dodge, and I did, but only just. If anybody knew my taste in accommodation, Leona did.

"How's it feel to be so predictable?" she said, standing up.

"Good," I said. Leona was a counsellor in Smithers, but four years earlier, we were both teachers at the same school in Victoria. I caught the waiter's eye, made the international sign for coffee and walked with Leona over to a table by the window.

"Nice day for a deposition," I said.

"Days, you mean," she said

"I was hoping you wouldn't say that." The waiter brought two coffees and a couple of menus.

"There's thirty-five of us on the list, Tony. You'll be lucky to see Doreen by Christmas."

"I don't have that much to say," I said.

"You'll say whatever it takes," she said. "I've been waiting ten years for this."

I ordered huevos rancheros. Leona had the waffles. Rain slipped down the glass. The summer drought was finally over. Two kids were looking under the hood of a car in the jobber's parking lot on the corner. One of them was holding a set of ignition wires and pointing, while the other one twisted something back and forth.

"Doreen's doing another burn," I said. "She was going to come with me, see some old friends, but the boss phoned her when his bid was accepted."

"That's too bad," Leona said. "I guess you'll just have to make do." The people at the next table settled into their sausages, eggs and pancakes; aromas mingled in the air.

"I'm not looking forward to this," I said.

"You'll be fine, Tony," she said.

"That's what Doreen said." On the far side of the room, a large-screen television flickered silently.

"Did you hear they found the guy who fell off the ferry?" she asked.

"I was just telling Doreen on the phone I thought I saw him. It was in the paper," I said.

"Oh, yeah? They had him on the news. He said God saved him from drowning."

"Funny how God saves drunks, but forgets about the starving in Ethiopia."

"Same old Tony," Leona said.

*　　*　　*

With the fire on Mason Street, Doreen knew she had overtime for weeks. It became clear I'd have to testify on my own. Work is work and when it comes, she has to take it. I'm a teacher. I stand up all day in front of an audience, but still I was nervous about what lay ahead. Anybody who thinks it's easy should try it sometime.

We were out to dinner at the Cohens, friends through Doreen's book club who live off West 13th in a trendy brick walk-up, when Doreen got the call. Half the time Ellen Cohen never makes it to the club. Her kids are young; it was just wishful thinking. She has no time to read. Doreen says Ellen hasn't finished a book yet. Every so often, we bring over a lasagne, a casserole or a big salad from our garden. It's the least we can do, Doreen says, not having any kids ourselves. We didn't decide not to have children, but it was our decision not to make fools of our-selves tracking down every herbal remedy and surgical option on the market. People say children are the glue that keeps a couple together. Maybe we're all the more amazing, then, living under the same roof without the benefit of adhesives. Or maybe it's just a matter of time.

Dinner was finished and Doreen was giving me her look, the one that tells me I'm dominating conversation. I was telling Sam about a boy in my class who'd found his older brother shot in his living room. "The news said the kid shot himself 'to death,'" I was saying. "Have you ever heard anything so stupid?"

"Well, he did, didn't he?" Sam asked.

"That's not the point," I said. "You'd think the guy was just sitting there on the sofa plugging away until he was so full of lead he finally died. All they needed to say was he shot himself."

"What if he shoots himself and misses?" Sam asked.

"First they told us he committed suicide," I said. "Then they told us he shot himself to death. It's just a bit much. That's all I'm saying."

I didn't tell Sam it was Doreen who had cleaned up the living room after the boy's brother shot himself. It's not the sort of thing people think is covered by insurance, but it often is. After the police give the go-ahead, a counsellor informs the family that they're free to call in professionals if their policy allows for it. If not, it's out of their own pockets, or they do it themselves. Doreen was there for three days. The carpet and sofa were too far gone, but even if they hadn't been, nobody would have felt comfortable in the same room with them again. What took her the time was the other furniture: the big English sideboard, the walnut coffee table, all the end tables and paintings. You can't be dusting and come upon a splotch of blood. And the walls and ceiling weren't easy, either. Blood goes right through most paint, so all of it had to come off before they could spray. She found bits of bone and brain all the way into the dining room.

When the pager beeped, Doreen excused herself to use the phone and gave me "the look" again. She does it while fixing her hair. She's never really said, "When I do this, you stop talking," it's just that she gets so fed up, she has to do something. I shut up and let Sam talk about his boy's soccer game. In the car on the way home, Doreen said, "You'll be fine."

"Like a rock," I said.

*   *   *

Four years ago, Doreen was with Clean All Services in Victoria, doing flooded basement suites ruined in the big rains of '92. I was a substitute with the district, teaching a "Gifted Eights" program at Douglas Junior Secondary. When I got offered permanent work with a school in Vancouver, we moved. We were still thinking about kids of our own and a permanent job was part of the plan.

At Douglas, two teachers ran the outdoor education program as well as taught drama classes. One was lean and tall, meticulous, the other squat like a bowling ball and very casual. Everybody called them Abbott and Costello. I didn't know them well, but occasionally I had coffee with them in the Green Room before classes. They'd fixed the place up with some worn-out living room furniture, a few dusty armchairs and a long chesterfield. The atmosphere was more hospitable than in the staff room, which still reeked from years of smoke. Drama students came and went, hanging out, doing their homework, reading magazines. Leona and another counsellor had been telling the principal for years the whole thing was a scam. They said Abbott and Costello had their own female fan club, that the drama was just an excuse to stay after school. They said the outdoor education kids went on field trips to a cabin and ate popcorn and massaged the teachers' necks. When the principal retired, the district started asking questions. Anybody who'd seen anything got a call. The formal depositions were the last step. Both of them were going to be in the room with us while we told the jury what we knew. That was the part I wasn't happy about.

*   *   *

Doreen's fire turned out to be a bad one: nobody hurt, but plenty of water and smoke damage. We'd seen the headline and driven by the next day. For Doreen, every fire's a potential work site— a black job, they call it—so she takes an active interest. The flames had blown out a basement window and a screen door was off its hinges. The owners, a couple, were standing on the front lawn. The woman was holding a sweater with a black line right across its front.

"I'll be back," Doreen said as we drove off.

"You think so?" I asked.

"If I'm lucky," she said.

Doreen's is the biggest cleaning contractor in the southern mainland, used by all the insurance companies. She's done everything from sewer ruptures to multiple murders in the past three years and her reputation is stellar.

When I phoned her from the Scotsman's Palace to see how things were going, she said, "It's not the write-off the owners want it to be. Yesterday, they came in to look at a fridge I'd cleaned. They said that it wasn't safe, that there were cracks in the lining and to move it to the discard pile. They even tried to bribe me."

"Get out," I said.

"It's true."

They didn't know Doreen. She will clean a blouse ten times before she gives up on it.

"So, what are you going to do?" I asked.

"Don't you worry about that," she said.

Jerry, Doreen's boss, has more faith in her than he does in God and he's a Pentecostal. When she says something is safe, he doesn't need a second opinion. He tells the clients that, as far as he's concerned, the case is closed. Usually they back right down.

"Did you read about that guy in the paper?" I asked her.

"I'm a working girl, Tony," she said. "I don't have time to read."

"I saw him, Doreen."

"Saw who?"

"The guy on the ferry," I said. "The one who fell off."

"You saw a guy fall off the ferry?"

"No, I saw the guy before he fell off the ferry. I went back to my car to get my briefcase and he was standing on the car deck, leaning over the rail. He was throwing up."

"Nice," she said.

"Eleven hours he was in the strait. Can you imagine? The

paper said he'd lost his balance while he was throwing up. That's got to be the same guy."

"Eleven hours," she said. "It'd be ugly."

"He was still alive," I said.

"Lucky drunk."

"The paper said it was sunstroke. He'd been playing softball at a picnic."

"Sure," Doreen said.

"Yeah," I said. "His wife didn't sound convinced, either."

Doreen said the man needed to "dry out." She said she had to go to the warehouse even though it was a Saturday. Jerry's a slave driver when there's work on the table. The movers bring in the burnt goods and Doreen and the other staff clean what they can and put it in storage. More than three fires in one week and they're out of storage space, so Jerry likes to move things along pretty quickly. He gives them whatever they need to get the job done: industrial washing machines, rubber gloves, forty-five-gallon drums of carbon tetrachloride. Doreen lives down there when a whole house comes in. The only time she gets out is for floods or murders.

* * *

After breakfast with Leona, I walked up to the Executive House. The board had rented a couple of seminar rooms on the tenth floor for deposing witnesses. They also had a suite where people could wait until it was their turn. Leona was right. I'd been scheduled for eleven o'clock, but at this rate anything before two was out of the question. The suite was jammed with coats and briefcases. Somebody had thought to bring in a couple of Mr. Coffee machines, so the bedside tables were littered with empty sugar packets and spilled whitener. There were teachers from a dozen different schools, people who had transferred or moved out of town and returned to the scene of the crime. I moved to the window and looked out at the Empress, oak trees and Douglas firs in Beacon Hill Park. Behind me, the board rep was talking to the next witness, Wayne Evans, a science teacher.

"We'll be asking the questions," the rep was saying, "so there's nothing to worry about. We already know what you know. You just have to tell it the way you remember it."

"Do they ask questions, too?" Wayne asked.

"There is no cross-examination," the rep said. "We are just gathering evidence. They're allowed to be here, but they can't interfere."

A few minutes later, a clerk came in to tell us they were adjourning until two o'clock. Anybody who hadn't been deposed yet should return tomorrow. I put on my coat and left.

* * *

I walked down the causeway to Belleville and along the waterfront into James Bay. If the term had been further along, I'd have brought some marking. I was hoping I wouldn't need the substitute I'd booked for Monday.

I strolled out to the navigation beacon at the end of the breakwater. Two kids had planted themselves on one of its stone slabs and were casting their lines into a kelp bed. Somebody had packed them a lunch. Two bright orange Thermoses stood beside a tackle box and a couple of Tupperware containers lay next to them, the clean-cut corners of white bread sandwiches visible through transparent lids. They tugged on their lures, reeled in their lines, eyes fixed on the water. Seagulls bobbed nearby, jockeying for handouts. The remnants of a Friday night beach fire smouldered among some logs by the shore, its smoke married to the wind and the mist. I went back the way I'd come, past Chinatown and across Bay to the Scotsman's Palace, where I'd said I'd meet Leona.

I phoned Doreen that evening to tell her about the delay. She had taken the portable into the bath with her and the sound of water slapping against the tub made me think she was trapped in a bottle of pop.

"Some people should not have house fires," she said.

"Doreen," I said. "Do you know what you just said?"

"No, I mean it," she said. "These people are rude. They want the insurance company to buy them a whole new life. They're pulling garbage from the attic and want me to say it needs replacing. Jeans they wore out five years ago, junky old typewriters nobody'll ever use again. Garbage, in anybody's book."

"Some people are sentimental," I said.

"And some people are perverts," she said. "You don't want to know what kind of pictures I found in some of their books. I could go to the police with what I've seen."

"No, really?" I said.

"Some with kids," she said.

In one fire, the movers had brought in a couple's matching coffins to be cleaned, homemade ones from kits. They were covered in signatures and messages from friends. There were even circular wine stains on them, as if they'd been used as coffee tables for a party. Doreen is always coming home with this stuff. I thought about the small bag of dope I had tucked away in my desk drawer, sex toys we had tried and then relegated to a box under the bathroom sink. Would I want a cleaning contractor joking to his wife about that? I resolved to throw everything out as soon as I got home.

"I saw your guy, too," Doreen said.

"My guy?"

"Yeah. Your drunken ferry guy. He was on TV."

"You mean my Christian drunken ferry guy," I said.

"That's the one. He was going over his route on a map. Some cop fishing near the American border picked him up."

"What was he using for bait?" I asked.

"His wife was interviewed, too," she said. "She was holding her husband's pager up to the camera. The thing still worked after eleven hours in the water."

"He had his pager with him?"

"His wife tried to phone him when he didn't show up. He remembers the call, but he said there wasn't a lot he could do about it at the time. He was too busy swimming."

"Aren't we all," I said.

*   *   *

The next day, the inquiry was back on schedule. I went over early to look through my daybook again, the one I'd kept from that year at the school. There wasn't a lot of detail, but I wanted to be sure of the dates.

I knew what they would be looking for. That year my class was invited to participate in an orienteering exercise with the outdoor education kids. It was my first class, so I wanted to make it a year they wouldn't forget. We turned the outing into an overnight camping expedition. I divided the students into groups, made them responsible for their dinners, had them set up budgets, create supply lists. Doreen offered to come along. Every "learning outcome" was covered. The day of the trip, everything went as planned. We took the school bus along the Island Highway and up into the wooded hills behind Shawnigan Lake. When we came to a narrow gravel road, all of us put on our backpacks and hiked the last two miles to the cabin. It was fall, the mornings just turning frosty. Each group made a fire pit and sent foragers off for dry wood. In the evening, the students gathered for hot chocolate and cookies and one of the teachers, Costello probably, played guitar and sang. When it was over, I called lights out and the kids went to their tents for the night. Students weren't supposed to go into the cabin except for the evening singsong, but the girls figured out they could if they were pretty and if they didn't mind sitting in front of the fire with a teacher's arm draped over their shoulders. Plain Janes didn't make it past the front door.

The morning after, Doreen sat beside me and closed the magazine I'd been reading. She was the girls' chaperone. She told me she was going to walk back into town and phone every one of the parents and tell them to come and collect their kids right away if I didn't do something. She said she'd never seen anything so disgusting in her whole life and if this was an education it was the kind nobody needed.

In the week following the camp, I wrote down what had happened. I tore up what I had written and wrote it again. I tore that up, too. I imagined conversations between me and the principal, between me and the counsellors. Leona got it out of me in her usual way and she nearly hit the roof. She wanted blood. It was the last straw, she kept saying, but I wasn't so sure. In the end, I went and talked to Abbott privately. I told him what I'd seen. I said it was our job to be models of proper behaviour. He nodded. He agreed. He understood completely. He even thanked me for bringing the problem to his attention. He said it would never happen again.

Now it was my turn to give evidence. The board representative led me out of the suite and down a hall to the seminar room. He showed me to a chair at the front of the room. I sat down. A panel of people had taken up positions behind a table opposite me. A few of them stared at a point somewhere behind my head. Others kept their eyes averted and wrote on legal pads, their pens pausing the way birds pause from time to time when they're feeding, alert to any changes around them. To my left, behind a table of his own, stood Abbott, a lawyer at his side. He acknowledged me with a nod I did not return. The board representative read a prepared text for my benefit. It explained the purpose of the proceedings and the manner in which they would be conducted. Then, one by one, the members of the panel, as though they were speaking lines from a play, began to ask questions.

RIP, Roger Miller

Murray Logan

HE HASN'T COME RIGHT OUT AND SAID IT YET, NOT DIRECTLY anyhow, but John thinks I should be moving on. We go way back, me and him, but even so.

I'm all set up in an old barn of his. John's got this two-bit farm he's busy running into the ground and off in one corner of the lower field is what's left of a barn. I hauled in an eight-foot camper someone gave me, set it down and I've been there ever since. I guess more time than I thought has passed, because now I'm getting the pretty strong feeling that John wants me gone.

Or his wife does, and I can't really blame her too much. Me hunkered down in a travel camper in a barn with no running water and no power, well, some people might object. I've been happy, though. Happy enough.

. "Don't even think about it," he said to me when I first hauled up. "Don't even goddamn think about it." Maybe that was when I got off to a bad start with his wife, showing up out of the blue with nothing to my name but an old camper and a bottle of Lamb's Navy Rum. John and I got the camper tucked into a dry corner of his barn and then sat and killed the bottle. Maybe that was what got between me and his wife. This was two years ago. It doesn't seem that long, but John tells me it is.

I watch the stars a lot. I'll sit out behind my barn, facing nothing but scrub forest and field so long fallow it's gone back to whatever it was before, and watch the stars move around. It gets so dark that it's like sitting in a big sack of nothing at all, the only light the end of my cigarette. I sit with a glass of rum and a smoke, watching the stars, looking for comets or whatever, and there's nothing like it.

You can hear the coyotes. People will try to tell you they're wolves, but they're only coyotes. You can even see the odd one, if there's a moon and you're lucky and quick, slinking across an open space, headed from somewhere to somewhere else.

I had a dog once, Annie, an old hound of some kind. I bought a shotgun off this old fellow, a tiny little gun, a .410, and the dog sort of came with the deal. I didn't want her at the time but he pressed her on me. He couldn't get around so well any more, that was why he was selling the .410, and he didn't think it was right to keep a dog that he couldn't run. Anyway, she used to bark back at the coyotes, howl back at them. That wasn't here, of course. That was a while back, somewhere else. But all memories seem to happen in the same place, if you let them.

*   *   *

Monday is John's day to drive to town for supplies. He turns off his road and onto the secondary at seven-thirty in the morning, like clockwork, so I have to set off by seven at the latest. It takes me almost half an hour to walk to the road and then a little way along it. That way, I'm walking to town and if John decides to stop for me, well, that's fine. So far he has, every time, but this way we each have the option.

The truck stops, just ahead of me, the engine ticking from not being warmed up properly. I walk up, throw my sack in the box and climb in the cab with John. He puts it in gear and pulls out, shaking his head. I wait for him to say something but he doesn't, so I don't, either.

We make it all the way into town without a word, until John pulls the truck up and shuts it off. Then, just before I can open the door, he asks, "You making it OK?"

Yeah, I tell him, sure. I'm making it fine. He nods, like I've answered a real question, something he's been wondering about. Then he reaches into his shirt pocket, where he'd keep his cigarettes if he still smoked, and passes me a folded twenty-dollar bill.

"Here," he says, "don't let Gail know about this." Before I can turn him down, or before I can think of how to say thank you, he's hopped out of his truck and walking away.

* * *

I don't think I ever even fired the .410. Maybe once, just to see what kind of kick it had, but likely not. The old guy I got it from used it for grouse, used it for years until his body got so worn down he couldn't hack it anymore. You could tell he was crazy about hunting and all busted up by not being able to do it anymore. I had to sit around half the day listening to his stories, drinking his watery coffee, before I could get out of there. It seemed like the right thing to do, though, spend some time with the old guy. It was right at the end that he brought old Annie out, told me how he couldn't run her anymore. There were honest-to-God tears running down his face when I drove away with that dog.

* * *

I take care of my laundry. I drop by the fuel company and arrange to have more propane delivered. They'll do it, but they tell me they can only carry me one more month unless I make good on my bill. "You say hello to John for me," the fuel man says. "He's a good man." Meaning that some of us aren't, I suppose. I tell him I will.

I buy a few tins of this and that at the grocery and a can of loose tobacco. With John's twenty and what's left of my money,

I've got enough for a bottle of Lamb's and I pick that up last. It's criminal what they charge for it now. The clerk watches me from the second I walk in the door, all the way down the aisle to the rum and back again. Like I'm going to start stuffing bottles in my pockets and make a run for it. He watches my hands shake as I count out the change for him and doesn't say a word as he hands me my bottle in a paper bag. I thank him politely and leave. He has no idea who I am or what I'm all about and I'm not about to tell him. He can think what he wants.

In the truck on the way back, I notice that I'm humming under my breath, over and over, the same song.

*　　*　　*

Trailer for sale or rent,
Rooms to let—fifty cents.
No phone, no pool, no pets;
I ain't got no cigarettes.

*　　*　　*

"What is that, anyway?" I ask John.

"What's what?" he says, the first thing he's said since we set off.

"That song: 'Trailer for sale or rent.' Who sings that? I've had it buzzing around my head all day."

John thinks about it. "It's 'King of the Road,' " he tells me. "Roger Miller."

Roger Miller. Right, I remember now. I remember hearing it come over the radio, announced the way they do with his name. Years ago. "I sure like that song," I say. "What's Roger Miller up to these days?"

"Dead, I think," says John. "A couple of years ago."

So I've got a dead man's song rattling around my skull.

"Imagine that," I say. "You think I would have heard about it." John just grunts. "You'd think someone would have told me,"

I say. I stare out the window all the way back, feeling vaguely sad about the whole deal.

* * *

The old man, he claimed that a .410 gave the birds a sporting chance. Most yahoos, they charge around the bush with heavy artillery, usually a 12-gauge. But a .410, a little gun like that, evened things up, if only a little. He told me all this when he sold me the gun and threw in a box or two of shells, skinny little shotgun shells about as big around as your finger. 'Course, he told me, the real joy comes from walking around the bush country, you and your dog, just being out there. It didn't matter if you got your grouse or whatever, or not, the point was you and your dog being out there. Which brought him around to Annie.

The reason I wanted to buy the .410 was I thought it would be the right thing to do. I still had my little boy then. I had this idea in my head that a boy should grow up with memories of fall days spent bird-hunting with his father. God only knows where I got that from. So I wanted to get a little gun, something my boy would be able to at least hold, get the feel of. One that, when he fired it, wouldn't send him flying. That was why I bought it, so I could have this perfect picture of me and him, the two of us in this memory.

* * *

"I ever tell you about my boy?" I ask John. He's driven me all the way down to my barn, to drop me off before turning around and heading up to his house.

John shakes his head. "I don't think so. Not that much, anyhow."

"Well," I say, "you come on down for a drink sometime. Any time you want, you come on down."

"I'll do that," says John. "I'll have to do that sometime."

"Any time at all. You know where to find me."

It looks to rain that night, so I pull my chair inside the barn. The barn is missing patches of roof, lengths of plank siding from the walls, but it still keeps its insides mostly dry. There's a wild feeling to it, though. When you're in it you can still see out, still feel the cold and the mist from the rain, so it's a bit like you're not inside and you're not outside. I sit and sip at my rum and I'm still humming that damn song. For some reason I'm all sad that Roger Miller is dead, has been dead for a couple of years and I didn't know a thing about it.

And, try as I might, all I can remember is that one little snatch of the song. This is something I used to hear all the time, probably used to sing to myself, and now it's almost gone. I keep trying, though. I have the crazy idea that I owe it to old Roger, that the least I can do for him is try to remember his song.

*   *   *

While she was in the process of leaving me, moving from room to room, packing up clothes, knickknacks, our son's toys, I sat in my chair and smoked my cigarette. Not saying a word, not moving a muscle. She didn't say anything, either, just moved from one room to another, packing up. If I saw two people act like that on TV, it would look pretty funny. Two stubborn people, not saying a word. When she was done, she herded my boy to the door. It opened and then closed and that was the last I saw of them. I poured another glass of rum, rolled another cigarette and sat there in my chair. I didn't even turn my head to see the door close.

I don't know what happened to the .410. The last I remember having it was when Annie got really sick. No, what she got was old. So old I had to boost her up into the cab of the truck I had then, hoist her back out again. She got so bad that she'd walk five or six feet, then stop, panting, resting up for the next five or six.

A man's got to shoot his own dog. I'd heard that, I guess

I believed it, and that's what I set out to do. I took Annie and the .410 and a shovel and drove out in the bush. I hoisted her down out of the cab and then walked into the scrub a ways. I dug a good hole and then went back for her. She wasn't ten feet from the truck, her head down, looking beat to hell. When she heard me come out of the bush, though, her whip of a tail started slapping against her flank. She was a good old girl, was Annie.

I had to pick her up and carry her in. I set her down, right next to the fresh hole, and picked up the .410. Annie didn't even look up at me, just stood there, like she was waiting. And I picked up the gun and aimed it at her head, knowing I was doing the right thing, that I was doing right by her. But I couldn't do it, even if it was the right thing to do.

I swore at myself all the way into town to the vet's. I gave him twenty dollars and told him I'd bring him the rest if he'd just do this for me. He asked me if I wanted to stay with her while he did it, but I couldn't. I guess I let Annie down, but I couldn't stay there. I'll admit it: I was crying like a baby when I drove away from there, howling like a baby with its heart broken.

Maybe I left the .410 in the woods, beside that hole. I didn't have any use for it, so maybe I just left it there. And I still owe that vet the rest of the money. That's going back some time now and I bet he's forgotten, but if I'm ever back that way I'll try to pay him what I owe.

When I think of my boy, he's seven years old. He's wearing a striped T-shirt, red and blue, and he's just standing there, looking square at me. I last saw him when he was seven, and this is going on ten or eleven years now, maybe more, so I know he won't look like that anymore. And he never had a striped T-shirt that I know of. Memory is funny that way, filling in details, colours, T-shirts that never were. Maybe I picked up that picture from some TV show. I still think of running into him, though, meeting him on the street. And he's always that same age and he's always wearing that same damn T-shirt. It's like I can't imagine him any other way, like that's all I've got left of him, this memory that more than likely never happened. I wonder how he thinks of me, if he does. How I look to him in his memories when he thinks of me. I don't know if I want him to or not.

*   *   *

I'm sitting, waiting to catch a glimpse of a coyote, when I hear footsteps crunching on the gravel and dried grass. I check to see that there's still some rum left at the bottom of the bottle, so I'll have something to offer John. But it's not John who walks up and stands there, but his wife, Gail. John must have told her where to find me, since I don't think she's ever been down to this end of their farm, at least not in the two years I've been here.

I'm a little surprised but still manage to get up out of my chair and offer it to her. Even at the bottom of a dead field, sitting with no power or water, half in the bag from Lamb's Navy, I like to think I keep my manners.

And Gail keeps hers. She thanks me for the chair and sits down, like that's why she came by, to sit and wait for the coyotes with me.

I fetch my other chair, the one I've been saving for John if he drops by, and pull that up. I know what's coming, I know that Gail's going to give me my walking papers, but I also know that there's nothing I can do about it.

"How are you doing?" she asks me. "Are you making it OK out here?" Making it OK. So she and John have been talking about me.

She sounds genuinely concerned, though. She's a nice lady, after all, and she sounds worried for me. "I'm fine," I say. "I'm making it. I'm not making much of it, but I'm making it." I say this last bit as a joke and she's nice enough to laugh along with me, say, "Well, good, then."

My glass is empty and I wipe it clean on the tail of my shirt. "Can I pour you some rum?" I ask, holding up the glass and what's left of the bottle.

"Thank you," she says, "but just a little." So I do, splashing a couple of fingers into the glass for her. I keep the bottle, since I don't have another glass. There's not much left covering the bottom and I don't think Gail will object to me nipping at what's left. I'm not hiding anything from her.

She sips at her rum and looks out over the field. I'd expected her to mention that it was awfully strong, or that she usually took mix, something like that, but she doesn't. She hunkers down in her chair and sips at her rum like she's been doing this all her life.

"John's worried about you," she says. "It's hard for him to say things straight out, but he's worried about you."

"Well," I say, "John doesn't have to—"

"I'm worried about you," she says.

I don't have an answer for that one. Instead I take a pull at the bottle and squint out into the dark, pretending to myself that I saw something move.

"Do you know how long you've been here?" I don't say anything, because I know what's coming. "It's coming up to three years you've been sitting out here, living on rum and cigarettes, and ..." She trails off. I should probably say something, tell her that I'll be pulling out, it's something I had planned to tell her, I'll be leaving early next week, tell her something like that. But I don't. I roll a cigarette and light it, take another mouthful of rum from the bottle. Rum and cigarettes, like she said.

"John tells me that you were married. That you had a little boy."

I nod, not looking at her. "That was a long time ago," I say. "A long time."

"Oh," she says. Then, "Have you seen him lately? Your boy, I mean."

I shake my head. "Not in a little while," I say. "Listen, Gail."

"Yes."

"Have you ever heard of Roger Miller, the singer?"

She thinks about it. "No, I don't think so. Why?"

"He sang 'King of the Road'? Roger Miller?"

"No, I don't think so," she says again. "Is it important?"

No, I tell her, it's not important. Just something I was wondering about. About how someone can be alive in your mind, you might not even know who they are, or their name, but they're alive in your mind, them and their song. And then, poof, you hear that they're not alive. That they're dead and have maybe been dead for a long time. It's a strange way to be thinking, I tell her, but it's the kind of thing that rattles around my brain. I'm aware that while I'm telling her all this I'm talking faster and faster, trying to use words to fill up all the space in the barn, in my head, in the world.

"What was your boy's name?" she asks me. Like she hasn't paid any attention to all the things I've just been saying. And I'm scared, I'm honest-to-God scared to death that she's going to make me tell her, when I see a flash of movement, a quick blur of shadow against some other shadows halfway across the field.

"You see that," I say, pointing. "A coyote just ran across. If we wait we'll likely see some more."

"Coyotes?" she says, her voice a little excited and a little disbelieving.

"You can hear them a lot of the time," I say. "Howling."

"I thought that was just some dogs at the next farm," she says, "barking at the moon."

I shake my head. "You can hear dogs answer back at them sometimes, but first you'll hear the coyotes." I pull at the bottle, but it's empty now. "I used to have an old hound that would listen for them with me. We'd sit out and listen to the yipping and howling and at some point she'd decide to join in. It was like she was letting them know she was there, and she understood, but she wouldn't be joining them. You know?"

Gail finishes her drink and puts the glass down next to the empty bottle. She reaches over and touches me, lightly, on my arm. "Listen," she says, "I think you need some help. We, John and I, we'd like to give you some if you'll—"

I shake off her hand and half turn my chair so she can't see that I'm crying, tears running down my cheeks like I'm a little girl. "Her name was Annie," I say. "She's dead now, Annie." I reach for the bottle and then remember that it's all used up. "I miss that old dog. I sure do."

The Blue Line Bus

Rick Maddocks

THE YOUNG WOMAN CAME IN OUT OF THE HEAT. SHE HAD TO shove at the door a number of times, working up a panicked sweat, before it finally gave. A knapsack weighed her down, along with a hardshell guitar case. And she was overdressed for the weather, a leather jacket hanging over her burgundy tie-dyed dress. She set down the guitar case and looked at the old man behind the counter. Nudging back her cap, she gazed around at the room. There were red naugahyde seats and plastic plants and the small upper window panes were grimy so they cast a yellow pall over the whole room. Its dark panelling and red shag carpet were thick with the smell of old smoke, humans and must. Two baroque metal ashtrays at either end of the ripped couch held permanent offerings of butts and ash. The laminated pictures of once gleaming Greyhound buses passing through the greatest hits of North American countryside were now sticky, faded yellow artifacts, as if they had spent long years hanging over stoves, greasy hot plates. SEE THE U.S. & CANADA THE GREY-HOUND WAY! WE'LL TAKE YOU WHERE YOU WANT TO GO!

"When's the next Victoria bus?"

The old man had been staring at her since she'd first struggled in the door. He stood silent behind the counter now, motionless save for his muddy grey eyes that blinked back at her once, twice.

She noticed how his hands, which were folded lifeless on the counter, were pale, more the colour of driftwood. As if aware of this, he lifted one of them and considered its yellowed fingernails, set it down again slowly, then turned his grey eyes up at her once more. "Eh?"

"Victoria," she said.

"No local buses here, missy, let alone a Victoria Street bus."

"No," she said. "Victoria, B.C."

"British Columbia?" he squinted. His was not a gruff voice with the jovial dance behind it. It was gruff and hard, period. "What, can't you fly, girl?"

"Can't afford it," she said.

"Shit. Bus'll cost you more'n flying, you ask me."

"I didn't. How do I get to Victoria?"

The old man supped on his gums, as if he had a mint in there, a habit that perhaps he'd perfected over many years, since his cheeks were now drawn in, puckered, even when he spoke. "Now, what's in Victoria that's so damn special?"

"Stuff," she said. "Trees. Water. Mountains ..."

"Oh." He spoke without humour. "There's none of that here, I suppose."

"Not much here at all," she said. "Except tobacco fields."

"Must be something here," he said. "Otherwise you wouldn't be leaving it."

She eyed him, mistrustful. "Listen," she said, "I just—"

"How about Lake Erie? There's your water. And Hamilton mountain ..."

"That's not a mountain," she said. "That's an escarpment." She shook her head quickly. "Look, man, all I need is—"

"Seems to me," he pressed a thinking finger to his nose, "you'll have to take a Toronto bus first. Then ..."

Impatient, she peered over the counter, then turned and surveyed the walls, flung her arm out at them, sending a waft of patchouli oil into the close, musty air. "Don't you have charts or something?" she said. "Any cross-Canada maps?"

He brought the finger from his nose to the side of his head and tapped. "Keep it all up here."

"So?" She let her mouth hang. "What do I do after Toronto?"

"Take another bus, I suspect. Ask in Toronto. They think they know everything up there."

"Thanks a lot," she muttered as she turned away. "Jesus. Who the hell do you think you are?"

"I'm a sumbitch," he said calmly, almost cheerfully. "Just an old sumbitch. How about you?"

She gathered herself, let out a long, tremoring breath. "Look," she said, the cuffs from her jacket rattling their plastic buttons on the counter. "When's the next Toronto bus?"

"It'll be along shortly."

"When?" Her tongue stayed pressed behind her teeth.

"A quarter to five."

She looked up at the clock; the hands read quarter to five. "That clock slow?"

He turned round awkward, contemplated the time, than blinked back at her. "Nope."

"Shit!" She rifled through her woven purse. "Whyn't you tell me?!"

"Just did."

"Fuck. Forget it. Just get me a one-way ticket."

"Toronto?"

"Yes, Toronto!"

He turned from the counter, not before gathering something from underneath. He moved slow as history and before long she could see he was walking with two canes and that, for some reason, the canes had been painted red. Such was the slowness of his walk to another counter at the back wall of the room that she stuffed her money back in her purse. She let her knapsack slump heavily onto the naugahyde couch and paced over to the window, where she tapped at the glass with her purple-painted nails and looked out across the street. The old man paid her tapping no mind. He continued at the same doddering pace as if all his concentration and energy were thrown into the pained movement and the rest of him, for that time at least, was nonexistent. His feet stutter-stepped until he reached the counter, where he hung his canes on a large hook, steadied himself before a machine at the back wall. He threaded a slip of paper into it and typed slowly, deliberately, at the numbered keys with his index fingers. The paper ratcheted through. The young woman flinched against the noise; she blew at her straw-coloured bangs and studied the street once more. It was Sunday and so the street was quiet. Shadows careened from parking meters, heat hummed off car hoods. The bus stop was still empty. She shook her head in contempt for all she saw out there. "They got computers that do that, you know," she said. "In other bus stations."

He spoke to the wall. "That right."

She nodded. Her eyes blurred as a truck grinded by.

"And I suppose," he paused to punch the last digits through the ink ribbon, "you've seen a good many in your time."

"Sure," she said absently. "Hamilton, Buffalo, Rochester."

"Hm," he grunted, whipping the receipt out of the machine. "And what's a young thing like you doing gallivanting all over in those places?"

She smiled. "You didn't say pretty."

"Eh?"

"You said *young thing like me*, but you're supposed to say *pretty young thing.*"

"Sorry," he said. "Can't do that."

"Why not?"

"Young ladies like you don't like being called pretty nowadays," he said. "I read it in the paper. Feller in California went to court for calling a lady pretty."

She laughed. "Just 'cos it's in the paper doesn't mean it's true. Specially if it's a shiny paper."

He nodded. "Yup. That's another thing I read about you. You don't believe in nothing, neither."

"Is that right," she said.

"It was in the paper," he sniffed. "So basically you unpretty young folks are running all over the place with your not believing in nothing and doing what else all over Hamilton and Buffalo and wherever, I want to know?"

"Following the Dead," she said.

He took his first cane down from a hook on the counter, propped himself against it, slipped the receipt into his shirt pocket, then grabbed the second cane and started to squeak back across the eternal linoleum. "The dead?"

"The Grateful Dead," she smirked, watching his hard complication of wrinkles work without changing expression.

"Now what on God's green earth," he said, "would possess you young folks to go following any kind of dead, let alone a grateful kind of dead? Seems to me they'd be the worst kind to be associating with."

She smiled. "They're a band."

He didn't do what she expected of an old man. He didn't throw back his head, mock theatric, and say, Oh! Why didn'tcha say so in the first place? and follow it up with a wink or quick, knowing smile or maybe nothing at all, just deadpan. He merely shifted on his canes, shook his head and looked past her at the sunny street. "Nope. Don't get up to Hamilton much nowadays. Forget the States." And when he finally returned to the front counter he didn't hang up the canes, but instead leaned over and nodded down at the receipt, which furled out of his pocket, quivering just below his chin. His shirt was cream-coloured and may well have been white once upon a time, subject to the same yellow weather as the posters. Through the cotton she could see a white vest with sky blue trim. A cleft sagged there in his loose chin, its folds ungathered, a C-section belly. "Self-serve," he said.

She flexed her fingers first, tickled her own palm as if sand was caught there, and plucked the receipt from his pocket. A shiver went through her as her fingers brushed his shirt. The ink had stained the receipt and she noticed there was ink smudged on his shirt as well, clear through the pocket. Though from the angle, she knew he wouldn't see it till he either looked in the mirror at his implacable face or took the shirt off that night.

She picked up her belongings and left the office without a word. The door was stuck again; she had to use all her weight to force it open. "You've got to learn to be responsible," the old man said.

She spun around, speechless and furious as he lifted the counter gate and now, taking up his canes again, started toward her across the shag carpet. "Comes a time people like you've got to stop running around and face up to things," he said. "Even a pretty young thing like you." His mouth was pursed and in this perhaps she could have read a smile, a concession of sorts. But she turned away quickly instead and pulled the door shut before he could get any closer.

He locked the door behind her and flipped over the sign and she stood on the sidewalk and watched him make his stubborn way back across the red shag and lift the counter gate and then cross the linoleum. She thought she heard the sound of his canes clear above the sparse, lazy traffic on the street. She watched until he stopped and picked up a bunch of papers, flicked off the light at the back. "What the hell do you know about anything, anyway?" she muttered. "Old bastard."

She crossed the street. A horn blared at her; she didn't notice the car till it passed, its blue hide glinting in the sun. She would've given it the finger, but her hands were full up. There was no one else at the bus stop. The sidewalk on this side was stifling, the sun still had work to do before it sank down behind the Greyhound office and the other faded, forgettable buildings across the street. Her straw hair could ignite, she thought, flare up like a candle, just like that. She took her jacket off. She lit a cigarette and stood with her hip cocked beneath the baggy dress. The smoke was unbearably dry. After four drags or so, she butted it out on a pole. At least the bus would be air-conditioned. She sat down on her knapsack and pulled down her cap against the sun. This not enough, she took her shades out of her purse, the ones with the narrow plastic frames and yellow lenses—she had others— and put them on. But they were for looks more than use.

There was a dog tied to a parking meter across the street, out-side the Salvation Army. It was a tawny cross, probably between German Shepherd and Lab. Circling the metal post, it got its hind legs tangled in the leash and then finally, dejected, crossed its front paws and lay its head on them, whimpering. The young woman was fixing to cross the street and release the dog, but there was a man approaching, walking crooked down her side-walk, so she stayed with her belongings. The man, his stride faltering, stopped in front of her. His face was in shadow. "Hey," he said, pointing at the guitar case, then letting his arm drop heavy against his leg. "Play us a tune there, darlin'."

"Sorry," she smiled tightly, as much from sun as discomfort. "Not today."

His figure remained standing there, swaying, apparently com-fortable in its shadow. "I know a thing or two 'bout guitars," he slurred. "Got some right around the corner, at my place." He sidled up closer, his zipper inches from the peak of her cap. He stunk of beer. "How 'bout you, darlin'? Whatcha got there?" he said, toeing at her dress. "What model d'you got packed away in there, eh?"

She stood and picked up the guitar case. "Winchester," she hissed. She tried swinging it at the man, but she nearly threw herself down on the sidewalk with its weight. "Fuck off!"

He danced away, giggling like a child. He was shorter than her. In sunlight he was pale, with curly hair and a Blue Oyster Cult T-shirt. "Tha's pretty good. Winchester," he scoffed, grabbing his crotch. "Me too. Me too." He rubbed his stubbly chin and staggered away. He looked back at her a couple of times and grabbed himself again, twirled around, then kept on crooked down the sidewalk.

"Asshole." She sat back down, breathless and shaking. "Nothing but fucking assholes here." She fumbled for another cigarette, but her hands weren't obeying her so she cursed the pack and stuffed it back in her purse. When she looked up, the dog was gone. She scanned the sidewalk over there: deserted. There were only the dark windows of the Greyhound office and the Salvation Army, a gutted-out store between them, its floor piled up with a riddle of oil cans and car parts, a motorcycle chassis, an old COKE THE REAL THING sign faded into pink. And yet there, too, behind the store buildings, she saw trees mushroom up into the sky. When traffic lulled, she could hear the rustle of leaves above the street, see their pale undersides turn over and shiver in the sunlight. So many trees here. She remembered thinking this back in high school, kicking leaves home on late October afternoons, a crisp sky and her knapsack full of books seldom opened, the dry rustle of yellow brown red underfoot, thick dead smell of them. She remembered the trees down in the gully behind her subdivision when the boy put his hand down there and she soared inside and the trees flew away with the sky and his face and then she held his penis like a lighter, pulling at it with her thumb till he rasped that it hurt but he was laughing and stiff, too, and a minute later she watched it spray across her jeans, the slow slug shine of it spread across her knuckles. That little scar on his upper lip when they were full and guilty but flying inside as they walked home under the trees.

Half an hour and still the bus hadn't come. The sun baked. She picked up the rank, cutting smell of the Nanticoke Co-Op grain silos slugging across town. "Get. Me. The-fuck. Outtahere," she muttered to herself. Dry, bleached weeds poked up out of cracks in the sidewalk. Saplings, with candy wrappers and pop cans scattered about them, runted out of the gravel around the planted maples. How's that possible? she thought. Cars and trucks rattled by, belching slow, tired exhaust at her. She could make out a young boy watching her through the tinted window of a slowing family van that was looking for an address maybe. She smiled and the kid frowned back before turning his hard face and saying something into the front seat. She gave the van the finger.

She contemplated going and knocking on the office door again, waiting forever till the old man opened the door, and nodding past him at the big yellowed Greyhound poster on the wall: "Didn't take me where I want to go!" Instead she picked up her things and lumbered down the block to the old diner. She had worked as a waitress here some time ago. Today the place was empty. Pre-wrapped sandwiches and submarines sat on barred shelves in a refrigerated glass display case where a counter once stood, dotted with red leather stools. Along a wall long ago shared by milkshake machines and soda fountains there was now a fridge, with a sliding glass door, full of pop and fruit drinks. Above it, fixed to the wall and ceiling, was a black steel frame which once held a television. She ordered a coffee at the counter —the girl there must've been new; it took forever—then paid and took it and sat at a window table in the corner. In the short time she had been outside, her skin was mottled pink, already giving off a raw sun smell. It was unbearably hot there behind the glass, but it was the only spot from where, just in case, she could see the bus coming up the street. The floor's black and white diamonds were cleaner here, untouched by years of grease and sun, and there were rivet holes in the floor from where booths stood once upon a time. Beside her, along the west wall there was another, smaller clean square on the floor where a jukebox once whirred. She sipped on her coffee and thought herself stupid for ordering it in this heat.

She was half done her coffee when—a hard, low swoop inside, up and under her ribs—she saw them walk by the window. A young man and his wife, a little boy swinging his weight back and forth between their hands, singing. The wife was dressed all in black like the man and, like the man also, her hair was dyed black. The boy was blond, almost white blond. He wore a striped T-shirt. Seeing them, the young woman slid down in her seat and lowered the peak of her cap, but it was the cap that signalled it was her in the first place. When they came in the door, the boy ran across the tiles to the counter and the young man said get back here, but ended up following the boy, black boots clopping over the tiles. She pretended not to pay them any mind, though their progress across the floor pulled on her attention like hooks, marionette strings. It was the wife who noticed her first. A stiffening of the shoulders. Purple lips spread thin across a white face and small teeth said, "Oh. Hello, Marie. Didn't think I'd see you again so soon. Why are you sitting right in the sun?"

She didn't answer.

The wife looked down at her things on the floor. "Going somewhere?"

"Victoria." She sipped her coffee. "Bus is late."

"A bus? To B.C.?" the wife said, already turning around, her cheeks pinched around a cigarette. She blew smoke up at the ceiling. A fan demolished it into the hot air. She called to the man at the counter. "What's he want? Juice?"

"Yep," the young man said shortly. He didn't turn around. He stood akimbo, his black clothes absurd in this heat, and his one foot tapped as he watched the girl behind the counter work the coffee machine. The boy was absently bodychecking his legs.

"Juice juice juice." The wife rolled her eyes and smiled at Marie, but Marie was watching the street.

"So," the wife said, taking a seat diagonally across from her at the next window table. "What's in Victoria?"

Marie craned her neck to see past the parked cars. "Oh," she shrugged, "I don't know. Stuff."

A minute passed. The wife spent it looking her up and down. "I like your dress," she smiled, ashing her cigarette in the tin tray. Her arms were thin as bamboo. Little blue veins networked at her temples.

Marie nodded. "Thanks."

The young man came to the other table with two cups of coffee and sat beside the wife, across from Marie. The boy followed him carrying a glass of orange juice in both hands. He frowned down at the glass, his feet pacing out steps slow and careful as if on a tightrope, his tongue sticking out the side of his mouth. Juice still managed to lap out the sides. He was concentrating so intensely that he walked past the couple's table and came instead to Marie's. When he set the glass on the laminated tabletop, a thick orange ring puddled instantly around it. He climbed up in the chair next to her. Looking up, he took in her face and his surprise didn't know itself from joy. His smile was a rat-tat-tat of tiny teeth.

"Over here." The wife eyed the boy gravely. She dragged a chair around the side of the table so he could sit close to her. "Marie's going to Victoria," she said, chipper, her eyes still serious on the boy.

"Oh yeah." The young man looked at Marie blandly over his coffee. Setting the cup down, he fumbled with a pack of cigarettes and looked out the window. He had pale blue eyes, full of yellow from the sun. His ears were red, transparent when the sun hit them. His black hair was tied back in a ponytail, wisps of it lifting from the fans dotted round the diner so that, except for the hoop earring, he was a burly white samurai. She could see his old, lighter brown hair poking up from scalp. She remembered how, once upon a time, his hair was almost as blond as her own. Her face reddened at the thought of it.

"I think that's great," the wife said. "It'll be good for you. I had a friend, Jody, who was out there. She just loved—"

The man reached across her and slapped at the hand of the boy who was pouring salt into his orange juice. "Quit it right now," he said, his eyes two full stops. He took the saltshaker and clapped it down in the middle of the table.

The boy slumped back in his chair and pouted. "Don't."

He shook his head. "It doesn't work that way, buddy."

But the boy's mind had already butterflied on to something else, his eyes flitting all over the room. His legs kicked under the table. Marie watched him intently, the happy globe of his face, yellow-blue eyes of his father.

The young man gazed over at her gear on the floor. "You never played guitar," he said. "Not far as I can remember."

"Leave it alone," the wife said, snatching the saltshaker from the boy's hand.

"What are you gonna do this time?" the man said. "You gonna busk out in B.C? On the street?" She didn't answer. "No, I know," he said. "You're going to be a star, right? Make it big and all that." Marie sat back silently and folded her arms under her loose breasts. The wife regarded her cleavage out of the corner of her eye. "You know what you need that you don't got?" the man said.

Her head bobbed side to side as she spoke. "No, Thane. Please tell me. What do I need?"

He leaned forward and spoke slowly, patronizing, and cupped his palm as if holding the word: "Talent."

She, a child under his gaze, sullenly fingered her coffee cup.

But unable to sit back any longer, she waved her arm—another waft of patchouli oil—in a vague motion over the faded, obsolete menus pressed below the laminated tabletop, across the window with its streaks and ghosts of handpainted signs, taking in the sidewalk and parked cars and traffic, the Salvation Army. "What's here for me anymore? Shit, what's been here for me the last couple of *years*?"

"Nothing far as I can see," said the wife.

"It's been three years," the man said, idly plucking a vinegar bottle from the boy's hands and setting it down again in the middle of the table. "Three years, almost to the day."

Marie settled back in her chair once more and punched back her cap. "I know how old he is," she said quietly.

The man's eyes lazed from the boy to Marie. Smoke scrolled from his cigarette. "OK," he said. "So tell me this: what's out there for you in the land of milk and—" He made a bitter, disgusted face. "Take those stupid fucking things off, would you?"

After sitting stubborn for a moment, Marie whipped off her yellow sunglasses and glared, not at him, but down at the shades, the orange puddle on the tabletop beside them.

"Do you got any jobs lined up out there?" he said.

"Well," she pulled a stray hair from her tongue, her eyes still not meeting his. "My friend Ange, I met her at the Rochester show, she's an amazing person. She's going out there, too, we're meeting in Regina. Friend of hers works at this big fancy hotel right by the parliament buildings in Victoria, can get us jobs, she says. And the first week I get there, there's a show down in Seattle and then—"

"What kind of show?"

She started, frowned quizzically at him. "Dead show." Ignoring his rolled eyes, she resumed, "And afterward we're coming back up and hitching across to the west side of the Island. Clayoquot Sound. They're clearcutting there, these trees that are hundreds,

hundreds of years old, and there's all these people protesting. It's old growth," she said, excited now. "They're these huge, fucking beautiful—"

"So you're gonna be a tree hugger," he said, studying her over his canoeing cigarette.

"Yeah, right," she said, cold. "Sure."

"Pfff." He looked away. "Flavour of the month."

"I think it'll be good for you," the wife said, her mouth pursed as she butted out her smoke. When it didn't go out, she ground it into the ashtray with her thumb. "Good for you to get out of this town. I envy you."

"Yeah," Marie smiled, insincere. "So you said."

"Look!" The man pointed his cigarette at her, his face shook. "There's certain responsibilities here still," he said. "Loyalties. Unlike you, I can't afford—"

He checked himself just as the bell clanged above the door and two teenage girls breezed in and crossed the floor's black and white diamonds. All tanned, smooth legs and short shorts and hair up in ponytails wisping at their necks. Their voices rang sharp and confident in the air, owning it. They grabbed two Cokes out of the fridge and teased the counter girl about a boy and she told them to fuck off. Laughing, they waltzed back out across the diamonds and out the dinging door without paying for the pops. Marie watched them walk by the window; the one girl was talking and the other grinned and pressed a sweating Coke can to her forehead and in a vague, empty moment her eyes caught Marie's then sparked away. When Marie turned her eyes back to the man, he was still pointing his burnt-down cigarette at her, as if the whole time he'd been frozen in that position. "Unlike you," he said slowly, "no, *because* of you, I can't afford to be a kid anymore. I can't be flying by the seat of my pants out into the wild blue yonder whenever shit doesn't work out the way I want it."

"Kid, you call me," she said. "Ha! After what we … Shit, Thane, we're the same age, and *she's*—" She waved her hand dismissively at the wife, then leaned forward and addressed him as if he were the only one in the room. "You told me, remember? How it didn't matter ... you'd take care, you know, till I got my shit together ..." She trailed off, her eyes wet.

"That was then," he shook his head. "That's history."

"No, it was always, you said, you know ... remember, how we—"

"No!" The wife slapped the kid's hand. Salt sprayed over the table. She pointed at his glass of juice. "Drink it."

The boy scowled. "Nooo."

"Drink it." The wife grabbed the boy's hands and clasped them tight round the glass. The juice shook. She poured in pepper. She snapped up a vinegar bottle and shook it until her knuckles were white, the veins at her temples swelled a little. "Drink it now." She tried to push the glass to the boy's lips and said to the man, "Tell your kid to drink it."

"Leave him alone," Marie said.

"You mind your own business, you," the wife whispered. "I wasn't talking to you. I'm his mother. He doesn't even know who the hell you are. You're some lady in whacked-out hats who comes breezing by every few months, or whenever she feels like, to smoke and drink on the back porch and yabber on about her next big thing. I'm the one who's had to feed and dress him for the last two-and-a-half years. What the hell do you think that meeting yesterday was, those forms we signed? One of your parties?" She laughed suddenly. "You weren't able to keep him for more than six months. It's a wonder you showed up at the woman's office yesterday." She fussed with the boy now, frenetic, combing his hair roughly with her fingers, her other hand still clenched around his glass. "He never was yours," she whispered. "You were always too busy being in love with yourself."

"Go to hell," Marie said. "You don't know anything about

love. It's just hate turned inside out for you. You're so scared to lose him and you lie to yourself that it's love that's keeping him with you 'cos you know it's always been me he—" She broke off and gazed into the young man's eyes, which were now riveted on her. She quickly looked down at her hands. "Ah, fuck it," she sniffed.

"Who's *he*?" the wife said, suddenly turning to the young man. "Which *he* is she really talking about?"

"Don't," the boy pouted. "Daddy … don't …"

But the young man was still staring across at Marie. Her bangled wrists, her fair skin mottled from sun, the loud, unashamed dress. She caught his eyes and they hurt, so she fumbled her sunglasses back on. She swilled back the last black puddle of her coffee as the boy started struggling back his juice. He sipped at it, but then let the liquid fall from his mouth as if a wad of gum. "Blecch!"

"You drink it all," the wife said. "Now."

The boy shook his head. Juice dripped sloppy from his chin.

"Drink it, I said."

Marie kicked back her chair and strode over to their table. She pulled some juice away from the boy's chin with her finger and licked it. Made a pleasant-surprise face at the wife. She picked up the kid's glass with both hands and raised it to her lips and began to drink, her elbows cocked up in the air. "Jesus," the man covered his face with his hands and laughed. Juice dribbled and then ran out the sides of her mouth, down to her chin. It was sharp and sick-tasting, but she gulped it back, ravenous. When she was finished she set it down slow and satisfied on the table.

"Mmmm," she smacked her lips. "Tha's good."

"There's your bus now," the wife said, without expression.

Marie started and looked out the window, but saw only the yellow and black abdomen of a school bus rumble by. "Yeah. Thanks."

"No, really," the wife smirked, leaning across the man to peer out the window. "It's stopped right across from the Greyhound office."

"Bullshit."

"No," the man said, looking out through his fanned fingers. "She's right."

"Shit!" She made for her stuff, but the boy had grabbed a hold of her dress. "C'mon," she said. "Let go, little buddy." But he sat back, tie-dye bunched up tight in his pink fist. He kicked happily, all bright eyes, his face crinkled. She looked down at him and her eyes softened, then broke. "C'mon," she said. "Please."

"Let go of her," the wife said. "She's got to go." She tried to pry the boy's fingers loose, but Marie picked up the chair, boy and all, and lifted it up over her guitar case and knapsack and away across the floor. She began to run, rocking the seated boy back and forth in her arms, leaning to his ear and going *vroom!* as she swooped between the tables, jostling chairs. The boy squealed with pleasure as he flew over the black and white diamonds. "You'll hurt him!" the wife cried. "Quit it! Thane, tell her to stop!"

But the man didn't seem to hear. "I give you six months," he said. "Tops. You'll still be the same person, you know. There, anywhere. It'll still be you." Marie made like she didn't hear, but her head was afire. She circled the whole diner—doing figure eights here and there, speeding past the counter so the boy waved over the cash register at the girl as he floated by—before Marie finally tired and set him down gently in the middle of the floor. He enjoyed the ride. She ruffled and then found herself kissing his hair. It smelled sharp, of vinegar and bleach.

"See ya, little guy."

"Bye." But he was more interested in his own travels. His head lolled about, gazed all over the room from his happy new spot.

"I say it's just a change of scenery," the man said, his face red.

The wife reached to stroke his cheek but he pulled away. Ignoring him, Marie strode back to her table and grabbed up her purse. She picked up the rest of her things and said bye again to the boy and lumbered out. The guitar case rattled the door as she shouldered into it, out of it. Yes, on the sidewalk she did turn, in spite of herself she looked back and saw, through the window, the man sitting alone at the table, staring back at her through her own reflection. Her silly bulbous hat, her spectacled face in shadow, the jacket draped over her arm, a bundle of black gear about her body, as if she was a magnet for such stuff. There were things she could've said to him, redundant things. Behind him the wife was lifting the boy out of the chair and saying something, softer now, but neither the boy nor the man paid her any mind as the wife jostled the chair back to their table. The boy twirled around under one of the fans in the ceiling, craning back his neck, entranced by the whirring blades. The wife grabbed his arm, her face drawn and pale. The man shook his head, ran his forearm across his forehead, rubbed at one of his eyes with the heel of his fist. Marie imagined the salt working in there, how bitter that salt would be, and her own eyes started to work. When he took his hand away, she half expected the eye to be gone, pushed back into the skull, but it was the same big, blue eye that stared back at her with its twin. The light, small scar on his upper lip. The wife said something, leading the boy toward the rear of the diner, then she suddenly stopped and petted the boy's hair, fawning over him, kissing him now, apologetic. Slowly, the young man turned and said something back to her. They picked up their things and walked back to the shaded half of the room where Marie could see them no longer.

She ran up the street fast as she could, her dress billowing a hot, dry breeze about her legs, her feet slipping in her sweaty sandals. The school bus was sitting at the stop, the engine still running. She set down her things and wiped at her eyes, the sticky mess of orange on her face. The door was hinged open and when she stepped up to the bottom step, the driver sat in his seat, a burly middle-aged man with dark three-quarter moons of sweat soaked through under his arms, shirt unbuttoned almost to the belly and hair stuck thick to his skin. His face a big bearded shine, rivulets of sweat caught in the laugh lines. He blew at his slick, matted-down bangs, glared dark at her and shook his head. "Fuck."

She had to bite her lip to stop from laughing through her tears at him when she handed him her ticket. "Hottest day of the year and my bus died on me," he said. "Just coming out of Port Dover. Nothing back at the shop. Had to go out to Blue Line Road to get one of these stupid things." He glared back at the regiment of green plastic seats, the black corduroy rubber floor, dust-caked windows in the back. He shook his head at her again. "Fuck."

There was no one else on the bus. Flies buzzed and razzled in the thick air. She walked up the wide aisle, wider than she remembered as a child, and dumped her baggage into a seat near the back. Her arms were light and hollow. A school bus, she thought. She just stood there a while, lost in a bubble of laughter, before she took her cap off and flung it onto the seat. She lifted her dress and let it fall, making a breeze. She began to turn around, once, twice, faster, until she was spinning now, twirling with her arms out like a helicopter skimming the tops of the seats, the skirt carouselling out all around her burgundy blue yellow green pink orange until it flew clear of her knees, her thighs, her underwear and swished over the dull green seats. "Hey, miss," the driver said. "Hey!"

She stopped in mid-flight, her blond hair lashed across her face, in her smiling teeth. "What?" She punched the dress back down as an afterthought.

"You want to help me out with the windows? Might be easier for ya. You're liable to get dizzy by the time we reach Hagersville."

They went from one end of the bus to the other—she rear to front, he front to rear—opening the top windows and letting them clap down so that, little by little, hot outside air came slugging into the bus. When they were done the bus driver smiled, tired and painful, and sighed thanks. "Twenty years I've been working for this company," he said, "and this is the shit I have to put up with." For some reason this made her want to laugh all over again. She slumped into a seat across from her stuff, kicked her legs out across the expanse of green vinyl and leaned her head back against the glass. A maple's red leaves leaned into the window, rustled at her ear. Cool, insistent, knowing. The driver settled back in his seat and shifted the bus into first and pulled out onto the street and she watched as their yellow and black reflection sailed loudly across the Greyhound office windows, the fake plants reaching out of the dark, pawing the glass.

The bus rumbled out of town, past a strip mall, a car dealership, the OPP station. It clattered over the train tracks which ran diagonal through town and away across the flat countryside. Passing by the small grass-runwayed airport, she saw a skydiver float into view, swinging gently back and forth beneath a red-and-white-checker parachute. She watched the small figure land nimbly on a clearing of bare earth and come to a running stop as the huge silk umbrella crumpled in slow motion in his wake. A small crowd of people gathered on the surrounding grass, ready to greet him. The bus passed a Baptist church, its parking lot filled with the cars of afternoon worshippers. Soon the highway narrowed to two lanes. Buildings gave way to yellow birch, hickory, sassafras. Out by the Blue Line Road they passed a man at the side of the highway. He was shirtless and tanned and squinting into sunlight, thumbing for a ride. The bus driver laughed as the bus coughed a wall of dust at the man. "Now what kind of a person do you figure tries to hitch a ride from a school bus?" he said. "A *school* bus."

The heat was more bearable now, the sun behind them. They passed over a creek bridge, sped above treetops, leaves reaching up through the guardrails. And in the distance, on the lakeshore, she saw the steelworks, its blueblack riffles of smoke luminous in the sun. She took her sandals off, pulled her dress up over her knees and let the air through the windows cool her stretched-out legs. She took off her yellow-tinted glasses, too, and suddenly the world was another, stranger and more real place. Tobacco fields floated past her bare toes, the new runt plants short and a pale, yellowish green in the sandy earth. On some farms tobacco had given way to ginseng. Kilns had been dismantled and where they once stood she saw hundreds upon hundreds of two-by-fours staked into the straw earth, propping up corrugated sheet metal roofs fitted together so low that a grown woman had to stoop to walk beneath them. The sun caught the sheet metal and glinted brilliant silver white across the flatlands, so brilliant that for a moment she was blinded.

And she opened her eyes to an October afternoon almost four years ago now when the water glinted silver over the white pebble riverbed. And he stood before her, his face in shadow, breath pluming, and he said something about the light on her face. "I've got to get home," she said. And he said, "Me too," as crows lit from the branches overhead and he picked her up and set her on a graffitied rock and she wrapped her legs round his and the stone grazed her skin, but it was good and they breathed into one another's mouth all teeth and tongue and she said, "I've dreamt about you, you know," and he said no and she said, "Yes, ever since, you know, that time," and he said, "You couldn't have 'cos there's only so many dreams to go round and I used them all up dreaming of you." She tugged hard on his coat lapels and his ear, translucent in the sun, tasted of cold smoke and she called him things she didn't mean, his hips viced between her knees. Her blond hair was in his face, between his lips, the scarred one she licked, and he said it meant one thing and one thing only and that was that they were soul mates and she said, "You think?" And he said yes, he thought so, "Oh of course, yes, always." She looked at him suddenly, so close, his face loose and honest and pricked with cold. "You're such an idiot," she said. And she was laughing up into the sky then up over his shoulder, his light brown hair, the branches bared themselves grey in the sunlight and leaves fell in the shushing water like yellow and red flakes of rain and got carried away on the water that shivered over the white stones.

"No smoking, Miss," the bus driver said.

"Not even cigarettes?"

He flashed a look at her in the large mirror. "Not even whacky tobacky."

She shrugged, flicked the cigarette out the window and watched it tumble and ricket into a bleached weed ditch. Then she took her whole pack out of her purse and threw it out of the window, too. The little white sticks went laughing out in all directions. She smiled to herself, pictured kids happening upon the smokes sometime in the next few days, ecstatic, scrabbling about after them in the gravel as highway traffic whizzed by, and smoking each and every one of them down to the filter, one after the other, throwing up in a field on the way home, lit smokes dropped in a field of chaff. She saw these fields ignite behind the silhouettes of running children and saw the fire rage across the flatlands, burn up ribbons of trees like hair, the wildfires raging for days, flames licking the blue sky until it turned black, the outskirts of the town charred and deserted, smoke rising slow. And she saw two figures walking through the rubble, their faces blackened except for a ghost of orange around the smaller figure's mouth. And as he stopped to pick up some charred, wretched thing the man beside him said, "Don't now, leave it alone."

So she found a new vision and in this vision she saw herself out west. Smoke scrolling up from a hillside campfire. People dancing in colours and swirls and shared food and clotheslines and clean water lapping, bluegreen from the trees surging down out of the mountains to the shore, cool air falling infinite from pine needles and arbutus leaves, and she would be sitting on a quiet strip of sand with the Pacific lapping at her feet and sand in her toes and there she would learn to play the guitar. Her name would be shouted and she would think of her name holding many things that it did not hold two, three weeks ago, before the three thousand miles of country she saw for the first time and drank in, drank up full. The cottonball clouds hanging, almost within reach, over the first farmlands of Manitoba. The yellow yellow brown yellow of Alberta. The Badlands. The trail of rainbows in the Rockies. And here, on the edge of the world, there'd be a man walking out of the trees down to the water with a couple of cans of beer and she'd know already it was his step, by its weight and speed and music, and she'd smile and keep playing —maybe Neil Young, or Joni Mitchell, maybe even "Ripple" by the Dead—like she didn't know he was there so that he would touch her in a soft, hesitant, tender way sure not to alarm her, but she'd jump anyway from his cold beer hands and when she turned round his face wouldn't be movie star handsome, no, that would be too much because with all his other charms it would just be too much. No, he wouldn't look quite like anybody she'd known before, no one from back home anyway. No, no one at all. And with her eyes closed but seeing him, she smiled softly and lulled by the heat and rhythm of the bus, drifted into sleep.

* * *

The old man locked the door behind the young woman and flipped over the sign. He walked back over the red shag carpet on his canes, which he had painted red some years ago in order to camouflage them against the carpet and give the impression, to any no-good who happened to be watching from the street, that he was walking of his own power and free will and just fine thank you very much. Of course, this hadn't worked. He'd been robbed twice in the last year, which meant he'd been robbed three times since he opened the place thirty years ago. The world was going to hell in a handbasket and sorry, his hands were full up. He lifted the gate and squeaked past it and, stopping at the counter at the back, hung up one cane, picked up a thin sheaf of papers, flicked off the light, tucked the papers under his arm, then took his cane again and made his slow, inevitable way to a side door. Before passing through that door he saw the blurred form of the young woman still standing out on the sidewalk, looking in.

He shuffled into another room which held a stove and chair, a sink and fridge, a TV against one wall and bed against another, with a low drop-leaf table at the foot of the bed. He'd had these things moved downstairs last year, when he finally admitted to himself it was too much for him to traverse the stairs day in day out. The upstairs rooms were vacant now, save for unessential furniture and stacks of papers and magazines and the ricketing of something or other at night. But he wouldn't rent the place out to just any come-lately. He'd offered it to his granddaughter, but something had gotten under her skirts and seeped into her brain since she'd left her mother's home and taken up with a lawyer up in Toronto; somehow she'd gotten her nose lifted up so high she'd developed the notion that her shit didn't stink. Never came down to visit, either. Not even when he was slated to get his cataracts done and they called off the operation last minute. Heart. Tests, they said. No, he didn't see hide nor hair of her. Just a telephone call, and not a word about what ailed him. "Get one of those motorized carts," she said. "They're cute." Dressed all in new ribbons and bows, she was, sitting pretty in the city and still not believing in nothing. Sure, maybe she'll have that lawyer guy pay her way, but to where on God's green earth? the old man wanted to know.

It was then—a dull, aching ripple through his chest—that he realized the young blond woman hadn't paid for her ticket. He stopped in his stuttering tracks. It was the third time in two weeks he'd made such a mistake. "That's all she wrote," he said, matter-of-fact. "All she wrote." He lit a gas burner then and, hanging his canes over the lip of the sink, filled a kettle and set it on the stove. A dog whined somewhere outside, but the sound soon melded with the hissing water. The old man sat down in the chair in front of the stove, rested his chin on his hands and watched the water boil.

He drank two cups of coffee in the same chair. When he was done, he got up shakily and swilled the cup under cold water and left it in the sink to dry. He took up the canes again in both hands and crossed the small room, past elaborate gilt frames that held portraits of men, women and children whose faces were no longer in fashion, pictures he had not looked at, not really, for some time. The white room was orange now, the ripe sun bouncing off the buildings across the street, its glow singing back through the small window in the wall. At the foot of the bed the old man slumped down, sighed, hung his canes on one of the hooks fixed here and there about the room's walls, sighed again and withdrew the sheaf of papers from under his arm. He shuffled through them, found a Greyhound map of Canada, one he'd never opened before. He dropped the other papers on the bed and set the map on the drop-leaf table, unfolded it, spread it out and turned it over to the side that housed Ontario. He took a red pen from his pocket and began drawing, freehand, a thick heavy line from right to left along Highway 3 to Jarvis. Beside it, in the margin, he wrote down the highway kilometres: 18. His hands, old and driftwood-coloured as they were, were steady, assured. Next he drew a line north along Highway 6, through Garnet, Hagersville, Caledonia, till he hit Hamilton: 58 kilometres. "The dead," he shook his head. "The dead. Now what in blazes ..." He kept drawing the lines, complete with small detours for village stops, and wrote down all the corresponding numbers until he reached Toronto. He pictured the landscapes she would pass through, most of them changed, almost unrecognizable since he himself had last passed through them. Leaves and grass and water now steel and glass and plastic. She would change in Toronto. And there would be many more miles to go. The old man would wear out the first red pen, already on its last legs, before she got there. He'd write down a lot of numbers, add up a lot of numbers, making subtotals every ten numbers, so he could make a list of the subtotals, too, so that the sums curled around the map's margin. When it was time, he'd turn the map over and start on the prairies, noticing how his previous red lines had seeped through the paper and thinking how in all his days he could never sleep on a bus. He'd draw the lines with such care and purpose, all the way across Canada to the ocean.

Letters to the Future

Andrew Gray

WHEN I TALK ABOUT SMALL TOWNS, I DON'T MEAN THOSE DOTS on the map that mark a clump of houses, a store or two, a service station. I'm talking about places with history, a courthouse, a school, a decent library, towns that were buzzing with civil industry in the fifties and sixties. True, now they have an uglier face—Taco Bells and car dealerships littering the highway—but each time I'm in a new one I look for the same things: faded civic pride, a collective memory eroded by satellite TV and big-box retail, a librarian. It's good to find a librarian who's bored, who's wondering if she's the only one who cares about books, ideas, culture. The only one who thinks high school hockey, drinking in the bush and getting married at eighteen aren't enough.

I read in a magazine once that all happy families are happy in the same way. I believe it's the same with these towns. The good ones are all good in the same way; the bad ones I just try to forget. They're like ghost towns to me, emptied of anything of interest—cars, people, insurance salesmen, motel clerks, birds I've never seen before singing their hearts out in the bushes outside my window.

*   *   *

It goes something like this: I put on my rumpled blue oxford button-down, a pair of faded chinos and a tweedy jacket I picked up at a Sally Ann. I sling a soft nylon bag full of papers, pens and manila envelopes over my shoulder. I go into the library and introduce myself to the librarian. I've thought of calling myself Thornwell Jacobs, but who the hell would buy that? Christ, even in 1936 people must have thought that was an odd name. So it's Jacobs, but I use my real first name, Ted, Theodore if they're old enough to have grandchildren.

The script varies, but the high points are usually the same. This time the librarian was younger than most, but the library had the look they all have: fluorescent lights, institutional carpeting, racks of well-thumbed paperbacks in the popular reading section.

"Good afternoon," I said. My bag thumped on the desk.

She looked up from her computer screen, chewing a lock of her hair, lost in something. "Hold on a second." She tapped a few keys and ran a barcode reader over the book that sat in front of her. "OK," she said.

"I'm a historian," I said, "here to do some research."

"A historian?" She looked behind her at the stacks of books for a moment. "This isn't a university," she said. "We don't have an archive or anything like that."

"That's OK. It's newspapers I'm looking for."

By this point they're usually excited—a real live historian rather than some Grade 9 student, or a retiree working her way through a mystery series.

"There's only one. It isn't exactly the paragon of journalism, unless you're researching the recipe-of-the-week column ..."

"No," I said, smiling encouragingly. "Not exactly. But if you have copies dating back to the forties, I'd be happy."

She looked to the rear of the library. "There's a room full of boxes back there. The *Courier* goes back to the turn of the century, but I don't know how far back our collection goes. They're not very well sorted. We're kind of a small operation here. They should probably be on microfilm, but we just don't have the money."

"That's fine. I'm used to it." In fact, I depend on it. Micro-film's spotty; details, pages, even entire issues, can be lost in the process. The pictures are bad and the text is sometimes impossible to read. Best of all, nobody else bothers to flip through the original musty piles of *Oakville Beavers* and *Saginaw Sentinels*. I wear latex gloves now, though I used to like having black fingertips. I used to get a hard-on when I smelled old newsprint.

"Harriet," she said.

"What?"

"I'm Harriet. If you're digging around back there, you'll be here for a while. You'll need to know my name."

"Of course." I do the Ted thing.

"If you don't mind, I'll call you Theodore, too. Ted sounds like someone you'd go hunting with and I don't particularly like hunters."

"You must be popular come deer season."

"I'm a librarian," she said simply, as if that explained everything. She stood up and turned off her monitor. "Come on, then, I'll find you a spot in the back." She came out from behind her desk and started walking toward the back of the library. "So," she said, "what's so interesting about the crappy old *Courier*?"

"I'm looking for stories about time capsules," I said. "I'm writing a book about hope, dreams for the future, what they tell us about the fifties and sixties."

"Really?" she asked, unimpressed. "Haven't we been hearing about their hopes and dreams all our lives? Don't you watch TV?"

I watch the news, the better game shows and history documentaries. Everything else is idiotic.

"Sorry," she said. "I don't mean to give you a hard time, but you know the Boomers recycle the fifties and sixties every chance they get. The Cold War, Sputnik, the Summer of Love. *Leave it to bloody Beaver*. What are you going to find that hasn't already had its two hours on the History Channel?"

"You're not like the other librarians," I said.

"It's a long story." When we reached the back of the stacks, she pulled a set of keys from her pocket and opened the door next to the washroom. It was the usual: the employee lunchroom with literacy posters on the walls, a white microwave, a coffeemaker, a cylinder of non-dairy creamer. There were stacks of envelopes, paper for the photocopiers, boxes of new books. Another door, another key and then a room full of stacked storage boxes on metal shelves.

Harriet gave some strict instructions and then I was alone with piles of newsprint, the familiar smell of it rising from each of the cardboard boxes. People used to think old papers wouldn't last, that their wood pulp fibres would turn into dust after a few years. It fuelled the mad rush to microfilm everything, but they last, all right. I reached into my bag and pulled out a pair of latex gloves.

* * *

What I didn't say: I didn't say that every time I stop at a library with its tattered paperback romances, garage sale signs on the bulletin board and lonely librarian, I dream. I dream on a lumpy mattress in my suite at the Red Flag Inn, when I'm driving inter-states and Queen's highways. It's a simple dream: all I do is turn a page.

I didn't say: "I said you weren't like other librarians, but I say that to all the librarians. Every town has its own Harriet, and if you drove the roads I've driven, you would see yourself at forty, at fifty, at sixty. All these paths leading to the desk and the cardi-gan and the books and a town lousy with insurance salesmen."

Finally, I didn't say: "I know deep in my bones that it will come to pass that no matter how you feel now, you will marry a hunter, because in the end we are all hunters."

*   *   *

I lay down on my lumpy Red Flag mattress, still smelling newsprint and musty air, and thought about the Crypt of Civilization. Laid to rest in 1940 by Thornwell Jacobs, the father of them all, it sleeps under Oglethorpe University, Atlanta, Georgia. DO NOT DISTURB UNTIL 8113, which is about as far from today as we are from the start of the Egyptian calendar. The man wasn't fooling around.

What will those big-headed creatures of the ninth millennium think of the array of objects stored in the vault? There are six hundred and forty pages of microfilm, a windmill to generate electricity so they can play the phonograph recordings of Hitler, Mussolini and Popeye. There's a quart of beer, for God's sake, a package containing six miniature panties and five miniature shirts, corn plasters and eyebrow brushes, dentures, ladies' stockings, an original script from *Gone with theWind*, a Donald Duck doll.

In 1996 Sotheby's sold Clark Gable's leather-bound copy of *Gone with the Wind* for two hundred twenty thousand dollars. A mint quality Donald Duck doll from the thirties doesn't fetch quite the same premium, but it's still worth a few thousand to the right person. *Superman's Christmas Adventure, a* comic book from 1940, goes for four thousand dollars. The market in vintage movie posters is brisk. I could go on and on.

Westinghouse may have coined the phrase "time capsule," for the 1939 World's Fair, but it was Jacobs who started it all with his 1936 article in *Scientific American* and the building of the Crypt. Jacobs really thought someone would wait until 8113 before cracking that seal, that crowbars and shovels would fall out of fashion. He forgot that most of the tombs in the Valley of the Kings have been empty for a thousand years.

* * *

The fourth morning, a bird I'd never heard before sang from the bush outside my window. It had a long, liquid call that rose and fell and rose again. It was the sort of sound that might tug at someone's heartstrings in a country music song or paperback romance. I peeked out the window, half expecting to see Harriet out there singing away. It was a bluebird, with a long, thin tail. I threw half a bagel at it from the bag on my bedside table and it gathered up its feathers like the skirts of a matronly woman and took its music elsewhere. Down at the Red Flag breakfast nook, I had cereal and toast, avoiding the $6.95 breakfast buffet of congealed eggs and fossilized bacon.

I had only made it through two boxes the day before. Fifty papers a year times twenty years equals one thousand closely printed issues. That's a lot of stories about weather and school board meetings and car accidents. I had become tired of the back room and started taking my papers to the stuffed chairs in the front and reading them there. I could see Harriet from the chairs, behind her counter. She didn't laugh much, but she didn't seem particularly sad, either. She had that look people have when they're listening for a footstep in the hallway, a knock on the door.

You'd think that after doing this as long as I have that I wouldn't be distracted by librarians, or by the papers themselves, that I'd fire through them like a speed reader, but it's a long and boring slog, so the interesting things stick in my mind. For instance, in three days of reading I discovered that until the end of the war there was a POW camp just outside of town. In a forties' issue I found a picture of a funeral service being held there, the casket flag-draped, iron cross prominent as German officers in greatcoats stood around with flowers in their hands.

Nobody remembers these things: the scandal involving the mayor in 1949, hints of sexual impropriety between the lines; the polio scare one summer that kept kids from local pools; civil defence meetings; the return of Korean War vets; a woman named Julia Casket who lived to be ninety-eight; a carpenter who installed peepholes in every house he worked on for fifteen years; the grade school that was built on a decommissioned army base, unexploded munitions heaved up by frost in the playground. These towns hardly deserve their pasts. The paperback romances must seem more real.

I was in the archive room reading about a series of mysterious sheep deaths in 1955 when Harriet knocked on the open door behind me and poked her head in.

"It's tuna salad today."

We ate our lunches together now. I had brought my own on the first day, but I'll admit it was a rather half-hearted attempt— a chocolate bar and a doughnut. She'd looked at it and said, "You can't be serious." Instead, she gave me half her roasted pepper, Asiago and pesto sandwich, laughing at my expression when I bit into it. She had a nice laugh, a slightly crooked smile, slightly crooked teeth.

"I'll bring you a whole one tomorrow," she said. "I can't watch you eat that crap."

Today's tuna salad was on thick multigrain, flecked with tomato, celery and green onion, layered with crisp romaine. "You've really got a way with sandwiches," I said.

"I'm sure you say that to all the librarians."

"You don't really seem ..."

"Like a librarian? You mean, what's a girl like me doing in a place like this?"

"I wasn't going to say *that*," I said.

"Close, though," she said. "Here's the condensed version. My mother was the librarian for years; I worked here through high school. Then I was off to university and halfway through my master's degree when she got sick. I came home to take care of her. I took on her work at the library because nobody else wanted to do it. The ladies who do the mystery book club and the high school girls who stack the shelves part-time certainly weren't interested. So I was here and didn't feel like going anywhere else. I'm still here."

I felt nervous for a moment. I touched the piece of paper folded in the front pocket of my chinos. "Maybe you can help me," I said. "I've found something."

"Better than the POW camp? Better than Julia Casket, unmarried until the age of ninety-six?"

"I've been bothering you," I said.

"You're kidding," she said. "What do you think I do all day once the books have been shelved and the ladies have their Agatha Christies?"

"I've found the story I was looking for."

"Oh. Congratulations." She took a bite of her sandwich. "So you're leaving, then?"

A poster on the wall that read HOOKED ON READING showed a trout with a fishing rod pulling a book out of a pond. It seemed to have captured her attention.

"I want to finish going through the rest of the papers to see if there are others. Then ..."

She tilted her head quizzically, reminding me of the bluebird.

"There's a time capsule I'd like to find," I finally said. "I'd like to dig it up."

"Can you do that?"

"There are thousands of time capsules buried around the world; most of them have been forgotten. If nobody digs them up, nobody will know what the people who buried it wanted to say. We're the people they wanted to find this stuff, after all."

"So you just start digging holes?"

"That's the problem. People misplace them. Sometimes

they're in building cornerstones, sometimes long paved over, sometimes forgotten entirely."

"I'm not much good with a shovel," she said.

I pulled a photocopy of the story from my pocket, unfolded it. "There's another way you can help."

The picture was of a group of people standing in a field. In front of them was a sealed time capsule the size of a child's casket. Low-slung buildings skulked in the background. There were shovels in evidence (always a good sign) and surveyor's stakes. The headline read: TIME CAPSULE TO BE BURIED AT NEW SCHOOL. Students and staff had written letters to the future, local businesses were involved.

Harriet squinted at the picture. "That silver thing is the time capsule, isn't it?"

I nodded. "They were going to call them time bombs."

She looked closer, her nose nearly touching the paper, staring at the halftone dots of the photograph.

"Half the school burned down when I was a kid. We were all pretty happy about it."

"It's still there, though?"

"They rebuilt it. It looks like they're standing on the playing field in the back." She looked thoughtful. "Did you like high school?"

"Sure."

"It's the interesting people who have the worst time of it in high school, the people who can't be the same as everyone else. Don't you think?"

"High school was fine," I said. "High school was a breeze."

I changed the subject, asked her about surveyor's plans, architect's drawings.

"The town hall should have them. They'll make copies for a small fee, but it might take a day or two."

"It's been waiting fifty years," I said. "I can wait a couple of days."

She knocked on my door at the Red Flag that night. The news was on.

"I know the clerk," she said after I let her in. "He told me your room number. I hope you don't mind."

"No," I said. I was suddenly aware of my toe sticking through the cheap cotton of my right sock, the small pile of dirty clothes by the bed.

"I thought maybe you'd be sick of the food here. You might want a real dinner."

Her house was small, on a well-treed lot. Buttery yellow light spilled across the lawn and the bushes in the front yard. She pulled her pickup into the driveway, gravel crunching under the tires. "I'm not really the truck type," she said as we got out. "My car's in the shop. This is my dad's."

Her father was retired, basketball-player tall, had to bend slightly as he went through doorways. When he sat on the couch, his knees were almost level with his head. I sat in the easy chair across from him and we both glanced at the pictures on the walls and the faded wallpaper as if they were deeply intriguing. Harriet was making cooking noises in the kitchen. Finally he said, "Historian."

I waited a moment, but that seemed to be all he was going to say. "Yes," I replied.

A minute passed. There was a small pile of dust beside the fireplace that someone had forgotten to sweep into the pan. "You fish?"

When I was a child there were days on the water with my father and his friends. I remembered the metallic sound of the bass they hadn't bothered to kill thrashing against the aluminum hull of the boat, the men pissing off the side as their empties piled up by the Styrofoam cooler.

"No," I said.

"You should fish. We've good fishing here."

There was a picture on the mantel of Harriet as a teenager. You could see the woman she was now latent in her younger face, though her hair was shorter, her cheeks rounder. For a moment I wished I had known her then, could have taken her out in my rusty Ford Escort. We would have driven with the headlights off down the rural routes past rustling fields of summer corn. Things would have been different.

We marinated in awkward silence and what felt like silent disapproval. Harriet came in to save me.

"Dad," she said. "For God's sake, get him a beer." She winked at me. "The poor man's obviously dying of thirst."

Harriet drove me back to the Red Flag after dinner and coffee and after her father had livened up enough to tell a few stories about his days with the Parks Service. There had been glances between us during dinner; she had shown me family photos. We sat there in the truck in the parking lot for a few minutes, a not uncomfortable silence between us. I should write this one off, I thought. I should pack my bags tonight and pay my bill in the morning and drive to the next town.

Instead, I turned and looked at her upturned face, the slightly crooked shadow of a smile. "Um," I said. "Do you want to come in?"

She nodded and I must have looked surprised, because she laughed. "Come here," she said and grabbed my ears. She tasted of coffee and burnt sugar, her skin faintly of popcorn.

We lay there on the lumpy bed in my room after the kissing and all the rest of it. I had filled the plastic ice bucket from the machine down the hall and she held a chip of it under her index finger and ran it down my chest in a cool line. I left my hand on the curve of her hip.

"I've been thinking about Julia Casket," she said, "who

married at ninety-six for the first time. What does that say to you?"

"What should it say?"

"Maybe it's never too late."

"To get married?"

"For anything," she said. "To change your life."

I thought about the other librarians I had known, the long ribbon of road that stretched behind and ahead of me. It was hard to imagine doing anything else.

"I think Julia wasn't like the rest of us," I said. "I think Julia is the exception."

She propped herself up on her elbows and looked at me. "You're the historian. You've been reading all about people's dreams. Didn't you ever look anyone up and see how they turned out?"

"No," I said. "I never looked anyone up. But I think we're probably all disappointed in the end."

She sat up, pulling the sheet around her. She suddenly looked vulnerable; it tugged at something in me. "I'm just saying that," I said.

"It's getting late," she said. "I better get home."

I stood in the doorway in boxers and a T-shirt as she drove out of the motel courtyard in her father's truck. She'd looked up at me from the parking lot and said something I couldn't hear. I waved, anyway.

*   *   *

"I've got a shovel and a spade," I said. "I'll use the spade to cut the turf, the shovel to dig out the earth."

"You sound like my father," Harriet said. She stood holding a flashlight, the beam pointed at my feet. We were behind the school, just beyond the edge of the playing field. Surveyor's flags bloomed from the grass, marking the squeals of my metal detector.

"Well, maybe it doesn't really matter what I use. I just haven't had an audience before."

"So you never ask permission to dig up someone's lawn?"

She had suggested we talk to the school board, or at least the caretaker, maybe even have a reporter there. "Most of the time I strike out. It's better to appear with a time capsule in hand than with a shovel and a half-baked idea."

I dug and Harriet held the flashlight beam on the ground and I started to hope we wouldn't find anything. Two hours later, the ground was pocked with small craters. I'd found an old beer can, unidentified rusty chunks of metal and a handful of nails. Cinders a bit below the grass gleamed darkly, remnants of the fire. I stood there for a moment, leaning on the shovel, feeling the sweat trickle down my side. Harriet scrutinized the site plans, the light from her flashlight yellowing as the batteries faded. "I was sure this was the spot in the photo," she said.

"We've still got two markers left." But I could feel the empty ground below us, the secrets it would not give up. I would dig twice more, come up with a handful of nails, then I could just drive away without looking back. I could start again somewhere else, anonymous again.

At the next flag the capsule announced itself with a hollow clank. My shovel blade hit it, about half a metre down. I stood there for a moment, the shovel still deep in the earth.

"Bingo," Harriet said. "Jackpot."

It looked like an ancient artillery shell, the metal marked with soil, stains and a long scratch from my shovel. It took the two of us to lever it out of the hole.

"I feel like a grave robber," Harriet said. We were both dirty, sweating, perched by the unearthed capsule and the hole it had left behind.

"More like an archaeologist," I said.

"They're not really that different, are they?" She rubbed her hands together, working a cramp out of her fingers. The flashlight faded and winked out, leaving us in the dim light of the half-moon and stars.

"So we fill in the hole and then what? Some sort of celebration?"

"I'm usually by myself," I said.

"We should celebrate," she said. "Doesn't your room at the Red Flag have a tub?"

Her face was turned toward me, a pale smudge in the night. I was unsteady. It felt like the sea was about to sweep my little boat out from under me.

Back at the Red Flag we splashed around in the narrow tub, my legs tight around her hips. I soaped her back. A cold beer wept condensation on the toilet seat by the tub. The remains of a pizza littered the countertop; green pepper and olive debris spilled from the box. I rubbed shampoo from the tiny bottle into her hair. The things we do when we're trying hard not to think.

Well-scrubbed, we tumbled around on the sheets for a while. It was better than the first time. Half-asleep afterward, I felt her pull her arm out from under me, a kiss on the temple light as the footsteps of a mosquito. "I have to leave again," she said.

"Run, run, run," I mumbled as she dressed.

I dreamed about coffins and dead people. I woke in the small hours and searched around the room, feeling hollow as a straw, before I remembered we'd dropped the capsule off at the library after we'd filled in the holes. It was safe, tucked away in the back room.

There was no birdsong in the morning. Its blue source had left for parts unknown. Consequently, I slept late, missed the breakfast buffet, the insurance salesmen who had checked out en masse that day, the opening of the library. When I finally arrived, a knot of people were gathered at the time capsule—my time capsule.

Harriet approached, eyes bright. "People love it," she said. "I cleaned it up this morning, put out the word."

They were running their grubby hands over its surface, chattering excitedly.

"Here," Harriet said. "I want you to meet someone."

"It could have been damaged," I said. "You should have talked to me first."

"I thought you'd be happy."

"Oh, I'm happy," I said. "I'm over the moon."

She gave me a strange look and then tapped the shoulder of a woman standing near the capsule, interrupting an animated conversation. "Mona," Harriet said. "This is Theodore, the historian I told you about."

Mona beamed at me, her grey hair in tight curls around her head. She clapped me on the shoulder. "Great going, Indiana Jones." She motioned to the capsule. "I'm in there, you know. My Grade 7 class wrote letters to the future and sealed them inside. I'd completely forgotten until Harriet told me this morning." She touched the top of it lightly. "You wouldn't believe the memories . . ."

"That's fantastic," I said. "Really." I smiled tightly at the two of them. "I'll just be a second."

I went to the back of the library, opened the door with one of the keys I'd copied from Harriet's set one day while she was out and went into the storeroom. There were two unread boxes of Couriers. I sat on my chair and started sorting through them. I'm supposed to be discreet; I'm supposed to keep my distance. It was remarkable how much I'd screwed up.

It took twenty minutes before Harriet came back. "People want to talk to you," she said.

"So I gather."

"The mayor wants to do a whole opening thing tomorrow night for the six o'clock news. The TV and everything. They want you and me to say something."

"Did I ever tell you about the bluebird?" I asked her.

"What?"

"Every morning it sits outside my window at the Red Flag and sings. The first time it's OK, the second time, too, but not day after day. Who can take that? The same sad little song day after day after day."

She didn't look very happy, but I hadn't asked her to go to all this trouble. I hadn't said a thing about it. "What's really going on?" she asked.

"How is this research? This dog and pony show, these people running their hands over an *historical artifact*? What do they know about history?"

"It's theirs, isn't it, the people of this town?"

"They don't deserve it."

"Jesus, Theodore. It *is* theirs." She spoke slowly, as if she were piecing something together. "This is their town, their time capsule, their mayor. They buried it and they're the ones who are supposed to open it. You'll still get to look through the contents."

The capsule was slip, slip, slipping away. "You're right," I said, conciliatory. "I get carried away sometimes. It's hard for me, when I've spent so much time looking. I've been disappointed before."

"You had me worried," she said. She smiled. "So you'll talk to the TV people, tell everyone about your research?"

"I'll put on a show," I said. "Don't worry, I've done this before."

*   *   *

What makes one person able to do something others can't? Julia Casket getting married at ninety-six, for example, or a bank robber sticking up the local credit union. It's a matter of will, being able to cross the line. The difference between a bank robber and yourself is not the gun, the note, the ski mask—these are props. The difference is that standing there in the lineup for the teller, the bank robber has the will to pull out that gun and make his demand.

That evening after Harriet went home, I drove over to the library and parked by the dumpster in the back. I put on my carpenter's belt, clanking with tools, and opened the back door with one of my copied keys. The time capsule sat on the table mid-room, gleaming in the light of my flashlight. I had a closer look at it. The case was in two halves, held together by a line of bolts. Fifty years underground had left the bolts pitted and scarred, though the whole thing had survived remarkably well. I treated each bolt with penetrating oil and pulled up a chair while I waited for it to work.

I once found an x-ray of a child's foot. A holy relic from back in the days when they x-rayed everything, when the shoe store in the city had a fluoroscope and you could wiggle your toes around and see the bones move. The bones were striated, ghostly, flesh just a shadow on the film. Something about it made it hard for me to throw away, though it wasn't worth anything.

The bolts came off. Wrench, hacksaw, small drifts of metal filings piling up on the table. More than enough evidence to convict, certainly. But who really cares about a time capsule?

I pried the top cover open like a coffin; for a moment I envisioned a skeleton, hands folded across its chest, a toothy grin. But the light of my flashlight found only a scattered mess of paper, some boxes. I smelled the scent of the past released.

Sometimes I pick through looking for choice morsels and leave the rest for whomever might find it interesting. This time I took it all. Paper, disintegrating plastic dolls, cardboard tubes and boxes. I left the plaque TO BE OPENED OCTOBER 12, 2052 inscribed in tarnished silver with the names of important people. Idiots put the date on the inside, not the outside.

Back at the Red Flag I spread the contents on the bed. One box held children's letters. I tossed it aside. One had letters from the old mayor, town council, various important, and probably dead, people, also worthless. Next some newspaper photos, including the one with everyone standing by the time capsule. Then there were samples from various merchants: squares of cloth, beauty supplies, a glass bottle of Coke, dolls from the toy store, tacky to the touch. They were just dolls—no Minnie Mouse, no Donald Duck. There were also magazines, a book with a garish dust jacket, some movie posters.

In the end I set aside five comic books in brown paper, a package of baseball cards, a Roy Rogers and Dale Evans lunchbox and Thermos and three movie posters in cardboard tubes. It was a good find, not the best I'd had, but good.

I packed my clothes and the collectibles in the car, settled my bill with the night manager. I felt clumsy putting my bags into the car, like I didn't quite fit into my skin. Then I realized I could take the leftovers and put them back into the capsule, seal it up again, stay for the opening, make up some stuff for the TV people. It wouldn't be hard.

I took the back way to the library, car tires crunching up the lane, headlights off. It took three trips to move the leftovers into the building. I left them by the capsule and went to dig through the trunk for my tools.

When I came back in, the pile had been moved and there was a pool of light at one of the reading tables. I stood holding my flashlight and tools, the door clicking shut behind me.

She didn't look up. She sat at the table.

"I'm bringing them back," I said. My voice sounded too loud. Harriet didn't look at me. I went over to the capsule and put down the tool belt.

Then she looked up. "Whatever you took isn't worth what you think it is."

I started to say, "I didn't—" and then I thought better of it.

"I know you're dropping these off, that they're worth nothing to you."

I didn't say anything. She didn't sound angry. I couldn't tell what she sounded like.

"I was excited. I couldn't sleep. I wanted to come out and look at it. So, naturally, I was surprised to find it open and empty. I went to find you, to tell you. Then I saw you loading your car at the Red Flag." She looked up. "So what did you get?"

"Some comics," I said finally. "A lunchbox. Stuff like that. Collectibles."

"And you've done this before? You're not really a historian?"

I nodded.

"It's funny," she said, "what has value and what doesn't. Those things you took are meaningless, pop culture crap. But the letters, the photographs, these pieces of people's lives. Nobody wants to pay for these."

"I'll return the other stuff," I said.

She shook her head. "No, you take it. Like I said, it's not worth anything to us." She held up a letter. "This is Mona's letter, written when she was twelve. Her whole life waiting to happen. Have you ever read any of these letters? Or do you just throw them away?"

I started to answer, but she interrupted me. "No," she said, "I don't want to know. I don't want to hear anything else you have to say. Go find another town. Go find another librarian."

If I had said anything before taking my tools and getting into my car and driving away, I would have told her I had read the letters. I would have told her that they're all pretty much the same, that I doubt Mona would have said anything different from any other twelve-year-old. *I was here. Remember me.* Some crap about world peace, that the people of the future will be wiser and kinder. All the things we never are and never will be no matter how long we wait to open the time capsule.

* * *

It wasn't the last time I saw her. A year later I was up at the university, deep into the library stacks, when I heard a voice I recognized. I looked around the corner and saw her sitting at one of the study tables with some students. They were laughing and there was a boy who couldn't have been more than twenty-five or so next to her, his arm casually around her shoulders. He obviously thought he was pretty smart.

I could have gone up to her, said Hello, as if we were old friends. I could have asked if she was finishing her master's degree. I could have told her that she had been wrong, that the things from the time capsule really *were* worth something, that collectors paid nearly a thousand dollars for them. I thought about it, but my meter was running out and I had to go.

You Would Know What to Do

Anne Fleming

LIKE A STATUE OF A PRIME MINISTER, LEGS APART, SHOULDERS square, eyes in the distance—George stood outside the bank. He was not yet ready to do the thing he meant to do and standing still for a stretch of time seemed important for some reason. Luckily, it was not too cold for February, or he would have had to go right ahead.

As he stood there, a picture was taking shape in his mind, the warmth and clarity of which reduced the street and dull parkette across it to two dimensions and made him forget what chill there was. George found himself doing this often these days, giving equal weight to visions that came from inside the brain and outside it. Memories, one could call them, but the word would never do them justice and was not quite accurate in any case. This was the realm, he was starting to think, of the artist, of the mathematician, the physicist, those who leap into whole new ways of thinking. The world he had formerly inhabited was small, so small, and the worst of it was he had thought it next to infinite.

In the picture, the memory, his wife, Penny, is reading to their children. She did this every Sunday night from the time they were babies until they left home, sitting in her big, puffy armchair, her feet up on a small ottoman.

In the picture, the motion picture now, the children are young and she is reading *Peter Pan*. Dorothy, the oldest, is nine or so and sits on the couch doing something with her hands. Knitting, perhaps. And kicking her legs, always kicking her legs. Edmund lies on his back on the floor beside Penny, listening intently and idly running his hands back and forth over the carpet. Alice lies under the piano, pretending to be a dog. She pants and scratches herself with her foot and laps water from a bowl Penny lets her keep there. Dorothy and Alice don't always appear to be listening, but every now and then they smile or laugh, or join in on a favourite line. It's a trait they share with their mother, the ability to concentrate on more than one thing at a time.

Alice barks every time the dog in the story is mentioned. She tries for a deep, gruff bark, because the dog is a big dog, but Alice is only six and her deep and gruff is not really either. She gets into a frenzy when Peter lures the children away while the dog is tied up, helpless, in the backyard. Only here can George place himself in the scene. Here he looks up from the *Scientific American* he is reading at the dining room table and roars at her for quiet. Then he takes his magazine to the kitchen. George likes to think that after this departure he puts down the magazine in the kitchen and listens surreptitiously to the rest of the story, a smile of whimsy playing at his lips.

George had remembered that the readings happened, but he hadn't remembered the books they'd read, hadn't remembered that *Peter Pan* was a favourite of Penny's until the children were reminiscing about it after the funeral.

"What would you say, Ed, once a year?" Dorothy half-shouted from the kitchen where she was wrapping up the sandwiches and crudités left over from the reception. "Keeping Saran Wrap in business," George would have said another time.

"At least," Ed said, sprawled in the living room with everyone else.

Alice, slouched in Penny's chair, was looking intently out the window as if trying to identify something outside, a bird, perhaps. George expected her to get up any minute and pluck one of the guide books off the shelf. One of the few things the whole family had in common was liking to look things up. Penny and Alice did it for a living—they were librarians, Penny at a public school, Alice at the university.

"Remember how she'd make a big deal out of Tinkerbell dying?" Alice said. George wouldn't have known she had been listening and he felt suddenly like he didn't know his children at all, like they were Penny's, they belonged to Penny, and he was just a sort of difficult pet they had let tag along from time to time. "And we'd have to clap and say we believed in fairies or Tinkerbell would die. Remember, Dad? And you wouldn't clap."

"Wouldn't I?"

"Oh, we kept bugging you," Dorothy said, leaning in the doorway, wiping her hands on Penny's happy-face apron. "'Come on, Dad, clap your hands, clap your hands,' but you wouldn't do it, you said something like you didn't believe in fairies, so it wouldn't be right to clap ..."

"And anyway Tinkerbell would never die because she only ever existed in a book in the first place," Edmund said. "Quote, Tinkerbell has life everlasting in print, she doesn't need me to clap for her, unquote."

"Long memory, Ed," Dorothy scoffed.

"I kept a diary."

Alice started quietly to cry.

"I still believe in fairies," Edmund said.

George got up abruptly, taking the last stack of dishes into the kitchen. He could hear Dorothy and Edmund in the living room.

"Jesus, Ed."

"What? It's true."

George leaned into the counter and took deep breaths.

Downstairs he could hear the rise and fall of the television. His grandsons, Dorothy's boys, watching videos.

* * *

What George meant to do was to rob the bank he stood outside of. George McFee, a thin, wide-shouldered man of sixty-nine years, meant to walk into the bank and point the unloaded gun in his pocket at a teller and demand she fill his knapsack with cash. He had no idea how much money he would get and he wasn't sure to the dime what he'd do with it. Some grand anonymous gesture having to do, in a roundabout way, with Edmund. Something that whenever he thought of it afterward, would tug his lips in a mysterious smile, something that on his deathbed he'd crook his finger to draw them closer and confess in a sly, happy whisper. Something that would make a good story.

George was not a desperate man, not in the usual sense of bank robbers, and he was not particularly nervous, but he still needed this time to stand before the deed. Like Penny, that year she took yoga, saying she needed to feel grounded. "We're all grounded, that's what gravity is for," he'd said at the time, but now he understood. Penny was dead seven years to the day. That was part of it, too.

The bare treetops made a mat between the city and the sky. A teenaged boy passed in front of him, or was it a girl? He wasn't a teacher anymore; he couldn't tell. George set his eyes on the black web of the treetops. He thought of Birnam Wood and wondered if he'd receive a sign when it was time.

* * *

Penny had been only sixty-one when she was hit by a car while riding her bicycle to work. She rode every day, regardless of the weather. When there was fresh snow, before the streets had been plowed, she rode on the sidewalk in case she slipped.

George's usual birthday gifts to Penny were dull—pleated dresses he should have known wouldn't suit her, kitchen gadgets, cookbooks she used only once. So the year mountain bikes came out, he almost choked with excitement. Here was something she'd actually like. Here was something that would surprise her. He spent hours at different shops comparing models, prices and advice, and more hours at the library reading reviews in bicycling magazines.

The Saturday before her birthday he was very close to a decision—it was down to the Sierra or the Rock Hopper. He just had to finish raking the leaves, then he'd pick up the bike and take it to Dorothy's for safekeeping until Friday.

But while he was raking, Penny came pedalling down the street. "Look what I got!" she shouted, ringing the bell on her new mountain bike and grinning to beat the band.

"Oh, Penny!" George said, as disappointed as a boy.

Her face went tight. "Don't rain on my parade for once, George, just don't."

She got off the bike and stomped into the garage, not giving him a chance to tell her what he'd meant. George raked the lawn leafless.

When he came inside, she was on the phone to a friend. Laughing, not sulking or huffing. He decided to go for a run, forgetting she was going out that night to a play he hadn't wanted to see. Not till she was brushing her teeth did George get the opportunity to explain.

"You beat me to the punch," he said. "The bicycle. I wanted so much to buy it for you."

She spat out her toothpaste, took his face in both hands and kissed him on the forehead.

*   *   *

On the morning she was killed, they left the house together into four inches of soft snow and the first clear sky in three weeks—

she on her bike, he in the old jogging suit she'd given him one Christmas when jogging was in. She'd bought a matching suit for herself and matching shoes, but she never took to jogging. She used hers for gardening and bought George new shoes when the old ones wore out.

Penny was riding on the sidewalk as usual when a twenty-six-year-old mechanic with the rising sun in his eyes, late for opening the garage, slid his '76 Duster into her white Norco Stump Jumper as she crossed at a stop street. Penny flew for the first and last time in her life, thirty feet through the air, headfirst into a parked car. Her neck broke on impact. She did not suffer.

George loved running in the morning, in the park by the river, especially in winter, when he left clouds of breath behind him, when the sun rose clear and yellow over the eddying Speed, and everything, even the shadows, felt clean. He was ashamed of himself for having loved it that morning, too, for coming back to the house exhilarated and unknowing. For humming "Bolero" in the shower, for deciding to let the phone ring rather than dripping all over the carpet (at his insistence, they had no answering machine), for going to work as usual, for not knowing this morning was different than any other. As he lay on the couch that night, he ran it all over and over in his head, the run, the shower, his happiness, his oblivion. There was no reason on earth he should have known his wife was being hit by a car and yet the fact that he hadn't threw his world out of kilter. That was the reason he had to keep running.

Getting ready the next morning, each step seemed insur-mountable—putting his legs into his long johns, lifting his arms over his head to put on his shirt, pulling on the old track suit. When he came to the shoes, he kept turning them over, examining the worn sole, the flap at the back where the rubber was delaminating, the stitching across the toe that was starting to come away. Yesterday he hadn't needed new ones. Today he did. Everything had changed.

Where had Penny bought the shoes? How much did they cost? How could Penny not be in the kitchen in her housecoat, blowing on a hot cup of black coffee?

On the feet, he had to tell himself, *shoes on the feet*. He put the right shoe on. The lace was frayed, almost broken through. *If the lace breaks, I won't go*, he thought, closing his eyes and tugging.

A block away from the house, he almost turned back. His heart was racing, he felt shivery with foreboding. Alice had forgotten to pull the screen over the fire as she'd promised the night before and a coal was just now igniting the floor. Dorothy's boys had made a snow slide that ended on the street where they'd be run over. Dorothy herself had slipped on a bar of soap and was drowning in the tub. He forced himself to keep running.

George had expected to die first. That was the way it happened statistically. The husband first, and then the wife, and later, much later, the children. Edmund beat up in an alley. Alice hit by a truck. Todd daring Kevin to drink Drano. He gave in, he ran home. And there was Alice, looking out the kitchen window, a cup of coffee in her hand. They were fine, they were all fine, it was just Penny, it was just a fluke. Flukes had their place in statistics, too. Alice gave him a little wave. He ran on past the house, tears running cold into his ears.

Dorothy was there when he got home. "Jogging? Today? Dad—" Her voice was thick with emotions he couldn't interpret. He didn't bother answering. As he went upstairs, he could hear her talking to Alice. "What is he thinking? Jogging! Like it was any other day."

"Yesterday was any other day."

God bless Alice. He ran the bath and sank into the hot water, feeling his chest loosen and his heart contract. He wept until the water went cold.

Every day it was the same. He ran half his route, panic building in his chest until he could not bear it, then raced home to phone his children. He wanted to hear their voices, even on their answering machines. "Hi," he planned to say, "it's your dad. Just wanted to say—" But he didn't know what he wanted to say, so he listened to their "Hello? Hello?" or to the silence until the second beep sounded, then held the receiver to his chest, depressing the cradle with his finger. He knew he had to stop the day Alice said, "Dad? Is that you?"

George bought a Walkman to run with. He cleaned out the basement. He painted the living room. He wouldn't let Dorothy and Alice get rid of Penny's clothes. Eventually, he went back to work.

The first night that Dorothy and Alice left him on his own, he played all the glorious big music Penny had hated, played it so loud it shook the windows. Afterward, he stood for a long time before noticing the cold of the windowpane under his fingers and against his cheek. Before noticing the silence.

"You would know what to do, wouldn't you," he said out loud. "You would call your friends, the whole big noisy gang of them. They'd be over here night and day, they'd wrap you up like a big cozy blanket. One of them would take you to Florida for a month, and in Florida you'd forget because it's not a place you'd ever been with me. There'd be nothing around to remind you. It would be warm, that'd make you forget, too."

He felt suddenly that she was outside the house. Not in person, but her spirit, that her spirit was outside the house like a vast cloud snuggled up to the brick and glass and shingle and foundation and extending outward and downward like an aura. He stood right beside the front door with his head cocked, as if he could hear it. He flung the door open. Gone, as he'd known it would be.

In the kitchen he made himself an instant decaf and felt it again. She was out there, she was right there, and he would never touch her. He would never touch her again.

"Maybe you'd stay in Florida longer," he said, pitching his

voice louder without knowing why, then realizing it was so the chair could hear it, Penny's big chair in the living room. "Maybe you'd decide to move down there. And you'd meet a widower. Fun guy. Bit of a joker. Not like me at all and for that reason you'd marry him. You'd go on adventure cruises. Costa Rica. Alaska. He'd get you to overcome your fear of flying."

He went into the living room and looked at the chair while he spoke to it. "Eh? Would you do that? Marry him, the guy who's fun at parties? Sure you would. Go ahead. You deserve it."

Dorothy had given him *On Death and Dying*; he recognized the stages he was going through. It didn't matter. He liked talking to the chair. Before Penny's death George had felt closest to Dorothy. Alice's stillness, her soft deep voice with its hint of misanthropy, had put him off. But it was Alice he told about the chair. Dorothy was the one who would sooner or later put him in a home. Sooner, if she found out he talked to chairs.

"I can't bring myself to sit in it," he told Alice. "Like something would happen. It would swallow me up, or, I don't know. Silly thing to think."

"I sat in it once," Alice said. "The day of the funeral. I remember the light came in in a peculiar way. Not brighter or less bright, but—thicker somehow. More thick."

After a long summer, George was eager to get back to school, but when he stood in front of his homeroom class the first day, he felt none of the nervousness and enthusiasm of other years. He didn't care if these kids learned which gases are inert and which are volatile or how to make polyester or how the reaction of sugar and yeast combined with wheat gluten and heat makes dough into bread. He didn't care if he never again saw that moment of unveiling in their eyes when one of them got it, really got it, for the first time. Spring—retirement—rose in the distance like a mountain he was approaching on foot. When he finally reached the top, it turned into a plain again. He sold the house, which angered Edmund, saddened Alice, and was applauded by Dorothy. Of course he kept the chair.

*   *   *

When Edmund got sick, he lost something, some edge. George hadn't expected that. He wasn't surprised otherwise, that Edmund had it, that none of them had told him until they'd had no choice. Penny had set the tone for that when she'd lied about Edmund in the first place. Who knows what else she'd kept from him. The girls could have had abortions, for all he knew.

That first lie ... every time George thought of it, he shook his head. It still made him mad. He and Penny had been getting ready for bed after taking Edmund out to dinner for his twenty-fourth birthday. She lay in bed reading. And he, cautiously, as he took off his shirt and tie, had wondered aloud about Edmund and girls.

"When was the last time he had a girlfriend?" he asked.

"That we knew about?" Penny said without looking up. "I guess that would be Amy."

"Amy was a long time ago. Do you think ..."

"Mm-hm."

George cleared his throat. "Do you think he could be," he cleared his throat again, "homosexual?"

"Oh, I don't think so. I think he's just shy. I think he's still going through that separation stage, you know, when he doesn't want us to know everything about him." She turned the page, never having taken her eyes off it. George thought she was probably right. She generally was about these things.

But the minute George saw Edmund on the news holding another man's hand, he was never more certain of anything than that Penny already knew. Gay Pride Day. George had never heard of such a thing.

"It's an oxymoron," George said to Edmund the next Sunday. George had not told Penny he'd seen Edmund on the news. Instead he suggested they have Edmund over for dinner Sunday. Penny was delighted. She wanted them to have more of a relationship.

"The hell it is," said Edmund.

"It is. Morally speaking, Gay Pride Day is an oxymoron."

"Oh, it's morals, now, is it? We've moved on from science?"

They were just warming up. Penny was in the kitchen, crying. Not because of Edmund, because of George.

"I saw you on the news the other day, Ed," George had started. "On the *news*, for God's sake. It's not enough I have a faggot for a son, he has to broadcast it to the world. 'Look, everybody, I take it up the ass.'"

"George!" Penny said.

Edmund dropped his fork and threw up his arms.

"Oh, Ed!" Penny said. "Didn't you see the cameras?"

That was it: the confirmation George had been waiting for.

"Why don't you go read a book, Penny. Why don't you go read a goddamn book." George started mimicking her, pitching his voice high and shrill. "'You know Ed, he's just shy. Why, even if he did have a girlfriend, that doesn't mean he'd tell us about it, now does it, dear?' You make me sick, the two of you."

So Penny cried in the kitchen while her husband and son yelled at each other in the dining room. After the door slammed behind Edmund, George went to the basement to avoid Penny and then sat there, reorganizing his tool bench, hoping she'd come down. When she did, when she apologized, he couldn't keep from crying. They held each other, saying I'm sorry. There wasn't much else they could do.

* * *

George dimly registered that passersby were noticing him and thought he had better move from the side of the bank to the bus stop, a place where people are expected to stand still in the cold. He stepped back when the bus came and forward when it left.

George hadn't fooled himself with his Peter Pan scene—at the moment, he was keenly aware he had not secretly listened and smiled while Penny told the story. He hadn't done it because he hadn't understood the point of either the story or the telling. When he pilfered candle stubs as a boy, it was to read *Popular Mechanics*, not *Treasure Island*. Penny blamed his bewilderment with fiction on his deprived, bookless childhood. Deprived it might have been, compared to hers, but it had given him a practical and uncluttered mind, and he was thankful for that. Why would anyone spend hours, years, reading about things that never happened and people who never existed? It was all right for Penny, but George had a whole universe to explain. He didn't have time for fiction.

*   *   *

After their big blowup, George and Edmund saw little of each other. Edmund came at Christmas and Thanksgiving, talked volubly to everyone else, asked George a few polite questions about his work, answered George's few polite questions and then left early. Penny, on the other hand, saw him once a week for lunch. She was their unspoken go-between, their interpreter. George thought she was making some headway. He no longer felt nauseated by the thought of two men together, although he tried not to think of it at all; he accepted that maybe Ed was not sick, just different. And then Penny had died.

He didn't know where to go next. He didn't know what to do with Ed's comment about believing in fairies. He didn't know what to do about Ed, so he didn't do much of anything, except worry.

And still he got used to it. He just hadn't realized how until Alice called him with the news.

"We thought you should know. Ed has AIDS." Beautiful blunt Alice. He imagined Ed and Dorothy fussing behind her "Who's going to tell Dad? What are we going to say?" And Alice just picking up the phone.

George had been reading up on AIDS. It fascinated him. A brand-new disease. Its very existence was fascinating. And the kind of disease it was—one that let all other diseases have their way with the body. If anyone had thought it up, it would be brilliant. For years George had predicted new diseases to take the place of former population checks like polio and scarlet fever and cholera. That even they had not been entirely stamped out sustained his belief in a world seeking ecological balance. The battle was still Man against Nature, but unlike his bush-clearing forebears, George was rooting for both sides. Here was AIDS: advantage, Nature. Here was Man staging a comeback, scrambling for a cure.

"Where is he?" George asked Alice.

"Right here. We're at the hospital. You want to talk to him?" Alice was off the line before he had a chance to ask how bad it was.

"Hi, Dad."

"How are you feeling?"

"Ah, well, you know. Not so good."

"I'm sorry to hear that."

There was a long pause.

"I was hoping you'd tell me before it got to this," George said.

"You knew?"

"I've been expecting it."

"Right. Of course. I was bound to get it. Listen, Dad, I'm going to hang up now, OK?"

George went and stood behind Penny's chair. He put his hands on its back. He knelt down and put his arms along its arms. His son was going to die. He *had* been expecting it, because if he didn't, it would take him by surprise, and he didn't ever want to be taken by surprise again. From now on, he wanted to do the surprising.

"You'd be one of those women I see on the news, wouldn't you," he whispered to the chair. "Yes, you would. Out there with your placards, shaking your fist. I never knew what you were on about." He was quiet for a minute. "You must have hated me sometimes."

The next day he donated ten thousand dollars banked from the sale of his house to AIDS research.

* * *

Ed was only in hospital three days that first time. He always seemed to be sleeping or dozing when George visited and George wondered if that was real or put on so they wouldn't have to talk. George didn't want to talk, anyway, he just wanted to care for his son. He made a list of things to do and get for Ed's apartment— bath rails, toilet rail, bedpan, foam mattress pad, hemorrhoid cushion. Alice told him he was being premature.

On his way out on the second day, George passed a man he recognized but couldn't place. Usually he was quick to identify the adult incarnations of his students, and the fact that he'd missed this one kept him puzzling all evening. It wasn't until falling asleep that he realized it was the other man he'd seen on TV, the one holding Ed's hand.

The next day George saw the two of them holding hands again—or rather René holding Ed's hand between both of his. It looked different this time. A bit shocking, but not offensive. Nice, even. As soon as Ed saw George, he drew his hand away.

"I've heard a lot about you," René said when Ed introduced them.

"Yes," said George. "Yes." He cleared his throat. "You went to Mexico together."

"Beautiful place. Great trip." René recrossed his legs and flattened a pant seam. "The doctor says Eddie should be out tomorrow."

"Yes, I thought I'd buy some groceries."

René coughed. "Oh, really. That's nice."

George left quickly. Ed was uncomfortable with both of them there. More accurately, Ed was uncomfortable with him.

*　*　*

George decided he had to do now what Penny had wanted him to do six years ago. He had to get to know his son. He had to see him regularly and he was pleased with himself for thinking of a way he could combine this with something else he wanted to do—start Ed on a macrobiotic diet. Preliminary studies seemed to show it made a difference in the lifespan of patients with full-blown AIDS as well as in the HIV-positive population. George decided he would cook for Ed.

He got the key to Ed's apartment from Alice so he could drop the first batch of groceries off and see what staples he might need to get. She didn't say a word about the possibility of René being there.

"Uh ... hello," René called out from the living room as George let himself in. George wanted to disappear. He turned to leave, then heard René behind him and turned back.

"No one told me ... I didn't realize ..." He lifted up Penny's net bags full of food. "Groceries."

René slapped his forehead. "I thought you meant for yourself. I'm thinking, 'Grocery shopping, how nice for him, but how exactly does this relate to Ed?'"

"Well, I'll just ..." George gestured he'd leave the bags there.

"No, no, no, you take it home, we have lots of groceries."

"But it's macrobiotic. I spent an hour at the health food store."

René cocked his head, smiling. "Well, all right then, what have you got?"

They developed a sort of friendship, René and George, based on their discussions of Edmund's conditions, current research, experimental drugs, diets, mental health. René was also a scientist, a chemist. He ran a lab at the university.

He made George nervous at first. He did not look effeminate, but his voice and gestures regularly veered off into a language George had only seen in parody. He was not shy about it, and gave no sign that he noticed George's discomfort, but he must have, because early on he said, "You have no sense of camp whatsoever, do you George?"

"René!" said Edmund.

"Of course you don't. You're Eddie's father. Never mind, we'll let you make us dinner anyway."

Edmund looked apoplectic. René leaned confidentially over to George. "I adore making him twitch."

George laughed. He realized how much he and Edmund tippytoed around each other, trying not to give offence. René breaking their unspoken rules was a relief. He found himself telling René—and by extension, Ed—things he would never have told before, like how he was starting to see things that weren't there and how he felt like Penny lived on in her chair. How he'd appreciated her, but maybe in the wrong way, maybe for the wrong things, and how much that possibility pained him. Ed didn't contradict him or reassure him, but he looked him in the eyes for the first time in ages and George felt a lump in his throat.

Alice was right about George being premature with the sickroom paraphernalia. Ed got healthy again. Not completely—he still had night sweats and diarrhoea—but enough to work. Working made him happy.

George thought the distance between him and his son was closing. The nights he cooked for Ed and René were the highlight of his week. He spent the days leading up to it planning the menu, and whole afternoons hunting down unusual ingredients. He went to cooking classes at the health food store. The moments after they took their first few bites became moments of high drama: Will they stop to exclaim over the exquisite taste? Will they savour the taste wordlessly on their tongue? Or will they shovel it in like it was any other dinner?

Their routine was this: George arrived early, around five, and started cooking while Ed, depending on how he felt, either kept working or watched TV. René arrived at six, took a shower, then helped George with the salad while Ed read them choice bits from the newspaper. "Grey Panther caught," read Ed. "The Florida bank robber nicknamed 'the Grey Panther' was apprehended today while attempting to flee a St. Petersburg bank on a moped. Charles Panowski, 75, is in custody on six charges of armed robbery."

"A moped?" René asked.

"Apparently."

"My God, that's too beautiful."

"Wonder what he did with the money."

"Built a private shuffleboard court."

"Renewed his lawn bowling membership."

"Bought seven pairs of white shoes, one for every day of the week."

After dinner, Ed would always offer to do the dishes and George and René would always refuse. This was when they talked treatment. AZT was the big topic these days. The drug had just been approved in the U.S. after determined lobbying on the part of AIDS organizations and direct action by groups like ACT UP. George had reservations about ACT UP, but he admired their brashness and vigour.

After several weeks of discussion, George took the idea to Ed one night after dinner.

"You and René think I should go on AZT," Ed repeated back to him.

"Yes."

"Uh-huh, yeah, and what about my bone marrow?"

"You can stop taking it if you're losing bone marrow."

"Who's going to pay for it?"

"I am."

"That's what I thought." Edmund spun his chair away from George and stared at his computer screen for a minute. He spun back. "No," he said.

"No?"

"No."

"Why not?"

"I don't want your money."

"But …"

"I don't want your money, I don't want you making decisions for me, I don't want you making me dinner every week, I don't want to eat macrobiotics, I don't want this perfectly planned little healthy life. You and René, I swear, you look like you're having fun sometimes there in the kitchen with all your little debates, 'Have you read this article, Have you read that, What do you think about XXX, What do you think about YYY.' I've been trying to appreciate it, what you're doing—for Mom's sake, if for nothing else—but you know what I think in the end? I think it drives you nuts that this is something you can't control. And you can't. You can't control it."

"Maybe AZT can."

"What am I talking to, a wall? I'm dying. You can't stop that."

"Not me, personally, maybe …"

"Listen, Dad. Nice try, OK? You've done your little bit, you've shown you cared, now maybe it's time we go back to the way things really are. I mean, why pretend we like each other? We never have before. Let's be honest here."

George walked away from Ed's feeling like his heart was in his shoes, and his shoes didn't want to go to the apartment he now lived in, they wanted to go home to the place where once upon a time he had counted himself the head of a happy family, a confident man in a modest but important job, providing his three children with an honest, disciplined example of how to be a good person.

He turned down his old street with a sense of rightness. He thought he would stand in front of the house for a while and trace its outline with his eyes, run through its rooms in his head, but as he got close to it he saw the blue flicker of light from a television in the living room and kept walking. The house had no memory—it housed whom it housed and no more.

At home, he sat in Penny's armchair for the first time. An embrace. A bountiful, forgiving embrace. He fell asleep there. And dreamed. In his dream, he was a Member of Parliament with offices in a rich, stately chamber that he couldn't get out of because the door was barricaded by a group of militant feminists. Then he discovered if he lay on his stomach and licked the floor, the room became an elevator of sorts, descending into the bowels of the parliament buildings, a series of dank tunnels from which he could escape only by shutting his eyes and running as fast as he could.

When he woke up, he knew exactly what he was going to do.

* * *

George put his hands in the pockets of his blue trench coat. It wasn't suspicious, the trench coat. Men his age wore trench coats as a matter of course. He fingered the old army pistol in his pocket. Nothing about him was suspicious. It struck him as funny that any number of people could be walking around with pistols in their pockets and no one would know unless they drew them. He blew on his hands and rubbed them together.

Edmund really was dying. He'd never taken back what he'd said to George, but he didn't object when a month or so later

George phoned to say he wanted to start making dinner for him again. As he got sicker, Edmund stopped caring who paid for what. René took a leave of absence from his job. George paid for the AZT, and when Ed and René's savings had run out, he paid for the rent. He wouldn't let René cash his RRSPs.

By now George was part of the team: he, René, Alice and half a dozen of Ed's friends, who took turns visiting, amusing, lifting, driving, comforting, teasing, soothing. They were marvellous people. They loved his son. He almost thought they might love him, too.

In the evenings they started a course of reading Penny's favourite children's books. It felt absolutely right for George to sit in the next room with his journals, listening in. The few times that Ed took a turn reading, it sent shivers up George's spine. He read in exactly Penny's lifts and turns. It was a gift, bringing her back like that, a double gift, Penny's intonation in a voice like his own.

One night after Ed was asleep, George went into his room, took the book from the bedside table and read until he was finished. It was about another world, where animals talked, evil was evil and anyone could be a hero. It was the book Edmund was named for. George took the series home and read them all, sitting in Penny's chair, formulating his plan—simple is best; as simple as possible. Maybe he'd get enough money to start an AIDS hospice for the Guelph area.

The sign he'd been waiting for still had not come. For a moment he'd thought it had, a flicker of light out of the corner of his eye, but it was just the street signal, white walker striding, red hand flashing, over and over.

His feet were cold inside his brand-new running shoes. The shoes were red and white, like the street signal, purchased from a suitably anonymous discount store the week before. He would ditch the trench coat and the shoes down by the river where he had stashed his regular shoes and then emerge from the bushes, a regular jogger on his regular route. He knew from this morning that the path by the river had been packed down by hundreds of jogging shoes like his own. He wouldn't leave a trail.

He pulled down his toque and walked into the bank.

Something Blue

Alison Acheson

THOUGH NELLIE PERSUADED HERSELF THAT SHE WAS NOT UNHAPPY, one morning she awoke and discovered otherwise. She put her fingers to the cold outer layer of quilt, then retreated and thought.

She thought, *I'm tired of being alone. But even more, I'm tired of looking for someone and waiting for someone.*

She had been waiting, though of late, she rarely looked.

She curled her body under the quilts, stretched suddenly, pushed them away from herself all at once, felt the chill air. She reached for a long full skirt, shirt, vest, cardigan, warm socks for the cold wooden floor, and after coffee, honey and toast, she built a birdhouse. A feeder, really, with a large floor, wide sloping roof. She opened her file of newspaper clippings, found the diagram and photo she'd saved the spring before and for wood, she split an old apple crate.

Of course Sebastian heard her, hammering nails in the tiny backyard. He'd probably heard her sawing, but he came outside to witness her hammering.

"Nellie!" he shouted. He always shouted. "What are you creating there?"

She imagined other neighbours' heads out of windows to see what they could.

She held it up briefly.

"A bird feeder!" he announced. "Well, you know about them ..." He turned back to the door he'd left open.

"No, I don't. I've never had a bird feeder."

"Really," he said. "You strike me as someone who would know everything about birds and feeding them." He spoke over his shoulder.

She wondered why he thought that, but didn't ask.

She'd lived next to Sebastian for nine years. He wore too many Hawaiian prints in summer, shorts in late fall, indulged in magenta lights at Christmas, built plastic homes around his two living palm trees in terra cotta containers on either side of his carport. He took great delight in going out for the evening and returning early in the morning, with roars of Jaguar power and doors slamming. He was never out for the entire night. At about ten on Saturdays and Sundays, he would stroll onto his balcony, coffee in hand, and always that hair on his head. Though he must have been near fifty, his hair was so black and was patterned with cowlicks and whorls, so that in the morning—and often at other times of day—it stood in every direction and mostly up. For work, and his evenings, he controlled it with something shiny and wet.

"What is it I should know about bird feeders?" she asked.

He was almost through the door.

"Once you start feeding the buggers, there's no stopping, you know." His sliding door locked into position.

He was on his balcony when she took the feeder up to her own and fastened it to the railing. Still in his blue robe, hair in a peak.

She felt dismay, finding him there. Though the townhouses were staggered and allowed for privacy, Sebastian seemed intent on thrusting his broad shoulders over the railing, over her basil and mint, into her home. Even when he was on his balcony with a woman, he would include Nellie in their conversation. Of course, she was able to hear every word, then he'd check with her. "Isn't that so, Nel," he'd say, or, "How did that go again?" Sometimes she spied out of an upper-floor window to make certain that his balcony was empty and hers safe.

"What kind of birds are you going to attract?" he asked. He looked as if he could step easily over the railing that separated them with one stride.

"I don't know," she said. "I suppose I need some wild seed." She regretted the words.

"Sowing wild seed, are you?" His black eyes glowed. "Or just wanting wild birds?"

"Here," he said, leaving her standing on her balcony, waiting for him as he disappeared into his living room. "Here," he said again as he came outside. He handed her a book. "This was my mother's. Keep it."

Nellie didn't hear sentimentality or grace in his voice. He didn't seem to want her thanks and she was happy he left before she opened it. *Birds of the West Coast*, it was, with a chapter on feeding. She left the book on the chesterfield.

The day was warming. She took off her cardigan and went to the store, bought a twenty-pound bag of mixed wild seed and a wide pan for water.

The bag should last until September, the woman at the store said and she tried to talk Nellie into buying thistle seed and sunflower, but Nellie shook her head and returned home.

She set the seed out, filled the pan and went into her home.

What an odd place, she found herself thinking as she stood in her living room. Though she'd never thought that before. Now she thought, *This home is not meant for one person. Not meant for two, either, or a family of more. It is meant for visitors.*

The centre of the room was filled with the bulk of her mother's chesterfield and her father's old chair and two matching chairs she'd bought for herself, for guests. The coffee table was big and square, for board games, if anyone still played them, and end tables were scattered everywhere.

Nellie had worked as a researcher since university and her books were tucked on ugly shelves downstairs, and her papers were hidden in drawers in her study upstairs, though often she'd paused in the living-room doorway and thought how pleasurable it would be to have her desk there, before the wide glass doors, catching the morning sun as she worked.

That night she fell asleep on the chesterfield, as she had so often as a child, on a Sunday afternoon when the rest of her family was at the beach, or on December nights by the lighted tree, and the following morning she saw the first bird—a sparrow. Not a real sparrow, of course, but a house sparrow. They find everything before other birds. Nellie read that much in the book. The brown-and-black-striped head attacked the tiny mound of seed, spread it over the wooden floor of the feeder and onto the balcony. Through the open French door, Nellie could hear seed scatter to the ground below. Then the bird flew away with the news.

Next door, on the balcony, Sebastian discussed bagels with a woman and raged about white or poppy seed: poppy was his favourite. The woman's voice hummed through and between his words, and finally Sebastian was quiet.

Nellie watered her herbs. She watched them leave: the woman with a marching step and Sebastian silent, his hair shiny and restrained.

As he pulled away from the curb, Nellie couldn't hear the woman's words but could see her lips moving behind the glass of the car door. The car went down the street without its usual roar.

So that was how to beat the man, Nellie thought. *Drone.*

But she had no desire to beat Sebastian and so she finished her watering, set seed in the feeder and returned to the house.

In July the days were hot and in the mornings the sparrows

splashed and ate greedily. At noon, Nellie would put out several handfuls of seed and refill the pan and again at suppertime. She could see the sparrows in the fir by the street; in the heat of the day the tree was quite still as the birds moved in a comfortless shuffle. Every so often, briefly, they would skirmish, perhaps to create some bit of wind. It was too hot even for bugs and the birds waited for the day to cool again to feed.

Nellie rid herself of several end tables, relocated her father's chair to her bedroom and moved the bookshelves into the living room. She spent hours in that room and the sparrows came to know her movements, and she grew sensitive to theirs, and so it was that she forgot there were birds who weren't sparrows.

One morning there was a bird with a black hood and a cheering yellow beak, and at first she thought it was some kind of chickadee—her knowledge being the size of a grain of sand —and then she realized it was not and she took the bird book from the shelf.

The bird was an Oregon junco, she discovered. She watched each morning for him and the Oregon junco seemed content with the wild seed. Others came and as they did, she was forced to be still again. Other birds, she discovered, were not as curious or as brave as the sparrows and would flee if she stood suddenly or looked directly at them.

"The juncos," Sebastian nodded when, over the railing, he asked her what had been to her feeder and she told him and he said *juncos* so easily—as if he knew more of her new friends than she did. And he probably did, in his own loud, casual way and that made her uncomfortable. She wanted to correct him, *say Oregon juncos*, but she didn't.

*   *   *

Chickadees began to come, too. Black-capped chickadees, she learned, though she called them chickadees. They moved so quickly, never doubting their own bodies and they plucked the sunflower seed from the mixed pile. They were so cautious of the sparrows and circled, fluttered, never angry or defensive, just waiting. They were absurdly happy.

There was something satisfying to her simple judgements: sparrows, curious; juncos, self-assured; chickadees, happy. Then came a nuthatch—red-breasted, Nellie found.

The red-breasted nuthatch never let her know anything about him. He was quick and he didn't seem to like her feeder. He tap-danced the spine of the fir in his blue-grey uniform with the red umber cravat, and his made-up striped face, and he ignored her offerings.

Nellie tilted her head. "Acknowledging your freedom, Mr. Nuthatch," she said.

He skittered sideways and she turned away from the window, went back upstairs to her desk.

Sometimes, when her work was done, she spread a blanket out on the warm floor of the balcony—near the wall adjacent to Sebastian's so that, if he looked, he wouldn't see her—and she watched the seagull, silver and high in the blue above her. Round and round. Sometimes a flock. Sometimes she felt she was with them, but often it was one up there, circling, and then she felt alone.

She found her job unsettling—it was a puzzle of perfect-fitting pieces, except there were too many pieces. She'd find the pieces, every one of them, and then she would disk them or box them or put them in the form her employer wanted and that would be the end of it. She would rearrange her cupboard—all the pot handles to the right—or sort her cutlery tray or her linen closet, make sure everything was in order and then she would look at her client list to find who was next. She was always busy. She was good at what she did.

And now that she'd made the decision not to look or wait for someone, she was truly free.

Late September there was a week of storm—wind and rain—and the sparrows made quick flights between the feeder and the blowing fir in which they huddled. One sparrow spent an entire morning sitting by the wide post in the feeder, to keep from the wind. His feathers were bunched and his shoulders protected his head. He didn't look at Nellie, though she was certain he knew she was there, passing her hands over her books. At ten, she realized she'd accomplished nothing.

Her older brother's son was coming by that afternoon, as he often did. She asked him if he would help her move her desk downstairs.

"Here?" he asked, looking around the living room.

"We'll have to move these two chairs," was her answer.

"Where to?" he asked, hoisting a chair easily to his shoulder.

"Home—you take them," she said. She knew he wanted to leave his parents' house soon. He left with the pair sticking out of his car trunk.

The sparrow was gone from the feeder and she was sorry she'd missed his leave-taking. She hoped he was all right.

But her desk was moved and she on-lined the library and settled in to make up for the lost hours.

The rain finally stopped and Nellie was aware of a sound she'd not heard for some days—not since the fall rains began. No. Not since cool summer mornings.

The birds were talking after the rain.

Nellie felt their sound was something more.

She opened the door to the porch and at the sound, birds spread buckshot—from below the porch, from the railings—to the fir tree or over the street. Nellie walked to the edge and looked down and there was the sparrow, on the cement. She hurried down the stairs, out the front door. She knew without touching him that he was dead. She hunched over and could feel the tail of her skirt caught in a deep puddle. The fabric was heavy as she rocked forward to see the bird's eyes. His eyes were dull, though she knew they shouldn't be. He couldn't have been dead longer than perhaps three hours.

What was she to do? The other birds were filling fir and spruce with noise.

She tried to stand, but her left knee ached and she stayed where she was. That was when Sebastian drove up, climbed out of his car, with hands full of takeout bags.

"You killed one, did you?"

She tried again to stand. "No call to be cheerful about it."

He leaned over, turned the bird gently with his toe. "Poor thing. You had him for a while, though."

Nellie half-stood on one leg. Sebastian held out his hand to her, which she ignored as she straightened slowly.

"I didn't have him."

"But you did." He looked up at the feeder on the railing over their heads. "You were blessed."

Nellie stared down at the bird. She wouldn't have known him from any of the sparrows that visited.

"Why do you think he died?"

Sebastian bent closer. "Salmonella poisoning, perhaps." He was calm.

"Salmonella?" Nellie didn't want to crouch again. She was afraid her knee would never make it a second time.

"How often do you clean the floor of the feeder?"

What else did he know that he wasn't saying?

"It's all in that book I gave you. You did read it, didn't you?" His voice rose slightly and he reached into one of the bags and pulled out a deep-fried wonton. He held the bag out to her. Nellie shook her head. She had no interest in eating.

"Are you saying I poisoned this bird?"

"Could be," he nodded. "Don't take on now."

What was *taking on*? Had her voice risen? If so, only to match his.

"Why didn't you tell me?"

He was standing, another wonton in his hand, and he had a strange look on his face. Nellie looked down to see if the buttons of her shirt were fastened.

He pulled a hand through his hair and it peaked after a day of downtrodden work hours.

"I can't tell you everything."

Nellie hadn't yelled in years. She didn't trust herself, so she went into her home and sat at the kitchen table, away from the living room—though it was now hardly that—and away from the feeder.

And some time passed before she realized she'd left the bird and even as the thought passed through her mind, she heard a clunk of metal from out back and she went to the window to look. Sebastian was in his backyard with the light on and he had a shovel in his hand and was digging a hole in the grass. He moved the shovel in rhythmic arcs, as if he'd been digging that particular hole for some time now, though it was shallow and he'd opened the ground only seconds before. She watched as he lowered his hand in the hole for a moment before replacing the dirt and the bit of sod. The bird. He bent to press his hand against the earth and went quickly into his home without noticing her.

Who did he think he was? The bird was her responsibility—she would have taken care of him.

It was dark when she stepped out to bring the bird feeder in. She never should have done this. Why had she thought to build a feeder? She opened the front door just enough to push it through and left it in the carport.

There was seed scattered over the balcony and on the ground below. For two days that fed the sparrows. The juncos stayed away and the chickadees.

On the third day there was silence. A waiting silence. A brief movement in the fir, a black head, grey chest, then gone.

Nellie rattled at her computer, made more coffee, pulled her socks off, rubbed her feet where she imagined them sore from sitting all day. Wished she'd left her desk where it was, upstairs, facing a wall.

Instead it was the window she faced, and what was outside of that window, and what she saw was empty. Her boxes of plants with all their life drawn in, into the twisted roots, like cantankerous shopkeepers setting out the CLOSED signs and drawing the blinds, leaving behind dead-brown for winter months. And the cold rain splatted down.

She was waiting again.

Down to the carport and she fetched the bloody thing, put it back in its place, caught the roar of Jaguar and remembered the dead sparrow. She took it up again and to the laundry, where she scrubbed with cold water and bleach. In her head she could hear Sebastian.

"Be quiet!" she cried out and imagined a new stillness.

Back to the balcony, downstairs again to fetch the seed, and when she returned there was a flutter of grey-brown to the tree to safety. Their waiting she could live with.

Two handfuls and she knew when she turned her back that they were there.

The next morning the juncos and the chickadees returned, and the next, a black and white and red bird sat astride the roof, curious.

It had to be a woodpecker, though Nellie couldn't remember ever having seen one. A downy woodpecker, with his red patch and white freckles, she found in the book. She took a sticky-backed notepaper, scribbled the date on it and affixed it to the page.

She spent the day reading Sebastian's mother's book and note-taking.

Winter was coming. Seed was not enough. Suet —*go to butcher's*, she wrote—black oil sunflower seed, peanut butter, mixed fifty-fifty with cornmeal, broken dog biscuits, for chickadees. Dog biscuits. Chickadees. Really? *Raw apples, raisins, cut-up fruit, for waxwings.*

Waxwings. She looked it up in the index. Bohemian or cedar. Cedar on the West Coast.

Melted-butter bandits, she thought, as she looked at the photograph, the rounded-smooth body, the black mask. *Imagine one of those in my world*, she thought.

October was cold and Nellie wore her cardigan always, and early November there was ice and that silence that means snow.

The butcher gave her chunks of suet. "Render it," he said, "and it won't go bad."

Nellie read the book and rendered, mixed the suet with seed, set it out.

Sebastian heard her on the porch and came through his doors with a small box. "Grit," he said. "Broken seashells. They need it this time of year." He turned away.

"Good of you to tell me," said Nellie and her voice was loud. She couldn't recall reading about grit in the book.

"You're welcome," he said.

Her voice was louder. "I don't remember thanking you."

"You're going to frighten the birds."

"Fuck the birds!"

"They don't."

She was amusing him. She was sure. "Don't laugh at me."

He leaned over the railing. "I'm not laughing at you!"

How was it possible to yell without anger? she wondered after him.

She buttoned her sweater before she went in and when she was in, she found a scarf she wound several times around her neck and shoulders. It was brown and black, like a fall night, and warmed her. The box of grit she placed on her desk for the morning. She would read about it first. She must have missed it in the book.

The next morning the wood floor was colder and she slipped long johns under her skirt before heading downstairs. She was expecting a file and she huddled over the fax machine and blew on her hands. The file had not come. Coffee at the window while waiting. She crouched at the heat duct by the French door and was startled to see the wide back of some bird, whose head reached almost to the roof of the feeder. She fingered her own scarf when she saw his brown-and-black chevron stripes. He turned crookedly and she saw a flash of red at his neck as he poked at the suet, and her skirt filled with air warm from the duct.

Sebastian chose that moment to step out onto his deck and the bird was away.

"You scared him!" she called out even before she'd opened the door.

Sebastian knew what she was saying.

"Don't yell at me!" His hair stood morning-up.

"Don't frighten my birds."

"Are you going to curse at me again?" He was actually grinning.

"I might."

"I've waited a long time for you to care. Do you know what that bird was?"

There was a loud cry from across the street, in the maple, almost a crow sound.

"A northern flicker."

Another cry swallowed his next words, but Nellie caught something about grit.

"Grit yourself," she said.

"Nitty-gritty," he said.

Caw. Except the sound was more like *keeeer.*

There was an answer close by, but Nellie didn't see them until later, at dusk. Something blue and dark-crested and there were two. One landed at the feeder, played with the suet, called to the other, shimmying the tree. The second one waited for the first to move, then came and scattered seed over the porch. Both laughed and Nellie felt a sharp pain low in her belly.

Page 276. Stellar's Jays. She tucked the book inside her vest and went next door to show Sebastian.

Seven Years with Wallace

Adam Lewis Schroeder

ALI AND WALLACE STOOD TOGETHER AT THE RAIL, LOOKING DOWN
at the grey water of Singapore and the sampan bumping against
the prow of their steamer. One of the men in the sampan peered
up at them from under his hat and, as always, Ali smiled down.

The captain of the steamer approached the rail, carrying an
empty tumbler.

Mr. Wallace turned and shook hands with him. "It's been a
lovely voyage," Wallace said. "I prefer these big ships."

"What's your destination?" asked the captain. He was Dutch,
but his English was excellent after years of dealing with the
bureaucrats of Malaya. He was forever running his tongue across
his cracked lower lip. "Perhaps up to Malacca?"

"No," said Wallace. "I am finished. I am going home to
England."

"Finished? You mean sacked?" The captain gazed out at the
roofs of the shop-houses, then at Wallace's bearded face.

"Oh no, certainly not. I was never employed by any one person in particular, only myself. Though certainly I *was* dependent
on buyers in England to keep the money coming in. I collect
specimens of natural history, you see. Surely you saw my boxes
down below. Those reflect only what I have collected in the past

few months, in Sumatra. I have dozens more sent on, nearly two hundred, I should think. At least I hope so!"

One of the Javanese crew joined them and the captain told him in Dutch that if he wanted to shut the engine down it was all right and that coal couldn't be had for free besides. Then he went back to gazing at Wallace. If the gin hadn't run out, he would not have had to come out on deck and endure this conversation. "I saw your cargo," the captain said, "but I thought it was clothes. You like to look correct, I think."

"Well, this suit I only bought in Surabaya and let me tell you, up until then I had but two shirts and my trousers were in shreds. In Sumatra I had to find proper cases for my collections ... no, it has not been easy, I should say."

The captain nodded and wiped at his neck with his sleeve. He wore trousers and a shirt that was missing most of its buttons, both once white, but now speckled with grease and rust.

"How long have you been East?" asked Wallace.

"Thirteen years."

"Eight for me."

"Your boy, he's worked for you the entire time?" asked the captain. "Let me tell you, he's robbed you blind. Every one of them is alike. What is he, Ambonese?"

"Oh no, he's a Dyak, from Borneo, but perhaps you do not know the famous Ali, my friend, or you would not dream of speaking that way. Ali!" called Wallace.

The boy leaned an elbow on the rail and shaded his eyes to look at them. He wore a blue sarong and an old shirt, possibly one of Wallace's.

"How long have we been together, lad?" asked Wallace.

"Since 1855, sir."

The captain thought this sounded rehearsed.

"There. Seven years," said Wallace, with a grin. "And the most extraordinary discoveries I owe to him. Incredible specimens. You would think God was delusional when he fashioned them, you surely would. Birds with such plumes on their heads as you can't imagine. I would venture to say that God did not make them *at all*, but that they made themselves and the next variety along as well. That's my way of thinking."

"I'll see about your luggage," said the captain. He started down the passage, the tumbler still in his hand. He knew from experience that Wallace would gladly go on talking for days, despite the delights of Singapore spread before him—real white women only steps away. It was the same with all Englishmen, they thought it rude to do otherwise, and those who have spent years away from other white men are only *more* obsessed with propriety. They were forever bowing and scraping, these Englishmen, thinking him a man of some importance in the Indies because he'd been trusted with a new iron steamer. In truth it was the quiet of the old ships he longed for, those without clattering engines, only the creak of rope, the flutter of sails, the silent tilt of bottle and glass on his table. After thirteen years he hated the Javanese and other Dutchmen besides. He loved only the one thing.

* * *

Ali held the bottom of the rope ladder as Wallace climbed down and the two men with oars sat ready in the rear of the sampan, nearly hidden behind packing cases. Chimes clattered in the stern. A breeze across the water blew Wallace's beard against his cheek, so that several times he had to brush it down and hold the ladder with only one hand. The sampan gave a sudden heave and bumped against the steamer and Ali cried out. The tip of one finger had been crushed between the two boats; blood welled under the nail and trickled down his hand. Wallace stepped down into the swaying boat.

"Did something happen?" he asked.

Ali smiled and gripped the finger in his good hand.

"Right, let's get to shore," Wallace said to the men. "Town awaits."

A crewman stepped to the rail of the steamer and emptied a barrel into the water as the sampan pulled away. Wallace stared with fascination at a dead rat that bobbed to the surface. It was only a common rat, though, *Rattus norvegicus*; had it a furred tail or an iridescent coat, some uncommon trait, he would surely have leaned over and plucked it from the sea.

He estimated his collection after eight years in the Indies at one hundred thousand specimens, with very little repetition of species, save those he knew Europe would always have an appetite for: the orangutan and the myriad varieties of bird of paradise that had kept him crisscrossing the islands off New Guinea. Horrible days in little boats, with only himself and Ali and one or two natives as crew, waiting out a windless spell with the next island just out of sight, looking at each other, looking at the water, trying to keep calm. Wallace had occupied himself then by wondering whether the next island would be bereft of animal life or so thick with undiscovered species, crawling and climbing and fluttering about him, that he might work the rest of his career there, playing host to other scientists, perhaps to the Geographical Society. Surely, he had thought, if he spent so many years in one place, even old Darwin could be coerced into a visit.

He had never found one enchanted place, though—only the ten thousand islands of the archipelago, overpoweringly rich in fauna, collectively, but visited over many years and in precarious little boats. He had only the strength now for one last trip in a little boat, the sampan to the dock. He'd have no more praus or canoes or rowboats, travelling at the mercy of the tropical weather and the Sulu pirates. That was no way for a man to live. The only place for him now was England.

One hundred thousand specimens in eight years. If three years were more than one thousand days, eight years would be three thousand days, so he'd collected more than three hundred specimens each day. Now, suddenly, nothing—he'd taken nothing since he'd left Sumatra two days before—and nothing ever again. Once home, he would remember these eight years, polishing each like a gem.

The sampan slowly pulled its way between trading junks at anchor, their crews stretched out on their wooden roofs, catching the cooling afternoon breeze as it swept over their chests and shaved heads. The day was overcast and humid, but the wind skipped off Sumatra—the monsoon was not far off. The Chinese lolled on the sturdy junks and gossiped while pots of tea were served. A basket of vegetables was passed from one boat to another and a shirt flew off a clothesline into the water. Its owner groped for it with a boat hook and the other men laughed.

Ali watched as they drifted by. The language of these Chinese sailors meant nothing to him. They were yet another community, one of a hundred in the archipelago, which he simply floated past.

Months before, he had met a pair of fellow Dyaks working the port at Batavia. They had told him that there were a few others in Singapore, if he was going that way, headhunters ridding the seas of pirates for the English East India Company. They had found this arrangement most amusing, for there were no pirates more fierce than the Dyaks themselves, the Sea-Dyaks. They had laughed then and one had told a crude joke, but Ali had not understood it. He had not spoken his own language since Wallace had taken him from Borneo.

"Sir?" said Ali.

"What is it?" asked Wallace. He was brushing something off the arm of his coat; it seemed to be fish scales.

"Will we be very occupied in town?"

"I believe," said Wallace, "that the ship departs for England in two days. We will investigate, of course. I may have acquaintances to call on, you understand, if they are still in the East and not on leave. You know, as often as not, a man is not where you left him. With luck we can leave these things at the shipping office and will not have to bother ourselves with ferrying them to the hotel. Have you seen these rickshaws the Chinese have?"

"Pulled by a man," said Ali. "In Kuching we saw them."

"Oh, of course," said Wallace.

Ali dipped his hand into the water, thinking it might cool his poor finger, but the sea was warm. He sucked at the blood instead and watched the fish rush beneath the surface.

"Are there many others like me in England?" asked Ali.

Wallace did not care for riding in small boats. He glared at another sampan as it veered rather close off their stern.

* * *

"Thank you, no," Wallace said. The emaciated rickshaw men crowded them, shouting out names of hotels, banks, public offices, plantations, jostling each other and running their hands over Wallace's shoulders as though admiring his coat. Ali stayed close behind as they made their way off the boardwalk and onto the dirt streets. The men from the sampan were hauling the trunks up onto the pier, looping ropes through the cases' leather handles. Three rickshaw drivers stood by, cousins of the sampan men. They would follow Wallace to the shipping agent with shis collection of hornbills, pheasants, monkeys, lemurs, curious butterflies, emerald-tinted beetles and numerous other speci-mens that he had extinquished, dried and tacked into place while in Sumatra. Wallace did not concern himself with the unloading. He had seen the natives' habits where such things were con-cerned and found that he only got in the way when he endeav-oured to direct them. Instead he and Ali wound their way through the markets along the waterfront, followed doggedly by a handful of rickshaw men. It was worth their trouble to persevere; Europeans never knew how much to pay.

Singapore was rife with voices, like a forest full of birds. Arabs shouted and held bangles out to Wallace; Japanese held up writing paper and string; Malays sang as they sat gutting fish; Mohammedan women pushed past in tawny burkas, haggling with the vendors, baskets under their arms; excited Chinese children held the hands of their mothers, who yelled for their own mothers, shuffling behind; a Hokkien shopkeeper stood in the doorway, shouting angrily at the neighbouring merchant.

Ali looked everywhere, but there were no Dyaks.

Wallace turned back to him and pointed out a sign written in Portuguese. "Before I know it," Wallace said happily, "every signboard will be in English."

They had lost the rickshaw men. A Bengali squatted against a building, razors clattering in his hand, inviting Wallace to have his beard shaved. Piles of rubbish that had earlier been swept under market tables now tumbled back underfoot, so that bones, rinds and feces were crushed into a sort of carpet Ali padded over with bare feet. Wallace started to feel weak and an ominous feeling came over him. His malaria had come and gone so often, he knew the signs only too well.

A poorly dressed European man came up and took Wallace's arm. "Good day," he said. He might have been German. "You speak English?"

"I do," said Wallace. "You have enthusiasm," the man said quietly, "for gentle ladies?"

Without a word, Wallace removed the man's hand and he and Ali pushed on. Soon the marketplace narrowed and they found themselves in a neighbourhood of stilt houses, built over another section of waterfront. Beyond the houses stood jungle.

"We have lost ourselves somewhat," said Wallace. "And not for the first time."

The vendors called to them again as they worked their way back through the tumult. The glow of the sea was visible far ahead. Wallace hummed a little. Ali recognized the song as the one Wallace sang on the open ocean to bolster their spirits, but Ali had never been told its name. They passed a stall where chicken roasted over open coals.

"Only a handful of meals left to me before I start home," said Wallace. "What do you suppose I should have?"

"Yams," said Ali. He smiled slyly.

"Oh no," said Wallace, with a chuckle. "Certainly not those."

*   *   *

The ship for England would be leaving in the morning. Wallace hesitated for a moment when the agent asked if he intended to be on board and gazed out the open door of the office and down the stairway to the street. He'd hoped to spend the next day rambling inland, perhaps have a look at the tiger traps near the Jesuit mission.

Then something in his chest began to rattle and he had to lean against the desk. He coughed for a full minute before his breath returned. He wondered what was the matter with him; a cough like that had nothing to do with malaria. Doubtless with every new species he'd handled, he had swallowed a handful of diseases.

"I certainly will be aboard tomorrow," Wallace said. His eyes were still watering.

The agent opened his ledger and began to write.

Ali stood away from them, studying the framed timetable on the wall. There was a steamer for Borneo every Friday, but he told himself that England was also a fine place. In fact, every person not already in England wished that they were. A moth fluttered beneath the glass.

"I've had some interesting clients come through lately," said the agent.

"Oh, who was that?" asked Wallace, leaning heavily against the wall. A Malay man copying letters cast him a sympathetic look.

"The Oxford Cricket Club," said the agent, "on their way to Australia. First time a club's made the trip."

"Wonderful."

"Good-looking men. Couple of them had really terrific beards. You'd have fit right in, Mr. Wallace."

"You think I would have?" He forced a smile.

"Oh, I know you would!"

* * *

Wallace was disappointed with the Royalist Hotel. The tea in the lobby was cold and the desk clerk was Chinese. Of course, he was still in Asia; Europeans were all managers at one post or another. But still, with the Royalist he would have expected a retired corporal out of India or even a cockney with side-whiskers — anything to demonstrate that, of all the hotels in all the outposts, this one was English. But he was not in England yet. He handed the teacup to one of the hotel boys and walked to the desk, Ali padding along behind. More boys stood swishing fans.

"I am afraid I have not written ahead. A room for Wallace and servant."

"Please sign," said the clerk, pushing forward the register. He wore a jacket and starched collar.

Wallace dipped the pen. "Alfred Russel Wallace, Naturalist," he wrote and then, "accompanied by Ali." He turned and winked at Ali, who was watching over his elbow.

"The hotel requests," said the clerk, leaning forward very slightly, "that the gentleman's servant be clad in better attire."

"I beg your pardon?"

"His clothes are not clean," said the clerk. "Perhaps ... perhaps he could be outfitted like a gentleman if you—"

"Really, like a gentleman? We have spent years sleeping on

beaches, my man, praying that another snake was not going to drop onto our heads. This lad was given a … a human skull to play with as a child. We have been in utter wilderness nearly every day of the past seven years and now I wonder if he would like to sleep in a proper bed. He is not the Duke of York, granted, but I would dare say neither are you!"

"In both sleeping out of doors and within a hotel, sir," said the clerk, "one may entertain certain expectations."

Wallace looked down at Ali.

"You could do with a new suit of clothes, couldn't you? In any case, we'll not be tricked out of our room."

The clerk watched as the Englishman strode away through the lobby, the boys with fans scattering before him and the poor servant trotting behind. Here was Singapore in a nutshell.

The clerk undid the clasp on his collar and set it down on the desk. One of the boys took the teapot away and the rest sat down cross-legged on the floor. The doorman would signal if the general manager or a guest was on his way in.

The general manager was having the clerk read Marlowe, because, he said, the clerks at every other hotel were reading Shakespeare. The clerk didn't enjoy reading Marlowe, though, because the words were too blurred; as he grew older, his eyesight grew worse. The general manager wouldn't allow him to wear spectacles. He said that a Chinaman in spectacles looked every inch a trained ape.

*   *   *

Ali knew that Mr. Roland the tailor was a terrible man, though Wallace did not seem to notice. The tailor shoved Ali around. He put a pin right into his arm.

"Lively smell the lad has," Mr. Roland said to Wallace. "Not much for baths, are they? Never seen one buy a cake of soap, have you?"

Wallace sat in a teak chair in the far corner, his head propped on his fist.

"They have always lived near water," said Wallace. "This far west I have not found that they have any smell at all."

"It's no wonder they have an odour," said Mr. Roland, taking the pins out of his mouth, "swimming in that filth."

The edge of the carpet was furrowed with tiny bites; Wallace contemplated what sort of insect might have been at work. He thought of the millipedes and beetles tacked into place in his collections, the crates he would have to unpack and finish classifying. That in itself could take years, and then to get all his findings on paper. But, for those necessary years, he would at last be alone with his thoughts, in the cool and quiet of England.

For years he'd been toying with titles for the book: The Land of the Orangutan and Bird of Paradise, or A Scientific Narrative, or Studies of Man and Nature. Yet none held the power of Darwin's The Origin of Species. None ever could. Such a title spoke of ... everything!

A trickle of sweat ran behind his ear.

"And the trousers, in velvet as well? A white cotton might be more comfortable but you want the best, I presume. Mr. Fullerton was in not long ago to have something done up in velvet."

"Fine," said Wallace. He gazed upward, watching the fan move across the ceiling; it was rigged to a cable through the wall and pulled, presumably, by a coolie on the street. The canvas sheet resembled a sail. Soon there would be no more sinking boats, no more sails sitting idle. He thought of the excellent sleep he would have that night at the Royalist, on beautifully white sheets, smelling so clean. He would sink into the soft bed as though to his death.

A woman passed the window, a white woman, followed by a boy carrying her parasol. Wallace watched the clean line curve up from her corset to her bosom, that long swoop that was so wholly feminine. He shifted in his chair to watch her, but she passed and was gone.

Once he had sat in a rocking boat and watched a volcano erupt off Mindanao. The horizon had filled with ash. He had wondered where the ash might travel on the wind, what species of bird it might choke, how his work might be affected. Then he had inexplicably thought of a woman's bosom and the perfect line of her corset, how a woman perfumed herself in a dark room. After a time his crew had asked where he intended the boat to go.

"I'll have my man start on the shirt, Mr. Wallace," the tailor was saying. "Do you prefer the low collar, or perhaps, if we have velvet for the suit, you'd like a ruffled shirt? It's been selling well here for a number of years. What do you prefer?"

"Ruffles," said Wallace.

Ali very much liked the ruffled shirt. He stood on a raised platform, looking into the mirror.

"He doesn't look like a Kling anymore, now does he?" said Mr. Roland. "He looks like a proper lad who's dressed up to look like a Kling."

"Klings are from India," said Wallace. "And this boy is from Borneo. He was a very good assistant to me, at harder work than you have ever done."

"There aren't any real Klings in Singapore, anyway," said Mr. Roland. "They're all half-English and half-Chinese and the Chinese all act like Malays and on and on. In my letters from home, they ask me to send them joss-sticks now. Joss-sticks! Like I was the Chung-King God of Rice! I feel sorry for these Klings of yours. No man of any race is a proper man of his own race any longer. Now you see what's missing on your lad? Shoes are what he needs. His feet look as wide as a couple of spades."

In the end, Wallace chose not to buy shoes for Ali. They both knew it would have been a waste of money. Ali reminded himself, though, that in England nearly everyone would be wearing them.

Ali walked through the dark, past the shop-house porches and silent men smoking long pipes. The docks stretched nearly the whole length of Singapore, but the hotel boys had said to go in this direction. Wallace had fallen asleep over his supper.

The evening was cool but, wearing the new suit of clothes, sweat ran down Ali's back and dripped from his fingers. He was accustomed to blending into his surroundings—though in the Papuan islands he had clearly been an outsider, with lighter skin and finer features, still, far less an outsider than Wallace—and there was no reason he couldn't blend in here but for the suit of clothes. The trousers were too long and already the cuffs were matted with dirt.

He walked past shops and food vendors. People bumped into him and walked without pause. Everyone was Chinese, walking with their families or chatting in front of the tea houses. Paper signs fluttered above them. Children played with metal toys on the pavement. A woman with a pole across her shoulder sold soup from the pots dangling at either end.

There were no Dyaks here, and for good reason. On such an evening, they would have dancing and stories, drinking palm wine called *arrak*, in a house with a fire on the floor. The whole village would be together. The smell of smoke would touch everything and the *arrak* would be powerful. Its taste filtered unbidden into Ali's mouth.

In the Aru islands all the men drank *arrak*, but Wallace did not let him. Wallace knew nothing about being a Dyak. At his age Ali should have been a warrior, been allowed to take an enemy's head to display with all the other heads his family had ever claimed. But he was not a warrior; he collected birds. When he was small, he and his friends had played at war, sharpening sticks and howling and tackling each other into the river. That was as close as he had come. He remembered how happy his aunt had looked when his cousin had gone to fight and how the other women had paid her their respects.

His father had been dead for a long time and, though every woman laboured in the field as she did, his mother felt that because she was a widow her children were poor and looked down on by other families. When Wallace came through the village and asked for a porter, his mother volunteered Ali. She saw the silver ornaments that Wallace carried and imagined her son returning with handfuls of them. But he and Wallace went overland instead, across another river, and spent several months gathering orangutan skins. Ali called them *mias* then, he did not know the word "orangutan," and Wallace had no beard at all.

In their first week together, Wallace shot an orangutan seven times, but still it did not fall from the tree. They stood on the forest floor, scratching their heads. After it had not moved for several days, Wallace thought it safe for Ali to climb up and get it. Scrambling far up into the canopy, he found it was a male, with a meaty face like a full moon and insects crawling out of its empty eyes and slack mouth. All of its flesh had been eaten away, so that when Ali tipped it out of the tree, it fell to the ground and broke open. Wallace found eighteen new species of insect inside the orangutan, and he complimented Ali, saying he was "a most rare specimen."

So Ali did not return home. He saw many other Dyaks as he and Wallace travelled around Borneo, but they were not his family and after a while he and Wallace left Borneo entirely. Ali did not question this because he knew he was a rare specimen. At the end of the crowded street stood a tall brick building, with lamps illuminating a sign over the door that read EAST INDIA COMPANY EST. 1600. A cripple was sweeping the steps. Ali waited for him to shuffle away and then tried the handle on the great mahogany door. It opened and he squeezed inside, stepping onto the cool marble floor. There were no lights inside, but a big white man with a thick moustache was coming toward him with keys jingling in one hand and a candle in the other.

"Out! You, out!" he barked. He was English.

Ali lowered his head reverentially. He had been practising what to say.

"Sir," he said, "I'm looking for the Dyak people, do you know of them?"

"Well, who are you, then?" The candle cast a white light under the Englishman's jaw and just above his eyes.

"I am assistant to Mr. Wallace, the naturalist."

"Kyaks? I don't know them. What are they?"

"They are from Borneo. I am also from Borneo."

"You don't look it."

"They have hair grown very long and a red cloth on the head." He did not think of his own people in these terms—in fact, this description was from Wallace's journal, with which he had first learned to read. "They wear a blue cloth about the loins. They are very strong." He squeezed his own arm to illustrate and was disappointed to feel the cloying velvet.

The Englishman cocked his head to study Ali.

"You're a more clever lad than usual. Have you been in England?"

"Not yet, sir. Perhaps I go tomorrow."

"Very good. The Kyaks, you say. They work for the Company? Go to the back, straight toward the water. You'll come across our warehouses and such. Some people are living in there—might be who you want. And when you get to England, tell them Matthew Brown said good morning."

"I am grateful," said Ali.

The lane through the warehouses was not lit. He ran his hand along a stone wall, feeling his way. Someone approached and Ali crouched in a doorway. It was a sailor with a bundle over his shoulder.

In the jungle Ali had nearly always been alone, spending days scouting for birds with his gun, meeting Wallace again in the evening, but in the towns they had always been together. They had stayed away from saloons; they had spent evenings at the homes of government officials, English or Dutch.

He wondered if Wallace had woken up and if he wondered where his boy was.

He crept from one building to the next, listening for his brother Dyaks, but listening for what exactly he wasn't sure. He remembered the melodies of their songs but not the words; the more he thought, the more vague his memory became, until all he could remember was the song Wallace always sang. He would sing the last line the loudest. It went, "Till we have built Jeruuuusalem in England's green and pleasant laaand." That was when the night was black, the waves were coming over the boat and they knew a reef lay ahead. Wallace had been brave.

Ali heard laughter and men talking. He stood and waited at the door, his head bowed. There were Dyaks inside, he was sure of it.

For a year he had thought of nothing else. But instead of sliding the door open, he toyed with the ruffles on his shirt while his heart pounded. His fingertip throbbed. He held it against his palm like a tiny jewel of pain.

The door opened with a screech, sliding sideways, and a man his own height leaned out, coughing and hiccuping. He spat a few times, then noticed Ali's splayed feet and looked up into his face.

"I am a friend," Ali said, in the Dyak language.

The man did not respond, but stood looking at him with a lopsided frown. Too late, Ali noticed his short hair and his flowered sarong, instead of blue and white stripes—perhaps he was not Dyak at all.

Another man thrust his head out, looking identical but with a red handprint on his chest. He glared at Ali. "What?" he said, in English.

"What do you want?" asked the first man, in Dyak. "What is your name?"

"Ali. I have not been home for seven years."

"We have not been home in a month!" said the second happily. "They made us cut our hair!"

"Come inside," said the first. He put an arm around Ali, who choked a little at the smell of *arrak* coming off them.

"Look at his clothes," said the second.

It was more like a cave than a building; it had no windows and fires were burning in two corners. Half-naked men crouched in groups, passing flasks of liquor. One man lay groaning on the floor.

"A brother!" said the second man, then shouted something too quickly for Ali to follow. The men all got to their feet. They crowded around him, touching his velvet coat, stroking it with the backs of their hands. It was strange for Ali to be with so many men his own height. One tugged at the shirt ruffles, but the others pulled him away. They were all giggling, their faces hot. Ali's hair was tousled and someone studied his scalp.

"Seven years," they said.

"With the white men," said the first man. He used *putih*, the Malay word for white. "All alone with white men."

"You work with us," said a young man. "Come tomorrow. We will all go home."

"Are you strong?" someone else asked. They began to clap their hands, everyone falling into a rhythm and backing away to make a circle around Ali. One man stepped up and knocked into his arm, hard, then kicked him several times in the leg. They were wrestling. Ali had forgotten. He ran at the man and grabbed him around the waist, pulling him down to the floor. Everyone yelled and the clapping intensified. Then his opponent was laughing, so it seemed the match was over.

Ali stood up, ready for the next challenge, but the men sat

down in their groups once more. One man turned from the fire and vomited, the liquid hot and white.

Ali stood near the door. The first man pushed past him and spat into the alley again.

"You work for the whites?" Ali asked.

"We work hard," said the man. "It never stops."

"You fight pirates?"

"No, no. We carry things from the boats, rice and guns and coffee. We all want to go home."

"Who fights the pirates, then?" said Ali.

"The pirates are all dead. Shot by the whites."

The man looked Ali square in the face, then spat on his trouser leg.

There was shouting behind them; his wrestling opponent was motioning Ali back to the fire. The man who had vomited dropped the flask, spilling *arrak* into the flames, and the men leapt to their feet in anger.

Ali stepped into the lane and walked away.

* * *

There were certain streets where only Europeans went, though often their servants went with them. But the clubs were for whites only, the shops exclusive, the hotels run by families who'd been in Singapore at least two generations. Gaslights had been put in on a few corners, policemen—Malays, mind you—walked their beats and many of the great English banking firms had offices facing one another. If not for the heat under your collar and the clouds of mosquitoes coming off the swamp, you might be in London, in the City. Fifty feet of cobblestones had been put in.

Thousands of insects circled the haloes of gaslight. Wallace stepped from one doorway to the next, peering into restaurants.

"A fine evening," he said to a doorman.

He rounded a corner and was disappointed to realize he'd

entered a Chinese neighbourhood and had still not found what he sought. The European quarter was only so big and he had covered all of it. He turned to retrace his steps and found her standing right behind him, leaning coyly on a folded parasol. He kept his head.

"A fine evening," he said.

"Are you English?" she asked.

"Yes."

"I am Belgian."

"I do not mind," he said.

They walked for a while into the Chinese neighbourhood, side by side but a few feet apart. She had her parasol over her shoulder. Wallace watched her closely; she was not the woman he'd seen at Roland's. The line of her corset was perfect, though, and the way her head tilted prettily as she looked at him filled his heart. She walked confidently past the shops.

They turned and went up a flight of stairs. An older woman wearing a wide hat greeted them at the door. They came into a carpeted hallway and for the first time the Belgian girl took his hand. They went through a door and sat on a divan. From another room Wallace heard a man howling.

"I will guess," she said and studied his face. She touched his beard. "Four years."

"I have been East eight years."

"Since you have been with a woman?"

"Ten years."

"You are sweating." She took out a handkerchief and wiped her hands. "You are very wet."

Sweat ran in rivers down his face and he leaned forward onto his knees. The man who had been howling moaned for a moment and then chuckled. The house went quiet. She tried to keep Wallace from falling to the floor.

"I so much want to be home," he said.

"There is another girl, who is English. Should I get her?"

"I want to be home."

The woman with the hat came in but she looked blurry to Wallace; she might have been a beetle standing upright. He slid off the divan to the floor.

"What's the matter with him?"

"He wants an English girl."

"Where's Bessie?"

"She is out."

They helped him into the hallway and back down the stairs. With his heavy arm around her neck, the Belgian girl planned where she would go next. The evening was just beginning. She could stay close to the good hotels. People treated you well in Singapore, they knew what a hardship it was for a girl to come all this way. Besides, it was better for the English and German and Swedish boys if there were white girls around, rather than having to go to the natives. The native girls were filthy and did not look after themselves, that's what she told everyone. Under their sarongs they crawled with disease.

At the bottom of the stairs, Wallace let go of her and took a few faltering steps up the alley. The woman in the hat tut-tutted.

"He wants to go home to England, you see?" said the Belgian girl, laughing a little. "He is on his way now. He has nearly made it."

There was a rickshaw at the corner and Wallace fell into it.

"The Royalist Hotel," he said to the man and though Wallace was twisted in the seat, he felt himself drift into sleep. "It's not a proper hotel, is it? Have you seen it?"

As they went under the gaslight, a handful of moths knocked against the seat and Wallace tried feebly to brush them away.

*　*　*

Ali left the lobby and stood in front of the hotel. Without Wallace there, the clerk would not let him into the room. Ali's eyes were drawn up to the sky: a black sea with a net of constellations cast over it, and bats and insects whirring in patterns of their own. Soon he would be in England and the stars would be different.

He inspected his finger; it was purplish now and much too big. The nail was loose and the skin radiated a queasy heat. He tried not to think about it, but he couldn't help remembering natives they had seen with legs and arms oozing infection. In England, he reminded himself, there were wonderful doctors. It would be so simple for them to heal it that it would be as though he'd never hurt it at all.

A rickshaw rattled up. Ali took the wallet from Wallace's pocket and paid the driver what he asked. Malaria had swept over Wallace. Ali called to one of the hotel boys to help him take Wallace to the room. It was on the third floor, and twice they had to lay him down on the landing so they could rest.

"Will he die?" the hotel boy asked. He seemed thrilled by the prospect.

"No," said Ali. "Once he was in a coma and he did not die then."

All night Wallace lay shuddering. Ali stripped off the bed-clothes and doused him with water. Wallace's hands and face were brown but his chest was terribly pale and so thin that the bones protruded. Ali put his hand over Wallace's breast and felt the beating wings of the bird trapped inside. The skin was as hot as iron in a fire.

Ali wondered what it might mean if Wallace died. Surely the clerk would not ask him to pay the bill for the hotel. Would Wallace want him to go to England by himself, to take his collections and classify them with Mr. Darwin? It seemed to Ali that Wallace would want that above all other things. Ali saw himself standing next to Wallace's coffin wearing his new suit of clothes.

Not long before dawn, a multitude of birds began singing outside their window, flying away in a cloud to another rooftop and back again. Ali went to the window to pull back the curtain and Wallace sat up.

"I'm thirsty," he said.

The desk clerk sent up water and soup. Strands of noodle stuck in Wallace's beard and Ali pulled them off.

"Today has arrived," said Wallace. "I'm awake to see it."

"England," said Ali. He knew how much the word meant to both of them.

"Home," said Wallace. He swung his legs out of bed. "Will you go home, lad, or will you stay here?"

"I will go home to England," said Ali, smiling.

"Someday, perhaps." Wallace was smiling, too. "You might enjoy yourself there. Someday I might come back to fetch you. We'll be old men then."

He slowly pulled himself up and took two steps to the chair where Ali had laid out his clothes. He picked up his trousers and found them still damp from his fever.

Ali sat on the edge of the bed, staring at him.

"I will go with you to England today," he said.

"You would be a great help," said Wallace, "but I suppose I will have to look after myself from now on. I never had a servant at home. It's difficult to picture, isn't it?"

"I will be your servant at home."

"No, I cannot take you with me, lad." Wallace stepped into his trousers. "It is not done."

Ali didn't know what to say. Surely Wallace was joking, but if he wasn't … his village in Borneo, slick with mud. Unloading ships with the other Dyaks. All without Wallace, never again Wallace. His heart beat fast inside his suit of clothes.

"I must not forget to pay you before I go. I have several years owing, haven't I? And a letter! I must write you a letter for your next job. Without your help, the obstacles would have been insurmountable. Insurmountable," said Wallace. He was buttoning his shirt. "And for our last breakfast? What about eggs? Do you fancy eggs? Wouldn't take long to cook an egg." He went to the mirror to tie his tie and stumbled a little. He leaned against the dresser, breathing fast.

Ali did not move to help him. He thought of lines of insects crawling over trees, lines of treasure moving through the forest. But it was no longer his place to discover anything new, that part of his mind he would forget about. The things that he knew now he would forget he had ever known.

"England," Wallace said, and stood straight again.

*   *   *

Wallace stood at the rail looking down at Ali, both of them waving, Ali on the dock in his new suit and Wallace in his own from Surabaya. At home he would hang the suit in his wardrobe and only take it out to model as a curiosity from the Orient. Didn't Ali look the little Englishman in his new clothes! But then the Company men in their white hats crowded around Ali and Wallace lost sight of him. The air was thick with moisture and ash; the monsoon was on its way. The crowd surged over Ali so that Wallace could no longer make him out.

A tall man in white linens stood nearby, waving a handkerchief down at the crowd. He grinned at Wallace.

"To whom are we bidding farewell?" he asked.

"Only my boy," said Wallace. "What about you?"

"To no one. But with everyone so gay, I felt I ought to take part."

"My name is Wallace."

"John Sparks."

After a few minutes the steamer moved out into the harbour and a forest of masts blocked their view.

"I have a friend who is in the saloon, I expect," said Sparks. "Shall we join him?"

Sparks' friend Hillyer leaned over and lit Wallace's cigar. On the first puff, a sweat broke out over his face, so from then on Wallace just rolled his cigar around the ashtray. Hillyer, meanwhile, smoked several. Like Wallace, he wore black; also like Wallace, he looked to have been out in the sun a great deal.

"There are tigers in the interior," said Hillyer. "Lots of tigers. But no one will beat the bush. Beaters can't be had for anything, not like in India."

"You couldn't engage the villagers?" asked Sparks.

"They all work for the Chinaman."

"What of your boy?" Sparks asked Wallace. "What was his asking price?"

"Ten pounds." Wallace held a brandy in his hand and watched carefully as Hillyer sipped his own. "I spoiled him."

"What, each year?" said Sparks. "It would cost me my whole pile to have a gang of them!"

"Ten pounds for seven years."

"Oh, well, that's quite different," said Sparks.

"The same boy for seven years?" said Hillyer.

"It is a specialized field," said Wallace. He fluffed his beard out from his chest. "Once the lad had his training, it seemed a shame to let him go. Most of the time we were out in the jungle and the only other people to be had were stark naked."

"Where was this?" asked Hillyer.

"The Papuans."

"Even the women?" said Sparks.

Wallace shifted in his chair and nodded thoughtfully.

"Were they nice-looking?" asked Sparks.

Hillyer smiled.

"No," said Wallace. "Goodness, no! They looked more like men than the men themselves." He waved his hands vaguely over his chest. "And their bodies had no, no support."

Sparks looked mesmerized. "Slack," he said.

"Exactly," said Wallace, and then paused for effect. "I did not envy those men."

Hillyer rocked in his chair and laughed. Wallace smiled and spun his cigar in the ashtray; he had told a fine joke. Sparks grinned down at his glass on the tray.

"It's a shame you didn't get on with your lad," said Hillyer.

"How do you mean?"

"Well, seven years, you either loved or hated one another. He's not on the ship, is he? So I reckon it's the latter one."

"Not at all," said Wallace. "Not at all."

He set his brandy down and stared across the room. Hillyer and Sparks went on talking without him.

Above the door was a painting behind murky glass: a dark hill, with a native village at its foot. Wallace looked at the picture for a long time.

He thought of Ali.

AUTHOR BIOGRAPHIES

Alison Acheson is the author of *Learning to Live Indoors* (Porcupine's Quill, 1998) and two young adult novels, *The Half-Pipe Kid* and *Thunder Ice*. Her stories have been published in literary journals and in *Carnal Nation: Brave New Sex Fictions*. She lives in Ladner, BC.

Kelli Deeth's short stories have appeared in publications such as *The Dalhousie Review* and *The Antigonish Review*. She lives in Vancouver, where she works as an English tutor. Her debut collection, *The Girl Without Anyone*, was published by HarperCollins in 2001.

Anne Fleming's debut collection, *Pool Hopping* (Polestar, 1998) was nominated for a Governor General's Award and for the Danuta Gleed Award. Her work has also appeared in *Vital Signs: An Anthology of New Canadian Writers* 1997 and in numerous literary magazines. She lives in Vancouver, where she is a lecturer at UBC and Emily Carr Institute of Art and Design.

Zsuzsi Gartner is the author of *All the Anxious Girls on Earth* (Key Porter, 1999; Anchor Books, 2000), which was nominated for a BC Book Prize. She has worked as both a senior and contributing editor at *Saturday Night* magazine, as books editor at *The Georgia Straight* and as a newspaper reporter and current affairs TV producer. She's currently a contributing reviewer for the *Globe & Mail*. Her short stories have been published in numerous literary magazines as well as in *Saturday Night, Geist, Toronto Life* and *The Canadian Forum*. Her story "boys growing" was recently optioned for feature-film development. She is on the faculty of the Banff Centre's Wired Writing Studio. She lives in Vancouver.

Andrew Gray is the author of *Small Accidents* (Raincoast, 2001). His stories have appeared in *Prairie Fire, Event, Grain, Fiddlehead* and *Chatelaine*. He was nominated for the Western Magazine Award (1999) and National Magazine Award for Fiction (1996/99) as well as being one of two finalists for the Journey Prize in 2000. Gray has twice been shortlisted for the CBC/*Saturday Night* Literary Award and won second place in the Eden Mills' Fiction Contest. His poetry was runner-up for the Leacock Award in 1995. He is the founder and director of UBC's Booming Ground summer writing conference, is the former executive editor of *Prism international* and currently teaches a course on small magazine publishing at UBC. He lives in Vancouver.

Debbie Howlett's short fiction has appeared in a variety of literary journals and has been anthologized in *Best Canadian Stories 1990* and *Words We Call Home*. In 1997 she won the Western Magazine Award for Fiction for her story "The Comfort Zone," which appears in her first collection of short stories *We Could Stay Here All Night* (Beach Holme, 1999). Howlett completed her undergraduate degree at Concordia University before moving to Vancouver, where she produced a festival of one-act plays for the Waterfront Theatre. During 1988–1990 she was on the editorial board of *Prism international* and was the editor in 1989. She has taught Creative Writing in Halifax, Nova Scotia, and her non-fiction has appeared in *Salon, Canadian Living* and *Today's Parent*. She currently resides in Montreal, where she is at work on her first novel and contributes to *The Montreal Gazette* and *Globe & Mail*.

Aislinn Hunter is the author of *What's Left Us* (Polestar, 2001) and has been shortlisted for a National Magazine Award (1996/2000) and the Journey Prize 1996. Her poetry collection *Into the Early Hours* (Polestar, 2001) and a novel are forthcoming. Her fiction and poetry have been published in numerous literary magazines and she has hosted and produced several shows and documentaries, including *North by Northwest* on CBC radio.

Nancy Lee has had fiction and poetry published in many literary magazines as well as the *Vancouver Sun*, *Toronto Life*, *Vintage 2000 Anthology*, *Fugue Anthology of Literary Non-fiction*, *Writers Under Cover Anthology IV* and broadcast on the CBC. She currently teaches fiction writing at the Simon Fraser University Writing and Publishing Program. She has twice been a finalist for the CBC/*Saturday Night* Literary Competition and was runner-up in the League of Canadian Poets' National Poetry Contest. She is the Associate Coordinator of the Booming Ground writers' conference. Her debut collection of stories, *Dead Girls*, is forthcoming from McClelland & Stewart.

Murray Logan is the author of *The King of Siam* (Porcupine's Quill, 1998), which was runner-up for the Danuta Gleed Award. His stories have been published in several literary magazines, nominated for the Journey Prize and have been featured in *Coming Attractions 96*. His story "Everett and Evalyne" was broadcast as a short radio play on CBC. A screenplay of "Steam" is in development with Los Angeles' David Lancaster Productions. He lives in Vancouver.

Annabel Lyon's first collection of stories, *Oxygen* (Porcupine's Quill, 2000), was shortlisted for the Danuta Gleed award. Her stories have been published widely in literary magazines and anthologized in *Fresh Blood: New Canadian Gothic Fiction* and *Carnal Nation: Brave New Sex Fictions*.

She lives in Vancouver and works as a freelance writer and book reviewer. She has taught a short fiction workshop at UBC and is past editor of *Prism international*.

Rick Maddocks' debut title, *Sputnik Diner*, a collection of linked stories, was published by Knopf Canada in Spring 2001. His writing has appeared in *Prism international*, *The Fiddlehead*, *Descant*, *Event* and *Prairie Fire*. His story "Lessons from the Sputnik Diner" was shortlisted for the 1996 Journey Prize. "Plane People" won *Prairie Fire*'s Long Fiction Competition and a gold medal Western Magazine Award in 2000. He's at work on a new piece of fiction and a collaborative multimedia project.

Eden Robinson's first collection of stories, *Traplines*, was awarded the Winifred Holtby Prize for the best first work of fiction in the Commonwealth, and was a *New York Times* Editor's Choice and Notable Book of the Year. Her first novel, *Monkey Beach* (Knopf, 2000), was nominated for the Governor General's Award and the Giller Prize. She lives in North Vancouver.

Adam Lewis Schroeder is the author of *Kingdom of Monkeys* (Raincoast, 2001) and has published in *Best Canadian Stories '99*, *Malahat Review*, *Geist*, *Zygote* and *Grain*. He has travelled to Thailand, Borneo, the Philippines, Malaysia and Indonesia, where his debut collection is set, but now lives in east Vancouver where he is at work on a novel.

Madeleine Thien's short stories have appeared in literary journals and anthologies, including *Best Canadian Stories '99* and *The Journey Prize Anthology 1998*. Her first collection, set in Malaysia and Canada, *Simple Recipes* (McClelland & Stewart, 2001), won the 1998 Asian Canadian Writers' Workshop's Emerging Writer Award. She is the winner of the CAA/Air Canada Award, the 1999 *Fiddlehead* short story contest, and has been shortlisted for the Western Magazine Award, the Bronwen Wallace

Award and the CBC Literary Award. Her story "Food for Thought" has been broadcast on CBC and she has published a children's picture book entitled *The Chinese Violin*. She has also contributed to a non-fiction anthology called *Nerves Out Loud*. Thien lives in Vancouver.

Terence Young is the author of the poetry collection *The Island in Winter*, nominated for the 1999 Governor General's Award. His fiction and poetry have appeared in numerous literary journals and "The Berlin Wall" was nominated for the 1997 Journey Prize. Young has won the *Fiddlehead* and Stephen Leacock poetry contests and *This Magazine*'s Literary Hunt. The title story of his debut collection, *Rhymes with Useless* (Raincoast, 2000), was shortlisted for the Writer's Union Short Prose Contest and "The Day the Lake Went Down" was shortlisted for the Canadian Literary Awards (CBC/*Saturday Night*). He received second prize in both the *Fiddlehead* and *Prairie Fire* fiction contests. *Rhymes with Useless* was nominated for the Danuta Gleed Award. He is co-editor of *The Claremont Review*, an international literary magazine for young writers in Victoria, where he currently teaches writing and English at St. Michaels University School.

OTHER RAINCOAST FICTION:

Sounding the Blood by **Amanda Hale** 1-55192-484-6 • $21.95 CDN • $15.95 US

Tracing Iris by **Genni Gunn** 1-55192-486-2 • $21.95 CDN • $15.95 US

Small Accidents by **Andrew Gray** 1-55192-508-7 • $19.95 CDN • $14.95 US

Quicksilver by **Nadine McInnis** 1-55192-482-X • $19.95 CDN • $14.95 US

Slow Lightning by **Mark Frutkin** 1—55192-406—4 • $21.95 CDN • $16.95 US

After Battersea Park by **Jonathan Bennett** 1—55192—408—0 • $21.95 CDN • $16.95 ¹

Kingdom of Monkeys by **Adam Lewis Schroeder** 1—55192—404—8 • $19.95 CDN
     $14.95 US

Finnie Walsh by **Steven Galloway** 1-55192-372-6 • $21.95 CDN • $16.95 US

Hotel Paradiso by **Gregor Robinson** 1—55192—358—0 • $21.95 CDN • $16.95 US

Rhymes with Useless by **Terence Young** 1-55192-354-8 • $18.95 CDN • $14.95 U

Song of Ascent by **Gabriella Goliger** 1-55192-374-2 • $18.95 CDN • $14.95 US

POLESTAR FICTION:

Pool Hopping by **Anne Fleming** 1-896095-18-6 $16.95 CDN $13.95 US

What's Left Us by **Aislinn Hunter** 1-55192-412-9 $19.95 CDN $14.95 US